W9-AEB-487

Christmas at the Shelter Inn

Also by RaeAnne Thayne

Sleigh Bells Ring
Christmas at Holiday House
Coming Home for Christmas
Season of Wonder

Haven Point

Snow Angel Cove
Redemption Bay
Evergreen Springs
Riverbend Road
Snowfall on Haven Point
Serenity Harbor
Sugar Pine Trail
The Cottages on Silver Beach
Summer at Lake Haven

Hope's Crossing

Blackberry Summer
Woodrose Mountain
Sweet Laurel Falls
Currant Creek Valley
Willowleaf Lane
Christmas in Snowflake Canyon
Wild Iris Ridge
All Is Bright

Cape Sanctuary

The Cliff House
The Sea Glass Cottage
The Path to Sunshine Cove
Summer at the Cape
The Cafe at Beach End

For a complete list of books by RaeAnne Thayne,
please visit www.raeannethayne.com.

RaeAnne Thayne

Christmas at the Shelter Inn

CANARY STREET PRESS

CANARY
STREET
PRESS™

Recycling programs
for this product may
not exist in your area.

ISBN-13: 978-1-335-00925-8

Christmas at the Shelter Inn

Canary Street Press
22 Adelaide St. West, 41st Floor
Toronto, Ontario M5H 4E3, Canada
CanaryStPress.com

Printed in U.S.A.

To Michelle Major, Molly Fader and Jill Shalvis for their brilliant help.
I love you all dearly!

one

Natalie Shepherd gripped the steering wheel of the rental car she had picked up at the Boise airport. As she drove slowly through the darkness, the sky spit more snow at her windshield than her wipers could beat away.

She had forgotten how much she really, really, *really* disliked driving in wintry weather.

She was going well below the speed limit on this stretch of road approaching her hometown of Shelter Springs, Idaho, but it still felt far too fast for conditions.

In the middle of what she could only term a blizzard, Natalie would have preferred to be driving a big honking pickup truck with four-wheel drive and steel-belted snow tires.

She wasn't.

The only available rental vehicle was this small, lightweight sedan better suited to driving to the beach on a sunny day in Florida.

It didn't help that she truly didn't want to be here. For years, Nat tried to avoid spending the holidays at home. She preferred to time her brief visits to see her family in summer, when the mountains were green and lush and the lake gleamed in the long, glorious stretched-out evenings.

She disliked the holidays anyway and she especially disliked being here, filled with memories and ghosts and regret.

Then there was the snow.

Oh, sure, during the holidays it could seem festive and charming, especially when it covered everything with a pristine blanket and sometimes fluttered down like glitter in a snow globe.

Snow lost much of that cheerful appeal when she could feel the tires of her rental spin and felt that dizzying churn in her stomach every time they lost purchase with the pavement.

No. She wasn't a fan.

Though she did not want to be here, she also knew she had no choice. When McKenna reached out to her three days earlier with a single-word text—Help!—Natalie had known exactly what she had to do. She quickly reached out to the agency she worked through so they could find another person to fill her job, packed up her luggage and caught the next flight out from the small Spanish island of Tenerife, off the coast of West Africa, where she had expected to spend the next few months.

McKenna needed her. For her independent, self-contained baby sister to reach out with that single plea, Nat knew things had to be bad.

Worry pressed her foot a little harder on the accelerator. She was driving as fast as she dared. When the lights of Shelter Springs began to appear in the distance through the thick evergreens, Nat let out a sigh of relief. Almost there. Soon this particular driving nightmare would be over and she would be safe and sound, tucked into the guest bedroom at the Shelter Inn.

She could do this. Her mother always used to tell her and her brother and sister they could do hard things. That mantra had been tested severely over the years. Compared to other things Nat had endured, driving a mountain road on a snowy December evening should have been a piece of cake.

Disaster burst out of the trees in an instant in the form of a mule deer, which leaped directly in front of her car. Too close for her to stop.

She screamed and hit the brakes out of instinct, turning the wheel in a frantic attempt to avoid the inevitable collision.

She managed to miss the deer, barely, but her evasive efforts proved disastrous. She hadn't been traveling at a high rate of speed, but her abrupt, instinctive jerk of the wheel to avoid hitting the animal was enough to send the sedan spinning, any notion that she was in control disappearing out the window into the night.

She tried desperately to regain control, pumping the brake and remembering to turn into the slide as panic washed over her like icy waves.

She was going to end up in the lake.

It was her greatest nightmare, being swallowed up by water, trapped and helpless inside a sinking vehicle.

Her sister didn't need one more loss. Poor McKenna.

That was her last random thought before the front passenger fender struck a small fir tree, the airbags deploying. The car spun a little more, then came to rest in a snowbank, only a few feet away from the water.

Natalie pushed away the airbag and fought to draw oxygen into her lungs, adrenaline pumping through her.

She was alive. She didn't know how, but she was alive.

She gave a small laugh, shaking her head. Now she only had to figure out how to get out of here.

Easier said than done. The car was high-centered on a rock or a log or something. She put it in gear and tried to reverse. The engine revved and the tires spewed snow and dirt, but nothing happened.

Okay. Great. Did she have a cell signal to call for a lift? Did Shelter Springs even have a taxi service these days?

Making a mighty effort to collect her scattered thoughts, she scooped up her tote from the floor where it had fallen off the seat and started to dig for her cell phone.

She was so focused on looking for it, she didn't hear the knock on her window. She glanced over in surprise and saw a man in dark clothing leaning down to peer in.

To her dismay, a small shriek escaped.

All the true crime podcasts she listened to seemed to flash a warning to her brain in neon lights. Don't. Open. The. Door.

She checked to make sure the locks were all engaged. When the man knocked again, obviously not going anywhere, she rolled down the window a crack, enough that she could hear over the howling wind.

"Is everyone okay? I saw you spin out. I've called the highway patrol. I'm a doctor. Can I help?"

The voice seemed to strike a memory chord, but she couldn't identify his features in the dark.

"No. I don't think so. I'm the only one inside the vehicle, and I'm fine. Except I seem to be stuck."

"What happened?" he asked. "Was it black ice? It's slicker than spit out here, and the wind isn't helping anything."

"Mostly a deer with a death wish that jumped out right in front of me. I think I missed him, but I probably still have hoof marks on the hood."

His teeth flashed in the darkness, and she found herself wishing she could see his features. There was something about that voice that seemed so familiar.

"I've got a truck back there, a three-quarter ton, and a tow rope. I can have you out in a jiffy."

Again, those podcast warnings rattled through her head. She almost told him thanks but no thanks, then discarded the idea. It might be hours before she could get help, and the alternative was walking two miles into town through the blizzard and with poor visibility.

She had learned in her travels the past five years that sometimes she had to reach outside of her comfort zone.

Anyway, this was small-town Idaho, where she knew most

of the people who lived here. Or at least someone who was related to them.

"Thank you. I appreciate that."

He seemed to peer in at her, probably trying to figure out if he knew her. She had the impression of strength, somehow. Though she knew that made no sense, it helped calm her nerves as he left her again. A moment later, headlights cut through the darkness as he pulled up behind her.

She heard rather than saw when he attached a tow rope to her bumper, then walked around to her driver's side again.

"Okay. Just put it in Neutral, if you would," he said to her.

She complied, remembering with stark clarity the month after she received her driving license when Jake took it upon himself to give her a few adulting lessons. How to fix a flat tire. How to jump-start a car battery. How to tow and be towed.

The reminder of her older brother was a sharp, twisting ache in her chest. He was one of the ghosts who stirred around her whenever she came back to town.

As much as she tried, Natalie found it impossible not to think about him here. Jake was the one who had taught her how to drive in snow, who had instructed her to carry a bag of rock salt for both weight and possible traction in the back of the little pickup she drove in high school.

Her rescuer backed slowly toward the road. With a loud grating noise, her car came free of whatever had been trapping it.

No other cars were in sight, probably because anybody with a shred of common sense was tucked up at home enjoying the lights of their Christmas tree and having some hot cocoa.

Her rescuer returned to her window. This time she lowered it a little more.

"That should do it," he said. "Your front bumper has a little crinkle in it, but shouldn't be too hard to fix. I know a guy, if you need someone. He won't overcharge you, and he does good work."

"I'm good. It's a rental and I took the insurance plan. I'll let them deal with it. Thank you for stopping. I wasn't sure my cell would have service here, and I really wasn't looking forward to walking into town."

"Where are you heading?"

She nodded toward that rim of lights in the distance. "Shelter Springs."

"Do you have family there?"

A serial killer might ask that very question to find out where he could find her later, so he could come slaughter her in her bed.

But so could a perfectly nice man trying to make sure she had somewhere to go out of the storm.

"Yes," she answered. "My sister."

While she had extended family in the area, her immediate family had been reduced to only that. Her mother. Her father. Her brother. All gone.

That familiar pain twisted again as the memories crowded back.

"I hope you have a good visit." He smiled in the darkness, and she had the impression he wanted to hold out his hand to shake hers through the crack in her window.

"I hope I bump into you under better circumstances. My name is Griffin Taylor," he said.

She drew in a sharp breath. Of course! She should have known. No wonder his voice had seemed familiar, though it had been years since she last heard it.

Griffin Taylor. How odd that he should be the first person she bumped into after coming back to town. What was he even doing there? Last she knew, he was living in the Los Angeles area, finishing his residency.

"Griffin. Hi. I hadn't heard you were back in town."

He frowned, and the moon came out from behind the clouds long enough for her to see snowflakes catching in his dark hair. "Sorry. Do I know you?"

"You used to."

He peered through the window. She finally opened her door and stepped out, giving him a rather shaky smile.

Recognition flared in eyes she remembered could be the very same blue as Lake Haven.

"Natalie? Nat! It's great to see you."

After an awkward pause, he reached to hug her. Taken by surprise, she waited a few beats before she hugged him back.

He had always been athletic, just like his best friend, her brother, Jake. But life and the years since she had last seen him had honed those teenage muscles to hard strength.

"How great that you could be home for the holidays to help McKenna. I understand she's having a tough time right now."

Surely McKenna didn't see Dr. Taylor on a professional basis. That would be just about the weirdest thing ever, to have the gorgeous Griffin Taylor looking at your girlie parts with a clinical eye.

No, thank you.

"It's been a tough pregnancy, from what she tells me."

"I heard she's been put on strict bed rest."

If he didn't know that personally, then he probably wasn't her sister's doctor. He was a family medicine doctor, she knew, but she was also aware that in a community as small as Shelter Springs, sometimes general practitioners did a little of everything.

"Yes. That's why I'm here."

"She does have her hands full, with those busy girls of hers."

Nerves jittered through her, anxiety that had nothing to do with winter driving conditions or almost hitting a deer. While she adored her two nieces from afar, she had no idea how she would manage for the next month to keep a five-year-old and three-year-old entertained.

"It's good you're here," he said. "I'm sure I'll see you around."

She nodded. "Thanks again for towing me out."

"Do you want to start it up so I can make sure everything's okay for you to drive the rest of the way to the Shelter Inn?"

"Good idea."

She slid behind the wheel again and turned the key. The car sputtered and hissed, and smoke began curling out from under the hood.

Great.

Griffin leaned in. "Looks like things are worse than we thought," he said, his tone apologetic.

"Doesn't look good, does it?"

"I'm afraid you won't be going anywhere else in this tonight."

Wasn't that just perfect? As if she needed another reason to question the wisdom of returning to Shelter Springs. She fought the urge to pound on the steering wheel a few times.

"What are my chances of finding a rideshare driver around here?"

"About on par with your chances of finding a gluten-free bakery on every corner. Hop in my truck where it's warm while we call a tow truck, and then I can give you a ride to the Shelter Inn."

She instinctively wanted to argue that she could take care of herself, as she had been doing that since she was about sixteen years old. But it seemed silly to refuse his help on principle when she could be much more comfortable waiting in his warm truck, especially when she might not have a phone signal to call anyone else for help.

"Grab anything you want to take to McKenna's place," he said.

She grabbed her big tote that held her laptop, then opened the back door for her rolling duffel bag, which held all the essentials she traveled with.

"Is that it?"

"I travel light."

"Must be nice not to have too much baggage."

Oh, she had plenty of baggage. Lucky for her, the ghosts didn't take up all that much room in her luggage.

"I've got this," he said, lifting the duffel from her and making his way to his big extended cab pickup. He opened the rear door and slid in her bag, then opened the passenger door for her and held a hand out to help her inside.

The vehicle was deliciously warm and smelled like cedar and fir and leather.

"I can crank the heat. It's nasty out there. You picked a lousy night to be stranded."

"Sorry. Next time I'll try to put more forethought into it."

He smiled. "Do you care what tow company we call?"

"Not in the slightest."

He scrolled through his phone and made a call and she listened while he arranged for a tow, explaining their location and the make and model of the vehicle.

With those particulars out of the way, he ended the call and finally turned to her.

"So. How have you been, Nat?"

"Oh, you know. Living the dream."

"That's what your sister says. You're a digital nomad, right? Last McKenna told me, you were in Croatia or something."

Her sister had talked about her to him? Natalie didn't quite know what to think about that. She wouldn't have thought Griffin cared about what she was doing. She was surprised he even remembered her. She had simply been his best friend's kid sister, who might or might not have followed Griffin around with stars in her eyes.

"I was in Croatia six months ago. The Dalmatian Coast. It was really lovely. I was staying at a beautiful house on a small island on the shores of the Adriatic."

"Sounds like paradise."

"Close to it. I've been a few other places since then. Ireland, northern England, Portugal."

"You get around. McKenna told me you stay at various places house-sitting and taking care of people's pets."

"When I can. It saves on rent. I pay the bills with freelance writing and editing, though."

Somehow, without quite planning it, she had carved out a life that fit her perfectly. She got the fun of taking care of animals, which she loved, without the long-term commitment. Plus she had the opportunity to explore places she once hadn't even known existed.

Natalie had caught the travel bug early, probably in those early days she spent living at the Shelter Inn when it used to be a hotel, watching their guests come for a few days and then move on to somewhere else undoubtedly more exciting than this sleepy Idaho town near Lake Haven.

She used to wonder where they had come from, where they were going and what sorts of things they would see on their journey. The answers were likely much more exciting than the life she lived here.

"Sounds interesting, always on the go."

"It works for me." She turned the conversation to him. "What about you? You could practice anywhere. What brings you back to Shelter Springs, of all places?"

He smiled, though she could swear it wasn't completely genuine. "I always planned to come back and open a practice here. The area has a shortage of good family medicine physicians, despite the new hospital between here and Haven Point."

He gestured out the window. "Anyway, what's not to love about living here? Quiet lifestyle, good people, gorgeous surroundings. What more could I want?"

She started to ask whether he had a wife and children, but flashing yellow lights announced the arrival of the tow truck.

"That was fast," Griffin said. "If you want to stay here, out of the weather, I can make arrangements with my buddy for the tow and then give you all the particulars."

She should assert her hard-fought feminist credentials, but after her very long twenty-six hours of travel, she had to admit it was nice to let someone else handle things for now.

"Thank you," she said, settling deeper into the heated seat while he went outside into the blowing snow.

She watched the tow truck driver hook up the rental car. He and Griffin exchanged a few words, obviously shouting over the wind. She couldn't hear what they said, but decided it didn't matter.

She would call the rental company in the morning to see how they wanted to proceed. For now, she had done her part by making sure the car was safely off the road.

After another shouted exchange she couldn't hear, the tow truck driver gave Natalie a nod and returned to his vehicle. Griffin climbed into the pickup truck as soon as the tow truck driver started back on the road, lights blinking in the blowing snow.

"I gave him my phone number and contact info since I didn't have yours. He's going to tow it to the garage and wait until he hears from you before he does anything."

"I hope it's not too complicated a repair."

"Sorry you'll be without a vehicle for a few days."

"I'm not worried about that. I can always drive McKenna's car while I'm here. I wouldn't have rented a car at all, but I didn't really have another good way to get here from the airport. Face it, Griffin. Shelter Springs is in the middle of nowhere."

He smiled. "And that's exactly why we like it.

After the tow truck's lights disappeared around the bend in the road, Griffin put his truck in gear and pulled back onto the road too. "Come on," he said with a smile. "Let's get you to the inn."

Right. The anxiety returned. Her sister needed her.

Natalie only hoped she would be up to the task.

two

This wasn't exactly how he planned to spend his Friday night.

If someone had told him an hour ago that he would be giving a ride to a stranded Natalie Shepherd, Griffin would never have believed it.

As he drove through the whiteout conditions on his way to her family's property, Griffin pondered the odd turn of events.

The last time he saw Natalie, she had been a teenager, at her brother's funeral.

He felt again the familiar weight of guilt and grief he had carried since that December day. More than a dozen years later, the pain was as fresh.

Seeing her again seemed to bring back all those emotions he had worked so hard to manage over the years. Natalie seemed to reach through the years to dredge up everything he thought he had dealt with long ago.

Her sister didn't spark the same reaction. While he always felt a little pang whenever he talked to McKenna, it was nothing like this—as if Natalie held the only key that opened the lockbox holding his memories.

He let out a breath, frustrated with himself. He carried enough on his shoulders right now, trying to establish his practice here in

Shelter Springs, where his family's reputation sometimes seemed damaged beyond repair.

"You probably had somewhere to go tonight. I'm sorry if I'm keeping you from something. Or someone."

She must have misinterpreted his sigh, he realized.

"You are," he said with a half smile. "I'm late for dinner with a beautiful woman."

"Really? Anyone I might know?"

"I think so. My grandmother."

Her short laugh went a long way toward helping him shove down all those raw emotions again.

"How is Birdie these days?"

"As feisty as ever. She's pushing eighty this year and decided to take up pickleball during the summer. She's kind of obsessed with it, which is funny because she has AMD, age-related macular degeneration, and can hardly see the ball."

"Oh dear. I'm sorry. I hadn't heard."

"For the most part, she manages well. She can still kick my butt at pickleball. She's always trying to drag me into playing with her. Good thing there's an indoor court at the apartment complex where she lives so she can play year-round."

"Are you serious? How many apartment complexes are there in Shelter Springs with indoor pickleball courts?"

"Only one, as far as I know."

"Birdie lives at the Shelter Inn?"

He nodded. "I told you I wouldn't be going far out of my way to take you to your sister's place. It's not out of my way at all, since I'm heading there."

"McKenna didn't tell me Birdie had moved to the Shelter Inn. How long has she lived there?"

"She moved in this summer. After her vision really started deteriorating, she struggled to keep up with the yard and the housework. For a few years, we hired someone to help her, but eventually I think she realized a smaller place made sense, especially where she could be surrounded by others who could watch out for her."

"That must have been tough for her. It's hard for me to picture her living anywhere but that gorgeous cottage on Huckleberry Street."

"Amanda lives there now."

"Does she?"

Her voice sounded a little odd, but he couldn't quite pinpoint why. He knew the two had been friends back in the day, though his younger sister, Amanda, was a year ahead of Natalie in school. He wasn't sure if they had kept in touch over the years. Amanda had never said if they had.

"Yes. For a while they lived there together and Amanda looked out for her. But Birdie broke her hip last winter trying to shovel the steps after a big storm and had to spend six weeks healing in a rehab facility. Now, with her vision so much worse, she finally decided it was time to downsize."

"She had a broken hip last winter and she's still a pickleball fiend?"

"That's Birdie for you."

She smiled at this, just a flash in the darkness, but it was like stumbling upon a mountain bluebird on a winter afternoon, cheerful and bright and lovely.

"I'm really glad to hear she's still going strong."

He didn't like thinking of the inevitable. Birdie, his maternal grandmother, had been a rock for him and for his sister amid all the ugliness of his parents' divorce and his father's struggle with addiction that had ended so tragically.

"She seems to enjoy living at the Shelter Inn, with the vibrant community there. Your aunt and sister have done a good job of creating camaraderie among the residents."

"That's nice to hear. I wasn't sure what to expect when they told me a few years ago that they wanted to transition the Shelter Inn from a hotel to senior apartments. I'll admit, I was skeptical it would work, but I'm happy to see their vision become a reality. I just hope McKenna can keep up with the demands of running things, now that she'll soon have three little ones running around."

"Those cute girls of hers already have all the residents wrapped around their fingers."

"I don't doubt it. They're adorable, if a little intimidating."

He smiled. "You'll be fine," he assured her as he pulled into the parking lot.

He had always liked the Shelter Inn, one of three grand historic brick hotels constructed in the early 1900s. At one point in the past, Shelter Springs used to attract people from around the world looking to partake of the reportedly healing waters from the many hot springs that flowed into Lake Haven.

Those days were gone. Only one hot spring outside of town was still in business for people who wanted to soak. The other grand hotel, The Haven, had been mostly torn down, except for one area that had been converted to a conference and events center a few decades ago, hosting concerts and sporting events as well as the town's annual Shelter Springs Holiday Giving Market.

A few years ago, Natalie's sister and aunt had made the decision to convert the struggling Shelter Inn to twenty-four one- and two-bedroom senior apartments.

His grandmother had a two-bedroom apartment on the first floor that offered a lovely view of the lake and the mountains beyond.

He pulled into the parking lot, currently being plowed by someone in a pickup truck, despite the snow still falling heavily.

"Thanks for the lift," she said when he parked in the covered spot allocated to his grandmother, even though she could no longer drive.

"Sure. No problem. Let me give you my cell number, in case you need a ride to the mechanic. If you need it, I can also give you a lift back to Boise to pick up another rental."

She gave him a startled look, but handed over her phone. Griffin quickly typed in his phone number and sent a message to himself.

"There you go. Don't hesitate to reach out if you need anything."

"Thank you. That's very…kind of you."

He wanted to tell her he wasn't being kind, that he owed her far more than a lift into Boise. He couldn't say that, of course. He didn't want to bring up Jake, though he knew it was a topic that couldn't be far from her mind.

"I wouldn't want you to head back to Tenerife thinking the people of Shelter Springs are as cold as the weather."

He climbed out before she could answer, walked around the truck and opened her door. He offered her a hand down, trying not to notice the warmth of her hand in his that made him suddenly remember that quick welcoming embrace he'd given her, when her curves had seemed to fit so perfectly against him.

He released her hand quickly and opened the back door for her rolling duffel.

"I can get this," she protested. "I'm used to carrying my bag from train station to taxi to airport."

"I'm sure you are. But if my grandmother saw me standing by and doing nothing while you carry that big bag inside by yourself, one of us would be in trouble. Spoiler alert, it wouldn't be you."

She laughed, though he didn't miss the note of fatigue that threaded through the laughter. In the overhead lights of the parking lot, he could see deep shadows under her eyes and lines of strain around her mouth. They left him feeling oddly protective of her, wishing he could carry *her* inside instead of only her bag.

"I wouldn't want to be responsible for you getting in trouble with Birdie."

"Thank you. I appreciate that."

He grabbed the bag and carried it to the outside door of the apartment building. While the crime rate in Shelter Springs was generally low, the outside door leading to the lobby area and large, open recreation room automatically locked from just after dark to sunrise. But he knew the code from his many visits with his grandmother. He quickly punched it in and carried Natalie's bag inside. She followed him down the hall to the first door beyond the lobby.

Before she could ring the bell to the same apartment where her family had lived when she was younger, the door opened and a curly-headed preschooler ran out wearing rain boots, shorts, a ruffly pink sweater and a sparkly cape over her shoulders.

"You can't catch me," she called out in a singsong voice.

"You're absolutely right," retorted a voice Griffin recognized as belonging to Liz Cisneros, Natalie's maternal aunt. "Hazel Jeanette Dodd. Get back in here right now."

The girl didn't appear to notice them as she looked down the hallway in the other direction. After a moment, she huffed out a breath and went back inside.

"Oh yes," Natalie murmured. "This is going to be great fun."

Griffin had to hide a smile at the slightly panicked note in her voice.

"You've got this. Don't worry. You just have to let them know who's in charge."

"The problem is, it's going to take them about five seconds to figure out that person is not me."

"You'll be fine. Trust me. I'm a doctor. And my prescription for you right now is to get some rest, if you can. All of this will feel less overwhelming in the morning, I'm sure."

"I'll have to take your word for that. Thanks again for rescuing me."

"You're welcome. Good luck."

On impulse, he gave her a quick kiss on the cheek, telling himself it was only a casual welcoming kiss between people who had known each other for decades. She smelled of almonds and some kind of exotic flower that made him think of warm beaches and ocean breezes, somewhere far away from this snowy Idaho December evening.

He walked back through the common area to the other hallway, which led to his grandmother's apartment.

Birdie answered before the echo of his knock even faded, her trusty golden retriever, Dash, at her side.

Dash wasn't a trained guide or service dog. Griffin's grandmother got him as a puppy as only a companion about a year before her AMD had grown progressively worse. Over the past few years, though, the dog had instinctively stepped up to help her with her new challenges.

The smell of tomatoes and cheese and bread wafted from the small kitchen, making his stomach growl.

"Hi, Gram," he said.

She smiled broadly. "There you are! You're late, young man. I hope you were saving someone's life. Barring that, I hope you were flirting with a beautiful woman."

He thought of Natalie's green eyes, wavy brown hair in a messy bun and the almond and flowers scent of her.

He would have liked to flirt with her, but knew it wasn't to be. He wasn't in a good place for a relationship right now with anyone. If things were different, if he were a little more settled in his practice and didn't feel this vast sense of obligation to the people of Shelter Springs, Natalie still wouldn't have been a possibility. No matter how lovely she was.

She was the sister of Jake Shepherd. His best friend.

One more person he couldn't save.

"Neither, I'm afraid." Griffin forced a smile. "I was on a rescue mission, helping dig out a stranded motorist after she slid into a snowbank while trying to avoid a deer."

"Oh my."

"She's fine. The car was damaged, though, so I had to wait with her until a tow arrived."

"Anyone I know?" Birdie's eyes crinkled at the corners with her smile. His grandmother seemed to believe it was her mission in life to set him up with every possibly eligible woman from here to Boise.

Birdie was under the misguided notion that his heart had been irreparably damaged after his divorce five years earlier and all the sadness and loss surrounding it.

"Yes, actually. Natalie Shepherd. McKenna's sister."

Her eyes widened behind the thick glasses that only helped a little. "Natalie is in town? Oh, how wonderful for McKenna and her girls, especially now while she's struggling so much with her pregnancy. We should have her over."

"I'm afraid she's supposed to be on strict bed rest."

"Not McKenna, silly." Birdie made a face. "I meant Natalie. As you know perfectly well."

Yes. He did know. He also knew he needed to nip in the bud his grandmother's matchmaking before it had a chance to take root.

"She's in town to help her sister and aunt with this place and with the girls. I'm sure she'll be too busy to do much socializing."

"Poor thing. It has to be tough for her, coming back to Shelter Springs for the holidays in the middle of so much chaos. Surely she can sneak away for a few minutes some evening when Travis can be home with the girls. I'll reach out and see if we can arrange something. Maybe I'll make a little party of it. Invite some of the other residents so they can get to know her."

Birdie had appointed herself the unofficial cruise director of the good ship Shelter Inn. She was president of the welcoming committee, chairperson of the community watch group, leader of the garden alliance. Despite her failing vision, or maybe because of it, she loved to be in charge of everything around her.

He wanted to remind her he was thirty-three and had been on his own a very long time and that she wasn't in charge of his life. He would never hurt his grandmother, though. Not for a moment, after all she had done to make his and Amanda's childhoods bearable.

"What's your work schedule over the weekend?" she asked him as they settled at the table over the dinner she had made of lasagna and garlic butter bread sticks.

"If you're planning a welcome party, you don't need to drag me into it."

Birdie chided him with a look. "Yes, I do. Why would Natalie possibly want to hang around with a bunch of old people like me and the rest of the geezers who live here at the Shelter Inn? She'll want to meet up with people her own age."

It was a bit of a shock to think of Natalie being considered in his age group. He had always thought of her as Jake's little sister, three years younger and an occasional pest when they had to take her along with them to the movie theater in town or a mountain bike ride on one of their favorite trails.

She would be thirty now, which wasn't nearly the impassable gap it might have been when he was eighteen and she was only fifteen.

That still didn't mean he wanted his grandmother to try throwing them together.

"You know how my schedule is. I never know exactly where I'll be."

"I thought the whole point of practicing here as a family doctor in Shelter Springs was so that you could maintain regular office hours. Instead, you volunteer to offer medical support to every possible sporting event, music concert and free clinic in the entire area."

"I'm trying my best to gain the trust of the community. That's not exactly an easy task, after everything that's happened."

"I know that." Her wrinkled features softened with sympathy, and she reached out a hand and laid it over his. "I wish you didn't feel like you had to try so hard. People should respect you on your own merits, because you're a good man and an excellent doctor. Not because they see you jumping through every possible hoop to prove you're not your father."

Griffin forced a smile. "That would certainly make things easier, wouldn't it?"

Birdie sighed. "It's not fair. You're not at all like Dennis. You're different in every possible way, and I only wish people could see that."

Though it was an inescapable part of living in Shelter Springs, Griffin didn't like thinking about his father, about all the harm and loss he had wrought in so many lives.

He quickly changed the subject. "How are plans for the holiday market going? Are you going to be ready to open the Shelter Inn kiosk?"

As he had hoped, Birdie spent the rest of dinner talking about the items that would be offered for sale, most handmade by residents of the apartment complex.

He listened to her, asking questions and commenting at the appropriate moments in the conversation, all while his mind returned again and again to Natalie Shepherd's arrival in Shelter Springs.

three

"Auntie Nat! Auntie Nat!" Hazel, the older of her nieces, and the one currently wearing the rubber boots, launched herself at Natalie as soon as she opened the door to the apartment where Nat had lived her first eighteen years.

Hazel's younger sister, Nora, three years old to Hazel's five, held back, looking anxious.

"Hello, my dear." Natalie, whose relationship with the girls mostly consisted of video call conversations and the occasional quick visit home, picked up the girl, boots and all.

"Guess what? I'm Super Hazel. I can fly through the air like Santa Claus and the reindeer and nobody can catch me."

"Aren't you lucky? Flying must be an awesome superpower."

"She can't really fly," Nora said, her lisp turning the *R*s into *W*s. Her worried look intensified, as if she feared Natalie might actually believe her sister's claims.

"Can too. You just never saw me do it," Hazel retorted.

Before the disagreement could devolve into a full-on fight, Natalie set Hazel down and turned to Nora. "What are your superpowers?"

"I don't have any."

"Not true." Aunt Liz, slim and lovely in her late fifties, with short-cropped silver hair and the green eyes she shared with

Natalie and McKenna, leaned on her crutches. "You give the very best hugs."

"Is that true?" Natalie asked.

After another nervous moment, Nora reached small arms around Nat's waist and hugged her tightly.

Natalie had to smile. "Aunt Liz is right. That's really good," she said, hoping she could set the girl at ease.

"How was your flight?" Liz asked.

She sighed. "Long. More than twenty hours, by the time we routed through Madrid and New York. But I'm here. Barely. I would have been here earlier except I had an accident outside of town. I swerved to avoid a deer and got stuck in a snowbank."

"Oh no! Are you all right?"

"I'm fine. I'm afraid I can't say the same for the rental car. But it's been towed to a repair shop in town, and I was able to catch a ride here so everything worked out."

Liz looked relieved. "I'm so glad you came home, darling. We're quite a motley crew, with me on these stupid crutches and McKenna stuck in bed."

"How is your knee?"

Liz sighed. "When it heals, it will be better than ever. It was horrible timing, though, a knee replacement during the holidays, especially with the giving market coming up. But that was the only time the doctor could schedule it until spring, and I didn't want to wait. If I had any inkling McKenna's pregnancy would take a turn, I never would have gone through with it."

Worry for her sister pressed in above the fatigue. Nat looked toward the bedroom at the end of the hall that had once been her parents' but now was used by Kenna and her husband, Travis. "How is she?"

"Stressed. Scared. Bored. All of the above. She will be so happy to see you."

"I'm not sure how much help I'll be," Natalie confessed. "If she wanted me to puppy-sit, I could absolutely handle that. Two small children are a completely different story."

"Contrary to the evidence in front of you, they're good girls. They've just been trapped inside all day with the storm and have a little bit of energy to burn. I was just about to take them swimming."

"You're on crutches. Are you supposed to be doing that?"

"Swimming is the one thing I can do with them. The doctor says it's good therapy for my knee. We keep the water extra warm for our residents, and it feels great on these old joints."

Though relatively young, Liz suffered from joint problems with her knees. Natalie knew this was her second knee replacement, and it wasn't healing as well as the first one had. Under normal circumstances, Liz could easily keep up with Hazel and Nora, but not on crutches and with a wonky knee.

"Can you keep track of the girls in the pool?"

"It's almost time for the swim-walk class. We do it after dinner hours and it always draws a big crowd. There should be others there to help me watch them."

Natalie could only imagine how much the residents probably did enjoy having an indoor swimming pool, as well as the indoor pickleball court Birdie favored.

When she had lived here, the indoor pool had drawn plenty of families. She and McKenna had loved it too, though she remembered they used to complain during the summers that they would have preferred an outdoor pool where they could get a tan.

Ridiculous, she thought now, when the gorgeous Lake Haven was only a short distance away, giving all the outdoor water fun they could ever want. Anyway, they should have been more worried about skin cancer and sun damage than having an outdoor pool.

"Go check in with your sister," Liz said. "I'll take the girls off your hands for a bit and try to work out some of their energy so they will sleep for you tonight."

"Thank you."

Liz hugged her. "It's really great to have you back. You're just the bright spot Kenna needs to help her through the final weeks of her pregnancy."

Natalie wasn't so sure about that. She worried her presence and her complete ineptness when it came to caring for children would only add to her sister's stress.

She would try, though.

"Come on, you two," Liz said. "Grab your towels and let's go."

"I'm a baby shark," Hazel announced.

"I am," her sister retorted.

They both clapped their hands together in front of them, elbows extended.

"You can both be baby sharks. And I'll be the auntie whale shark who likes to eat baby sharks for breakfast."

They giggled at that and raced away from Liz, heading toward the pool area with a speed that Natalie frankly found mind-boggling.

When the apartment was quiet again, she took a breath and made her way to her sister's bedroom. When she knocked, she heard a gloomy-sounding "Hello" in response.

She pushed open the door and peered into the dim interior. It took a moment for her eyes to focus enough that she could find her sister on the bed, covered in a red-and-white quilt.

McKenna squealed and switched on the bedside lamp. "Nat! You're here! I can't believe you're really here."

She moved closer to the bed to take her sister's hand. McKenna's features were swollen, her eyes exhausted. "Of course I'm here. Did you think I wasn't going to come when you needed me?"

McKenna squeezed her hand. "I thought you wouldn't be here until tomorrow!"

"I was able to find an earlier flight."

To her dismay, McKenna suddenly burst into tears, then seemed as shocked by them as Natalie was.

"Hey. It's okay. You don't need to cry."

"I'm...just...so glad...you're here."

Nat sat next to her on the bed and slung her arm around McKenna's shaking shoulders. Her own fatigue could wait. "I am too. I only wish I had thought about coming earlier. I guess I assumed you had a good support system and I would only be in the way."

"You're here now. That's the important thing." McKenna rested her head on Nat's shoulder. The gesture reminded her with painful clarity of other times she had tried and failed to offer comfort to her sister.

After their mother died. After their father left. After Jake's accident.

She had done her best to provide comfort and support during those times, but had felt as helpless as she did now.

"How are you feeling?" she asked, hoping to divert McKenna's attention away from her emotional tumult.

"Huge. Exhausted." She paused. "Scared."

Natalie hugged her again. While McKenna's face and her belly were swollen, her shoulders still felt thin, almost frail. Was she eating enough? Natalie did love to cook. She would do her best to provide her sister with healthy, delicious meals while she was here.

"Everything's okay, though, isn't it?"

McKenna plucked out a tissue from a box on a bedside table and wiped at her eyes and nose. "So far. My doctor is keeping a close watch on things."

"That's good."

Her sister shrugged. "I guess. Sometimes I think Dr. Reynolds has an abundance of caution. If not for the two miscarriages I had last year and Nora coming a month early, I don't think she would have put me on strict bed rest, just because my blood pressure was high at one appointment. It's been fine since then. My friend had mild preeclampsia at every appointment and they just made her check her blood pressure four times a day and take medication if it reached too high."

"Every woman is different, I imagine. Better safe than sorry."

"I just feel like I'm failing at everything right now," McKenna admitted, her eyes filling with tears again. "I can't be there for my girls, I'm not taking care of the apartment or our tenants, I'm no help to Travis. I'm not even doing a good job with this pregnancy. All I can do is stay on this bed like a lazy cow."

"You need to trust your doctor that you're where you need to be. And I'm here to help with the girls and the apartment building. You don't need to worry about a thing but taking care of that baby."

"I'm sorry to be such a whiner."

"You have every reason to be upset."

"I just hate being stuck here. It hasn't even been a week and I'm already tearing out my hair. I don't know how I'll make it until my due date in six weeks. And it's the worst possible time! You know how much I usually love this time of year."

That was yet one more way she and McKenna were different. Her sister had always adored the holidays, taking after their mother in that regard.

Jeanette Shepherd had been their own Christmas elf. She brought out the holiday decorations from the hotel storage room the day after Halloween and made sure the inn always crackled with holiday spirit, featuring a huge tree in the lobby and carols playing on the sound system throughout the building.

Natalie might have been like her mother and sister at one point, but she had not been able to truly enjoy the holidays since the year she turned fourteen, when Jeanette had been diagnosed with breast cancer. Her mother's first chemotherapy appointment had been the week before Christmas that year, and Natalie vividly remembered her mother's queasiness and how fearful the rest of them had been.

"I'm not even looking forward to the holidays this year," McKenna said. "I can't play in the snow with the girls or go Christmas shopping or even decorate a Christmas tree. It's pathetic."

"All those things will still happen," Natalie assured her. "Right now your priority needs to be resting and taking care of yourself. The rest of us will handle everything else. Even Christmas."

"You don't even like the holidays."

Though she couldn't honestly argue, Natalie still looked at her in mock outrage. "What are you talking about? I love the holidays! I'm so festive, I should have baubles coming out of my, uh, ears."

McKenna made a face. "Right. That's why you never fly home for the holidays. Why I practically had to beg you to come back and help me this year."

Funny, but as Nat recalled, McKenna had only sent her that one-word text—Help!—and Natalie had instantly called her and started making arrangements to return as soon as she understood the situation.

She wasn't going to call out a pregnant woman, though.

"You know the holidays have always been a little tough for me. They remind me so much of Mom and how much she loved them and that last Christmas when she tried so hard to be festive, even though she knew she was dying."

McKenna made a small sound, and Natalie covered her sister's hand with hers, wishing she hadn't brought up their mother. "That doesn't mean I hate them. I'm fully prepared to throw the most Christmassy Christmas of all the Christmases for you and your family until we can get little Travis Junior here safe and sound."

Her sister laughed, swiping at her nose again. "Not Travis Junior. He doesn't want the baby named for him. So we're going with Austin Travis Dodd."

"Cute. I like that one too. Travis must be over the moon about having another baby. A son this time."

"Sure. He's thrilled." She smiled again, though this time Natalie could tell she didn't mean it. Worry flickered through her. Where was her brother-in-law? She would have thought he would be here offering reassurance and comfort to his nervous wife and his energetic children.

"I'm so glad you came home, Nat. I know it was a lot to ask."

When it looked as if McKenna would cry again, Natalie squeezed her hand. "You've got this. *We've* got this."

"The Shepherd girls against the world."

"Darn right."

"I'm sorry. I'm so emotional these days. We just wanted this baby so much, especially after the two miscarriages. He won't admit it, but I know they were tough on Travis. I'm not sure what he would do if anything happened to little Austin."

"You won't have to worry about that." Natalie's voice was firm. "Everything will be fine. You're going to do exactly what the doctor has told you, and I'm here to make sure of it."

No problem at all, once she figured out how to handle two active girls.

"What time will Travis be home?" she felt compelled to ask.

McKenna looked away, but not before Natalie saw that hint of worry in her eyes again. "It's hard to say. Because he's a manager now at the delivery company, he has mandatory overtime and of course this is their busiest time. From now until Christmas, I won't see him much."

Natalie refrained from pointing out that her brother-in-law could have taken family leave to be here for his wife, which was more important than any busy season at work.

She was fond of Travis, but wondered why he couldn't tell

that his wife was frightened right now and needed him more than she needed a few extra dollars from overtime.

"He leaves by seven in the morning," McKenna said, "and usually gets home around eight or nine, in time to maybe read a story to the girls and tuck them in. It's been that way since the first of November."

"That's a long day."

"Things will be better in the new year. After the holidays, he can take time off to be home with us."

McKenna yawned suddenly, her hand resting protectively over her abdomen.

Natalie pushed away her own exhaustion. "Why don't you rest for a bit, and I'll go rescue Liz from the girls. Then you can supervise from in here while I get them to bed."

McKenna yawned again. "Thanks, Nat. I don't know why I'm so tired, when I've been doing nothing but sitting around on my rapidly expanding butt for a week."

"What you're doing is hard work," she said. It frankly astonished her that any woman could make it through the miracle of pregnancy and childbirth.

"I guess," McKenna said, looking doubtful.

Still, she rested back against the pillow and closed her eyes and Natalie eased quietly out of the room, back into the hallway.

McKenna had truly made the apartment their own. She had painted all the walls a warm white and hung pictures of the girls at various stages of life in black frames along the hallway.

It was a restful space, filled with toys and personal mementos. Nat's duffel was still in the hallway where Griffin had set it. Natalie quickly picked it up and carried it to the room that had once been her brother's, the smallest of the rooms, on its own across the hall from the primary bedroom and next to the one she had shared with McKenna until Jake left for college.

Her sister likely intended to make this the baby's nursery at some point. The walls had already been painted a pale green, and a picture of a calming pastoral scene hung on the wall.

Natalie really wanted to stretch out on that plump-looking taupe daybed and crash, but she forced her eyes to stay open. She took her duffel inside and set it in the closet. The room was cozy and warm, but didn't quite compare to the seaside villa where she'd been staying on Lanzarote, with the two elderly cats and a parrot that swore up a blue streak.

She had been looking forward to spending a month there. But life had a way of changing priorities. Right now, her sister and her nieces needed her, and she knew she was exactly where she needed to be.

four

She had been a traveler long enough to know that the worst thing she could do for jet lag was to nap, as much as she wanted to. It was far better to keep active and perhaps go to bed a little bit early to reset her internal clock. She pushed through the fatigue and left her sister sleeping to go in search of Liz and the girls.

She rounded the corner on the way toward the swimming pool that took up most of the space in the center atrium—which sounded more grand than it actually was—and nearly collided with an elderly gentleman sporting a shock of white hair and a courtly looking mustache.

"Careful there," he said as he steadied her by grabbing her elbows. "Good to know I can still sweep a woman off her feet."

He beamed at her, and Natalie couldn't help giving a reluctant laugh.

"Have we met?" he asked, forehead furrowed as he released her. "You seem familiar, but I can't quite place you. I'm terribly sorry. Used to be I never forgot a woman's name. Just one more miserable thing about getting old."

He sounded so disheartened, she was quick to reassure him. "I don't believe we've met. I'm here visiting family. McKenna Dodd is my sister."

He nodded his understanding. "Well, that explains it, then. You look a little like your aunt Liz, especially around the eyes."

She felt a pang in her chest at his words. Not that she minded being compared to Aunt Liz, who was lovely and graceful, but it reminded her how people used to often say she looked like her mother, Liz's older sister.

The man thrust out a gnarled hand. "Calvin Wiggins. Cal. I live with my wife, Barbara, in 224."

"Hi, Cal. Pleasure to meet you. I'm Natalie Shepherd."

"And you're here to visit our McKenna and her family for the holidays? That will lift her spirits. We're all so worried about her and the baby. I understand she's on strict orders to stay in bed."

She was touched by the possessive pronoun he had used regarding McKenna.

"Her doctor is being extra cautious."

"And a good thing too. We can't have anything happen to the little man or to his mama. We all love her. She's the heart of this place."

"I love her too," she said with an answering smile.

"If you're looking for the girls, I saw them at the pool. My sweetheart Barbara likes to go in the evening to get her swim steps in. It's better on the knees once you get to our age."

"Good to know. Thanks for the info."

"When I was your age, I would hear that kind of advice and think it would never apply to me," Calvin said with a rueful expression. "Unfortunately, the day comes too soon when you only wish you could remember the various health advice people have given you over the years."

"Maybe I should start writing it all down now so I don't forget."

He smiled. "Not a bad idea. Not bad at all.

"Barbara forgot her swim goggles so she asked me to get them. I'm headed there now." He nodded back toward the pool. "I'll walk with you, if you don't mind."

"Sure."

"I don't suppose you need directions from me. If you're McKenna's sister, you must have grown up here at the Shelter Inn too."

In some ways, her childhood had been idyllic. She and McKenna had always been close, and the two of them and Jake used to have the run of the place.

They had loved swimming in the pool, playing hide-and-seek in the stairwells, making friends with all the staff.

She had not loved all of it, though.

She had hated the lack of privacy, feeling as if they never truly had their own space.

She used to resent that she and her family never had the chance to go on a vacation and see a little of the world, since their busiest times of year at the inn were invariably during school breaks. It was so hard to look at other families having fun and exploring the area together when her own family stayed right here at the Shelter Inn.

And they could never have a pet. She had always wanted a cat or a dog, but her parents used to say it didn't make sense when some of their guests might be allergic.

Sometimes Natalie used to wish they could live in a normal house like her friends did, with a backyard swing set and a treehouse and a garden rich with vegetables.

She still didn't live in a regular house, but she had certainly explored the world. And while she didn't have her own pet, she loved caring for the animals of others.

"I do know the way," she said now to Calvin. "But I wouldn't mind the company."

That seemed to thrill the man beyond words. He beamed at her and walked down the hall with all the gravitas of someone leading her on an exotic expedition.

A few things had changed since she had been here last, the previous spring. The tired old dark carpeting and dated wallpaper had been replaced with what looked like wood flooring and a fresh light paint that brightened the space immensely.

When they walked into the swimming pool area, Charlie bid her farewell and headed toward a group of swimmers in the deep end. The echo of conversation and the squeal of children's voices seemed to bounce off the walls and ceiling.

The girls were both playing in the small kiddie pool, watched over by an older woman in a polka-dot swimsuit and flowered swim cap that Natalie didn't know. Liz, she could see, was in the regular pool, hands against the side and her face focused on her rehab exercises.

The girls both shrieked even louder when they spotted her, and Nora scampered over and wrapped wet arms around her leg.

"Aunt Nat! You should watch me. I can swim. Want to see?"

"Absolutely."

"You can't swim. You're only little," Hazel, all of two years older, informed her in a bossy tone.

"Can too. Watch me."

Nora jumped into the kiddie pool, plopped down with her belly resting on the bottom of the shallow pool and started waving her arms up and down.

"That's not swimming," Hazel retorted. "That's just kicking your feet and shaking your arms. Swimming is like this."

Hazel moved to a slightly deeper area of the pool, went on her belly in the pool and started moving her arms. The only difference was that the water was slightly deeper and Hazel kicked her legs, propelling herself forward almost by accident.

It was obvious they had spent considerable time enjoying the pool.

"You're both very good."

"You should put your suit on and swim with us."

"I'm fine watching for now."

Even if she had a suit handy, Natalie was afraid that if she slid into that warm water, she would fall fast asleep.

"Actually, you can swim for a few more moments, then I need your help back at home unloading my bag."

"Okay," Nora said happily.

They returned to splashing each other and being silly. Natalie had to smile, listening to them play. They really were cute girls. After a moment, Liz climbed carefully out and walked up the ramp entry to the pool, a towel around her middle.

"Are you good if I go change and take off back to my place?" she asked. "It's been a really long day."

No. She wasn't. She had no idea how to care for these two wriggly little girls who seemed to have far more energy than she did, even on her best day.

"That's fine," she finally answered. What else could she say?

Liz smiled. "Thanks, honey. I'll see you tomorrow after my physical therapy."

Assuming they all survived the night. Natalie fought down panic as she watched her aunt hobble with her crutches into the dressing room next to the swimming pool. She was just about to call the girls to come out when a woman with gray curls, thick glasses and a walker came into the pool area, took one look at Nat and made her slow way over to sit down beside her.

"It's about time you came home," she said, her voice gruff.

Natalie blinked at the presumptuous stranger.

Who wasn't a stranger, she quickly realized.

"Mrs. Mulcahy." She forced a smile. "I didn't know you lived at the Shelter Inn."

The woman gave a sour nod. "Six months now. My daughter made me sell the house over on Sugar Maple Drive. Said I couldn't handle all those stairs any longer and was likely to break a hip trying. Just shows what she knows."

She knew the woman's daughter, not a spring chicken herself. Janice Mulcahy had taught her in second grade. Mabel, Janice's mother, used to own the dime store and small grocery not far from the elementary school, where all the children bought soda and candy on their way to and from school.

Mabel had been their sugar dealer, which Natalie found highly ironic as the woman was about as far from sweet as she could imagine.

She used to glower at every child who walked in, as if she expected them all to fill their pockets with her merchandise.

"Your sister needs you," Mabel said bluntly.

Natalie let out a breath, too tired to deal with crusty senior citizens who thought they knew how the whole world should manage their lives.

"Yes. I know. That's why I'm here."

"I hope this means you're going to help out with running our booth at the Shelter Springs Holiday Giving Market."

"The what now?"

Mabel huffed out a breath. "The booth your sister usually organizes for us. You know."

McKenna and Liz had told her something about the Shelter Inn residents organizing a stall for charity at the town's holiday market. But since she hadn't been in town for Christmas in a dozen years, she couldn't be expected to know every detail about it.

"Does the stall do well at the market?"

"Yes. We raise thousands of dollars for charity. This year we're giving to Make-A-Wish."

"I haven't been to the market in years," Natalie admitted.

"It's nice, if you're into that sort of thing."

Natalie suspected Mabel wasn't into anything of the sort. The woman didn't strike her as particularly festive. If Nat remembered correctly, Mabel hadn't hung so much as a paper snowflake in her sweet shop.

"We work all year to make items for our booth. Ten percent of the sales from every single booth goes to a charity picked by the Shelter Springs Foundation, but we give a hundred percent of our profits."

That sounded very much like something Liz and McKenna would endorse.

"That's nice."

"Everyone needs to give back."

Mrs. Mulcahy glowered at Natalie, as if daring her to disagree.

"True," she said. How could she argue with that?

"Are you going to help us or not? We need more people to work at our stall, especially with your sister out of commission."

Mabel gave her an expectant look that had Natalie squirming.

"I expect I'll have my hands full with the girls," she finally said. "They are the reason I'm here, not to work at a booth at the Christmas market."

Mabel's disapproval seemed to splash over her like the noise from the pool. She sniffed. "I might have guessed you would say that. You never loved Shelter Springs like your mother or your sister, did you? That's why you were in such a big hurry to leave."

She had to admit there was some truth to that. She associated her hometown with loss and pain, memories that still made her ache. She had lost nearly everyone she loved here. Everyone but Liz and McKenna.

Mabel rose, as if she had said what she wanted to say and didn't want to waste another moment of her own valuable time with a loser like Natalie. She gave another sniff and stalked away, her walker thumping with force on the concrete.

Surely she could help a little bit with the Shelter Inn stall. Maybe she would have a few hours free after the girls went to bed. While she didn't really want to spend those free hours sitting at a noisy stall, it was for a good cause.

She didn't have to decide anything at this moment, when she was running on willpower and caffeine alone. After she had time to rest and form a routine with the girls over the next few days, she would have a better idea whether she could squeeze in some volunteer work.

Right now, she had to figure out how to get the girls out of the pool and back to their apartment with only a modicum of drama.

By the time she managed to get the girls fed, bathed and tucked into bed two hours later, Nat was about ready to fall over.

She wanted to crawl into her room and flop onto the bed for the next three or four days.

Too bad she still had things to do.

After closing the door to the girls' bedroom, painted a soft lilac color, with two twin beds separated by a charming dollhouse that looked handmade, Nat made her way through the apartment to the master bedroom. She knocked softly and heard McKenna's low-voiced response urging her to come in.

She pushed open the door and frowned when she found Kenna's eyes wet and her nose red. Rumpled tissues cluttered the bed next to her.

Okay. She wouldn't be able to sleep yet.

She hurried toward the bed. "What's going on? Is it the baby? Are you hurting somewhere?"

Kenna sniffled. "No. Nothing has happened. I'm sorry. You must think I'm such a mess. I can't even take care of two children, let alone three."

"Travis still isn't home?"

McKenna picked up another tissue and blew into it noisily. "No. Not yet."

"It's past eight." And she had now been up for thirty hours straight, except for a brief, fitful nap on the plane.

McKenna gave a helpless-looking shrug. "This time of year, it could be eight, it could be midnight. I just never know."

Was her brother-in-law really working all that time or did

he have another reason to stay away from his daughters and his pregnant, stressed wife?

She didn't want to think about the alternatives. From what she had always seen, Travis Dodd seemed to adore McKenna and the girls. She couldn't imagine him betraying her sister's trust by seeing someone else.

Still, she couldn't help but wonder.

"Is there anything I can do?" she asked. "Do you need anything? More water? A treat from the kitchen?"

"No. I'm fine." Her sister gave a smile that looked forced. "I feel so *extra* right now. The closer I get to having the baby, the more emotional I become."

"It's only natural, especially now that you're in bed. Don't ever worry about venting to me. I'm your sister. It's my job."

"It's not. None of this is. But I'm so grateful you're here. I don't know how I'll ever repay you."

Natalie sat on the edge of the bed. "Speaking of jobs, I got an earful tonight from Mabel Mulcahy about the Shelter Inn booth at the Shelter Springs Holiday Giving Market."

Kenna wiped at her nose, an expression halfway between dismay and begrudging amusement.

"Did you?"

"Yes. She basically told me I'm obligated to fill in for you while you're down with the pregnancy."

"Oh, that Mabel. She can be such a pistol. Whenever she gets wound up about something, I've learned to just smile and nod my head."

"Well, apparently I don't care about Shelter Springs as much as you and Mom did or I would step up to volunteer my time."

"Tell me she didn't really say that."

When Natalie didn't answer, McKenna rolled her eyes. "I'm so sorry. Mabel needs to learn to mind her own beeswax. You really don't need to volunteer. I'm sure the other residents can fill in for me."

"I don't remember the market being a big deal. It was around when I was a kid, but hardly anybody ever went to it. What's changed?"

McKenna smiled slightly. "Around the time I was pregnant with Hazel, a few members of the chamber of commerce got together and decided our neighbor to the south was outdoing us in the generosity and community spirit department. You may remember that Haven Point has a big gift fair the same weekend as the Lights on the Lake Festival, and then the town donates the profits to some organization or other."

"That's nice."

"Right. But you know how much of a rivalry we have with Haven Point. So the chamber of commerce decided we can do better. We'll show them. We'll have a European-style Christmas market for almost two weeks, before and after the Lights on the Lake Festival, with kiosks, concerts and food. It's become a whole thing."

"That's...nice?" She couldn't think of another adjective.

"I've been on the entertainment committee for a few years, helping to vet and hire performers for the stage at the market and a few other venues in town, like churches and the library auditorium. Amanda Taylor runs the whole thing now."

Natalie felt tension squeeze her shoulders again. This was the second time in one evening that Amanda's name had come up.

Griffin Taylor's sister.

The woman Jake had loved.

It didn't surprise her at all to hear that Amanda was busy behind the scenes of the town. She had always followed her grandmother Birdie's example, volunteering her time to help others.

Natalie remembered when they were in high school, when Amanda had always stepped up to lead some dance committee or school fundraiser.

She used to admire that about her friend. Now it just made

her feel guilty. Amanda always had been kind to her, yet Natalie had pushed her completely out of her life after Jake's death.

"What's Amanda doing these days?"

"She has a store over on River Road now. The Lucky Goat. They have the best lotions and bath bombs. I think maybe I sent you some for your birthday last year."

"Oh, right." She had been staying in a small Paris apartment at the time with a minuscule shower and no tub, so she had given the bath bombs to an expat friend.

"I still use the lotion. It smells delicious. Like vanilla pods and jasmine."

"She makes some of her own products, but then she also has a consortium of women around town who help her. Usually young mothers who need another income stream from something they can do at home. Some of my friends do it."

More guilt pinched at her. She had not treated Amanda well in those days after Jake's death, had chosen to shut her out instead of leaning together to share their pain.

"Anyway, when Liz and I decided to convert the Shelter Inn to senior apartments, our first residents urged us to host a craft booth at the market. Now everyone gets so excited, and they work on their projects all year. I'm usually in charge of organizing it and making sure we're staffed throughout the market, but I'll admit, I've had such a tough time with this pregnancy that I've kind of dropped the ball this year. I was hoping we could maybe skip it this year and let someone else use our booth space. Apparently, the residents revolted and decided to organize themselves. I think Birdie Lovell has kind of taken charge."

"Mabel apparently has strong feelings about it."

"Don't listen to her. I'm sure you don't need to volunteer."

Right now the idea of working in a hectic, crowded market listening to every possible rendition of "Jingle Bells" sounded miserable, but she might feel differently after she'd been able to rest.

McKenna yawned again, and Natalie took that as her cue to stand up again. "Can I grab you anything before I head to bed?"

Her sister shook her head. "I'm fine. Travis will be home any moment, I'm sure. I'll just read for a while until he's back."

All of her misgivings came flooding back. Why wasn't he home already? As busy as the man might be, managing a busy delivery service warehouse during the holidays, his pregnant, frightened wife needed him.

She said nothing, only smiled at her sister. "Get some rest. In the morning, you can walk me through everything I need to do with the girls in the course of an average day."

"Oh boy. That's going to take us some time."

"I'm ready," she lied.

McKenna squeezed her hand with both of hers. "Thank you again for dropping everything and coming home. You are the best big sister, Nat. Seriously."

She wasn't, or she would have come back before now. How could she be too annoyed with her brother-in-law when Natalie hadn't been here for McKenna, either?

"You know where to find me if you need anything in the night."

"I do. Good night. Try to get some rest. I'm afraid you're going to need it."

Given how the girls had worn her out after only a few hours this evening, she had no doubt that dealing with them all day would be far more exhausting than twenty straight hours of travel.

five

How did mothers do this day in and day out?

By noon the next day, Natalie had broken up five fights between the girls over toys, changed Nora's clothes twice—once for a toileting accident and once for a bloody nose—fixed lopsided Mickey Mouse pancakes that looked more like Mutant Mouse, cleaned syrup off the wall, washed and dried four loads of laundry and talked to the garage and the rental car agency about the repairs needed from her little escapade the night before.

She needed a nap…or maybe a monthlong cruise to Tahiti.

She wanted to think she was starting to get the hang of her responsibilities, but apparently things really could go from bad to worse.

"Sorry. Could you repeat that?"

Maybe she had misheard Hazel. *Please, God, let her have misheard Hazel.*

"I said," the older girl replied, emphasizing her words loudly, "Nora has a bloody nose again. I think it's from the jingle bell she stuck up her nose yesterday that won't come out."

Her sister stood beside her, holding a wad of spotted tissue to her nose and looking vaguely panicky.

"It hurts," she said, her trouble with *R*s making it sound like "Hoowts."

A jingle bell. Up her nose. Great.

"Where did she get a jingle bell?" Especially one small enough to fit up the tiny nostrils of a three-year-old?

Hazel looked away, not meeting Natalie's gaze. "We didn't steal it, I promise. We found it."

"Found it where?"

"Outside Mrs. Mulcahy's door. I don't think she wanted it. It was on the ground."

What on earth was the woman thinking to leave jingle bells around for anybody to find? Natalie suddenly remembered the evening before on her trip to the pool when she and her new friend Cal had walked past several apartment doors that sported holiday decorations. One of those must have been Mabel Mulcahy's, and the decor must have included at least one jingle bell that had gone astray...and ended up in her niece's nose.

"How big is it? Do you know?"

Hazel held her fingers about an inch apart and then drew them together to make a space that was roughly pea-sized.

"Not very big. It was silver and round and cute. Like a little jingle bell for dolls."

In other words, the perfect size to go up the nose of a preschooler.

"Did you try blowing your nose?" she asked the younger girl desperately.

Nora shook her head.

"Let's do that," Nat suggested, lifting out a clean tissue from the box she had noticed earlier on a shelf in the kitchen. She offered the tissue to her niece and Nora held it to her face, making a big noisy show of trying to blow her nose. Unfortunately, she was only blowing air out of her mouth, as far as Natalie could tell.

It was quite adorable, but not really helpful in their current predicament.

"Let's go see your mom. She can probably walk us through what to do."

The girls had spent time that morning on their mother's bed doing sticker books and watching a holiday movie with her, but McKenna had been tired and not feeling well so Natalie had rescued her about an hour earlier, taking the girls out so she could nap.

Now she rapped softly on the door and pushed it open to find McKenna still sleeping on her side, her hand cradling her swollen belly with a protectiveness that gave Natalie a sharp pang.

For most of her adult life, Natalie had told herself she didn't want children, a family, the whole traditional picture that McKenna had embraced so beautifully.

The idea of trusting someone else with her heart seemed completely impossible.

Every once in a while, though, she yearned for something... more. Someone to share her adventures with, to lean on when the world felt overwhelming.

Maybe a child to love, who couldn't leave her.

She pushed away the completely unrealistic ache as McKenna opened her eyes, still cloudy with sleep, and tried to sit up.

"I'm sorry to wake you." Natalie moved farther into the room.

"It's okay. I'm awake. What's up?"

"We have a little crisis that's way above my pay grade. Nora apparently has a jingle bell stuck up her nose."

McKenna stared, swiping at her eyes with the heels of her hands. "She what?"

"I know. I couldn't believe it, either. A jingle bell. A cute little one, just right for a doll, apparently. I tried to get her to blow it out, but we're not having any luck. I'm afraid to go after it with tweezers or something for fear I could push it up higher."

"That can happen," McKenna said. "Remember that time I put popcorn up my nose and Dad had to take me to our pediatrician?"

"Right. That was traumatic." For both of them, mainly because their mother had refused to make popcorn for about a month. A true tragedy, in Natalie's opinion.

"It's Saturday, though," McKenna said. "I'm afraid our pediatrician's office will be closed."

"Should I take her to the emergency room?"

"I'm not sure that's quite necessary. What about urgent care?"

"Does Shelter Springs have an urgent care clinic?"

"Yes. A great one that we share with Haven Point. It's next to the new hospital, between our two towns."

When she was a kid, they used to have to drive an hour away to the nearest hospital. As the community around Lake Haven started to grow, more medical facilities opened to serve the increased population.

"I would suggest starting at urgent care. I'm sure they can take care of it there."

"Good plan."

"You'll need our insurance info. It should be in my purse. I'll write a quick note saying you have my permission to seek medical care for her, but they can always call me if there are any issues."

How about the issue that Natalie really didn't want to deal with a jingle bell nostril extraction?

She told herself to suck it up and went in search of McKenna's purse. After she found it hanging from a doorknob in the master closet, she handed it to her sister, who rooted through until she found an insurance card in her wallet as well as a set of keys.

"Your rental is still in the shop so you'll have to take my SUV. That's better anyway, so you don't have to move any car seats."

"Sounds good."

"You can leave Hazel here with me."

"Are you sure you're up to that? She's been kind of restless for the past hour," she said, though privately she thought that was an understatement, rather like calling a squirrel who accidentally drank an entire can of Red Bull restless.

McKenna nodded. "We will be fine. Hazel is always much calmer one-on-one. Both girls are. I think they feed off each other."

She had to agree with that, given her experience that day.

After settling her older niece in with her mother, along with several Christmas storybooks, a tablet and the remote to the TV, she helped Nora into her coat. The girl's nose continued to bleed, so they packed along the entire box of tissues from the house.

It took a minute to figure out the car seat situation and which strap went where, as if she needed something else to make her feel inadequate.

Finally, Nora was loaded, still dripping away, and Natalie programmed her phone navigation to find the urgent care clinic.

When she reached her destination, she parked in front and helped Nora out. The girl handed her the bloodstained tissue.

"Um. Thanks," she said, plucking out a clean one from the box and switching it out.

When they walked into the waiting room, Natalie was relieved to find it sparsely populated, empty except for a teenage girl in a beanie and parka sitting in a wheelchair with her leg extended—ski injury, she guessed—along with an older woman next to her, knitting something in green and red.

A wall television played an animated holiday special, and a Christmas tree decorated with blue and silver ornaments took up one corner of the waiting room.

It was already the first Saturday in December and McKenna's apartment didn't have any Christmas decorations up, Natalie realized with some degree of shock.

That was something she and the girls could do to cheer up their mother. Maybe they could even find a little tree to put up in Travis and McKenna's bedroom, to help bring a little holiday spirit to her.

They would definitely not hang up any ornaments with small pieces that could become lodged in nasal cavities.

She and Nora approached the reception desk, the girl still sniffling into her tissue.

"May I help you?" The receptionist wore dangly earrings and a blue-and-white sweater. She matched the festive decorations in the room to perfection, though Natalie was quite sure that was unintentional.

"Yes. Thank you. I'm afraid we have a bit of a jingle bell emergency."

"A jingle bell emergency?" The woman gave her a blank look.

Natalie inclined her head toward her niece. "Yes. Apparently she shoved one up her nose."

The woman's eyes widened with a combination of surprise and amusement, though she quickly veiled her reaction. Natalie expected she might find the whole situation a little more funny if not for Nora's obvious distress…and if she weren't the responsible adult in this situation.

"Oh dear," the woman said. "Has she been seen at one of the facilities in our network before?"

"I have no idea. I'm her aunt. I do have her insurance information and a permission slip to receive treatment, signed by her mother. My sister is pregnant and on bed rest, so I'm the designated caregiver."

The receptionist took the card from her, gave it a quick look, then her smile widened. "Oh. Your sister is McKenna Dodd. You must be Natalie."

"I… Yes."

How did she know her, when Natalie had no clue who the woman was?

"I'm Jane Logan. I worked with McKenna last year on a couple of committees for the holiday market. She talked about you quite a bit. I understand you live all over the world. How exciting!"

Natalie wasn't sure how she was supposed to respond to that. "Nice to meet you," she finally said.

"Is this Nora or Hazel? I can never quite keep them straight. I'm sorry."

"I'm No-wah," the girl said through her tissue, sounding as if she was squeezing her nose shut with her fingers.

"Hello, Nora. We should be able to get you back to see the doctor right away. You've got good timing and are lucky you came when you did. We had a frantic morning, but things have calmed down considerably."

She looked around at the mostly empty waiting area. "Thank you."

"Go ahead and have a seat and a medical assistant should call you soon."

They sat not far from the door. A few moments later, after the girl in the wheelchair was called back, a woman in coral scrubs with a name tag that read Keri called out Nora's name.

After leading them to a treatment room, the woman checked Nora's temperature and blood pressure and entered some information into a computer monitor there.

"The doctor should be right in," she said with a reassuring smile. "He's with the patient just ahead of you. Hang tight."

"Don't want doctor. Want Mama," Nora said, sniffling, after the medical assistant left the exam room, closing the door behind her.

Poor little thing. Her entire routine had been thrown out of whack by her mother's precarious pregnancy, and now she had a medical trauma on top of everything else. Natalie didn't blame her for being done with it all.

She wasn't sure how to calm her. All her feelings of inadequacy came rushing back. Shouldn't this be instinctive? Maybe she was completely missing the maternal gene.

"Don't cry, sweetheart," she finally said feebly, pulling the girl onto her lap. "Why don't we read one of these stories? Do you want to hear the one about the dinosaur or the mouse with the glasses?"

"Neither," Nora said on a wail.

"But look how cute the mouse is. She's wearing a tutu like you have."

"My tutu is purple. That one is green."

"Is it?"

Nora nodded her head vigorously. "Hazel has a pink one. I want Hazel. And my mommy," she said, sobbing now.

Feeling wholly ineffectual, Natalie did her best to offer comfort, but the girl was still quietly crying when the door opened.

Natalie looked up and wanted to sob herself. She had never been so happy to see anyone in her life as she was to find Griffin Taylor in the doorway.

He looked tall and gorgeous, in a pale blue striped dress shirt and tailored tan pants, with an ID badge clipped to his pocket and a stethoscope around his neck.

She wanted to sink into his arms and sob like Nora.

He took one look at the situation, closed the door behind him and approached the little girl.

"Hi there, Nora. I'm Dr. Taylor. Griffin. Remember me?"

Nora stopped sniffling and lifted her face from Natalie's now-soggy shirt.

"My grandma Birdie is your neighbor," he said in a calm voice. "She lives at the Shelter Inn with you."

Nora swiped at her dripping eyes. "Birdie is my friend," she said, though it sounded like *Boodie is my fwend.*

"How about that? She's my friend too. She's the best grandma in the whole wide world."

"Birdie makes good cookies."

"She does, doesn't she? What kind is your favorite?"

"I like the stars."

"Those sugar cookie stars she makes. Yum. Me too. I also like the peanut butter cookies with the chocolate kisses. And the chocolate chip. And the lemon bars. Do you know that when I was away at school to become a doctor, Grandma Birdie used to send me a new box of cookies every month, because she knew how much I love them."

"Hazel and me like to visit Birdie because she always gives us a cookie."

"Can I tell you a secret? Sometimes that's why I go visit her too."

Natalie fell a little in love with him in that moment, not just because of his story, but because of the reassuring smile he gave to Nora and the slow, even tone of his voice, effective at calming scared little girls and their nervous aunts in equal measures.

"I didn't know you worked at urgent care," Natalie said after a moment.

"All the doctors in the area take a turn so we can keep it staffed. It works out to about once or twice a month."

He turned to Nora. "I understand we have a jingle bell causing some trouble."

"Bell in my nose. Hurts." Tears welled up again in those big blue eyes as she pointed to the general area.

"That won't do. Jingle bells aren't allowed in noses. Will you let me take a look at it?"

Nora turned her face into Natalie's shirt again as if to hide away from his attention, but after a moment, she turned back and nodded slowly.

"Do you need her on the exam table?" Natalie asked, pitching her voice low to match Griffin's.

"She should be good right there on your lap, at least for now."

He sat on the rolling chair in the exam room and slid closer to them. When he did, Natalie could smell him, that same leather and pine and cedar she had noticed the night before in his pickup truck. He had his shirtsleeves rolled up a little, and she could see a dusting of dark hair on his forearms that gave her a strange little tingle.

Natalie wanted to roll her eyes at herself. It seemed wildly inappropriate to be experiencing the yums for the medical professional who was helping out her niece.

"Can you look up at the ceiling?" Griffin asked. "I've got this funny flashlight that will help me take a look in there."

He pulled the tool off the wall and showed it to Nora. After she angled her head up, her hair brushing Natalie's chin, he leaned over closer to peer into her nostril.

"That's definitely a jingle bell. It's wedged up there pretty high."

"Will you be able to get it out?" Nat asked, envisioning the Jaws of Life or a major surgical procedure.

"Fingers crossed."

He offered up another reassuring smile, this one from so close to her that she felt ridiculously breathless.

The man was entirely too gorgeous for his own good. That smile probably sent the hearts of all the women in Shelter Springs aflutter. She wouldn't be surprised if every woman he treated ended up with situational high blood pressure. She could certainly feel her pulse in her ears.

She didn't draw in a full breath until he finally rolled away from them again on the stool and gave her niece a solemn look. "I am positive we can get it out without too much trouble. Nora, can you be super brave and lay down on my special jingle bell removal table?"

She could feel the tension tighten her niece's shoulders, and the girl trembled a little in Natalie's arms.

"It's okay. I'll be right here," Natalie said. "I can hold your hand, if you want."

She lifted Nora onto the table and helped her lie down. Her niece gripped Natalie's hand tightly in both of hers as Griffin reached into a drawer and pulled out a small disposable bin with a clear cover that he pulled back to reveal sterile tweezers, gauze and scissors.

"This won't take long," he promised Nora, positioning a flexible light overhead.

He picked up the tweezers in his gloved hand. "This won't hurt, but I need you to hold really still. Can you pretend you're a statue?"

Nora nodded and froze into an almost comical grimace.

"Perfect. Okay. You're going to feel a little pressure."

A moment later, he inserted the tweezers into her nostril, his brow furrowed with concentration, then he quickly withdrew them, the tweezers wrapped around a small metal circle covered in mucus and blood.

"Success!" he said. "I'm going to assume you don't want to keep it," he said to Natalie with a sideways smile.

"I would be happy if I never saw a jingle bell again," she answered truthfully.

He tossed it into a nearby garbage can, where it hit the inside with a clink.

"Your nose might be a little sore for a couple of days. Don't stick anything else up there, okay? Nothing belongs up your nose. Not even fingers."

Nora screwed up her face in disgust, which made Natalie laugh and hug the girl.

"Thank you," she told Griffin.

"No problem. I'm glad it was something relatively easy to handle. I have to admit, I've seen weirder things stuck in people's various orifices."

"I'm not sure I want to know."

"You definitely don't."

He helped Nora down off the table. "Because you were so brave, you get to pick something out of our prize basket. I can have Nurse Keri show it to you on your way out."

He led them out of the exam room to the nurses' station, where the same woman who had helped them earlier approached them carrying a basket overflowing with small toys and healthy treats.

Nora took a good five minutes to decide which she wanted, looking through every single offering before ultimately choosing a small stuffed puppy that Natalie was certain Hazel would covet.

"Thanks again," she said to Griffin, fighting an overwhelming urge to give him a hug of gratitude, which she knew would be inappropriate on several levels.

"All in a day's work. Again, it could have been worse. I'm glad it was relatively simple to dislodge. How's McKenna doing today?"

"I wish I could say great. I'm worried about her. She seems so tired all the time."

"I'm sure her OB is keeping a close eye on things. It's good you can be there to help."

She thought again of Travis, whom she still hadn't set eyes on since arriving the day before. She had been in bed when he came home, and he had left the apartment again before she heard the girls wake up.

She wanted to confide her concerns in Griffin, but that also didn't seem appropriate, here in a busy urgent care office.

"What about you? How are you settling in now that you're back in Shelter Springs?"

"Swell. I've been back less than twenty-four hours and we've only had one trip to urgent care. I'm taking that as a win."

His laughter warmed far more than it should have. For some ridiculous reason, she wanted to close her eyes and bask in it, like feeling the sun on her face after a long, cold winter.

She did her best to clamp down on her reaction. What was the point? Nothing would come of it, and she would likely end up making a fool of herself over him.

As soon as McKenna gave birth and didn't need her help anymore, Natalie was heading back to her nomadic life.

"That nose might be tender for a few days," he said. "Don't panic if she has another nosebleed. Or two or three."

"Got it. I hope we don't have to see you again."

"Ouch."

She felt her cheeks color. "I meant professionally."

"I'm glad you clarified that, since I'm sure I'll see you around."

He turned again to Nora. "Bye, Nora. Save a few of my grandma's cookies for me, okay?"

She smiled shyly at him. "Bye, Dr. Jingle."

His eyebrows rose at the name, but he said nothing, only waved at them both and headed off to his next patient, leaving Natalie feeling as if the sun had just gone behind the clouds.

six

After they left the urgent care clinic, she checked in with McKenna to let her know what had happened and then decided to make a stop at the grocery store.

While her sister's kitchen and pantry were well-stocked, she wanted to pick up a few things so she could whip up one of the foods that used to be McKenna's favorite, minestrone soup.

With Nora in the cart, she rolled through the aisles trying to locate items on her list. The grocery store had been built a few years ago and was larger than she expected, with a big selection of gourmet food items and a well-stocked deli.

She was checking out a section of ready-made items, trying to think of things her sister might enjoy eating, when she heard someone call her name.

She looked up to find Holly Goodwin, a dear friend, pushing a cart toward her from the opposite direction.

"Natalie Shepherd! It is you! I spotted you when I was going past the cereal aisle and thought I had to be imagining things. What are you doing in town? And why haven't you called me or Hannah to let us know?"

She hugged the other woman, who always reminded her of a blonde pixie with her short wispy hair and her custom jewelry.

They had once been a formidable foursome. Holly, her twin

sister, Hannah; Natalie and Amanda Taylor. Griffin's sister. Amanda had been a year older, but because she lived on the same street as the Goodwin sisters, they were all close friends.

In high school, they had played on the volleyball team together, worked on the yearbook staff, went on group dates to school dances, hung out after school.

They had been her support system, first when her mom was diagnosed with cancer and then when Jeanette ultimately lost the battle. They again had rallied around her and McKenna after her father walked away from his responsibilities.

She still stayed in touch with Holly and Hannah, though not with Amanda.

"I'm sorry. I've only been in town a day and it was a last-minute trip. I haven't had time to reach out yet, but I planned to, I promise."

"No worries," Holly said. "How long are you in town? We have to get together!"

"A while. Through Christmas, at least. Maybe into the new year. I'm here to help McKenna, who was put on strict bed rest last week."

Holly's gamine features twisted into an expression of concern. "I hadn't heard that. Oh man. How's she doing? That can't be easy with those busy girls of hers. Is she up for visitors?"

She wasn't sure if the doctor had given any rules about that, but decided to err on the side of what she thought would be best for her sister.

"I'm sure she would love it. She's feeling pretty down. A visit might help cheer her up."

"I just saw her a few weeks ago at the bookstore, and she didn't say a word about any problem with the pregnancy."

"This is a fairly new development, apparently. She's having some issues with her blood pressure that came on about a week ago. The doctor is concerned about preeclampsia."

"I'll pretend I know what that is," Holly said.

"Pregnancy-related high blood pressure, which isn't good for her or the baby."

"When is she due?"

"Not for another six weeks. The doctor wants to keep the baby in as long as possible. Even a day or two makes all the difference, apparently."

"Look at you, becoming a certified nurse-midwife overnight."

"I wish. I'm the last person a pregnant woman probably wants on her team. I've been here one day and we've already had to make an emergency trip to urgent care after an unfortunate jingle bell incident."

Holly laughed, reaching out to hug her again.

"Oh, I've missed you!" she exclaimed.

The physical contact unexpectedly made Natalie's throat feel tight.

She could tell herself she loved being on her own, living her best wanderer life and traveling from country to country. She *did* love it, learning about new cultures and enjoying food that she likely would never have heard of, living here in Shelter Springs, Idaho.

But there was something undeniably comforting in a hug from an old and dear friend. It connected her to the person she used to be, young and fun and filled with possibilities. Before grief and heartache had left its indelible mark on her soul.

"I've missed you too," she said.

"We have to get together while you're in town! Seriously. When can we hang out? I know Hannah will be thrilled you're back for a few weeks."

"My schedule isn't really my own right now. I'm here to help McKenna, and I'm not sure I would feel right about going off partying when she needs me."

"Then we should take the party to Kenna! Let me talk to Hannah and Amanda. We can all come hang out with her too. Nothing strenuous, just friends enjoying the holidays together."

Amanda again.

She wasn't sure she wanted to see the woman who had broken her brother's heart, when Jake had already been lost and struggling after their mother's death and their father's desertion.

She had a feeling Amanda and the Goodwin sisters were a package deal, though. They had obviously still stayed close.

"I'll have to let you know, once I have the chance to settle in a little more."

"I'm going to hold you to that. Amanda will be busy with the holiday market, but I'm sure she can squeeze out an evening to spend with you and McKenna."

"Aunt Nat," Nora suddenly interrupted. "I need to pee. Bad."

"Oh my." Holly grinned. "That sounds like an emergency situation."

"Yeah. I'd better…" She gestured to the girl and toward the store restrooms, which she had noticed near the canned goods.

Holly kissed her cheek. "I'll be in touch. I'm really so glad you're home, Nat. I can't wait to hear about all the sexy guys you've met on your adventures."

That would be a very short conversation. Natalie didn't like thinking that the sexiest guy she had interacted with in a long time just happened to be the newest doctor in Shelter Springs.

seven

The absolute last thing Griffin felt like doing after a long day in clinic was spending two hours being grilled by his grandmother's book club about all their ailments.

As he pulled away from the small building he shared with a pediatrician and another doctor of family medicine, Griffin reminded himself this was all part of living in a small town.

He had become the de facto medical adviser to most of the people he knew, who tended to ask him for free advice everywhere he went, from the gym to the grocery store to his rare outings to his favorite tavern.

He usually didn't mind, but he had worked a long shift at his own clinic that day after a stint at the urgent care clinic on Saturday and another long shift on Sunday, filling in for a friend in the emergency department at the hospital.

Hanging out with a bunch of older residents at the Shelter Inn, talking about the latest self-help book on how to live your best life into your seventies and beyond, wasn't his idea of a good time.

Maybe Natalie would be there.

The thought pushed at him as he turned onto Main Street, where a big sign encouraged people to attend the holiday giving market when it opened the following week.

Would he see her at the Shelter Inn?

Griffin was uncomfortably aware of a small tingle of anticipation. He hadn't been able to stop thinking about her since seeing her a few days before at the urgent care clinic with her niece.

He smiled, remembering the gentle, reassuring care she had provided her niece, exactly what the frightened girl had needed.

Natalie and her green eyes and soft, lovely features had haunted his dreams since he had encountered her on a snowy road outside of town.

He again felt that little rush of anticipation and did his best to ignore it. He likely wouldn't see her. Why would he? She didn't need to attend a book club with a bunch of the Shelter Inn residents, discussing how to create healthier habits.

He expected he would spend much of the night answering questions about bunions, high cholesterol and osteoarthritis. Definitely not topics that would be of interest to Natalie.

He found the depth of his disappointment disconcerting. If he wanted to see her that badly, he supposed he could always drop in at her sister's apartment, using the excuse of checking in on his patient with the extracted jingle bell.

The memory made him smile. Her niece was adorable. He didn't think he would soon forget her relieved delight when he had pulled out the bell and tossed it away.

Maybe if the book club finished at a reasonable hour, he could stop by quickly, if only to put his mind at ease that Nora hadn't experienced any further complications.

He pulled into the parking lot at the Shelter Inn and parked in his grandmother's spot.

When he walked toward the doors leading to the lobby, he spotted someone trying to stake down a small inflatable Santa Claus, aided by two small, bundled-up girls who were chattering away.

He made his way around several large plastic totes that lined the sidewalk.

He moved closer to her. "Need a hand?"

She looked up from the ground, a rubber mallet dangling from her fingers.

"Oh. Griffin. Um. Hi. What are you doing here?"

He gave Natalie a wry smile. "Birdie is hosting her book group in the common room. They read a book about living your best life and she asked me to come and talk to them about a few small changes they could make in the new year, especially when it comes to mental health and everyday stresses."

"Like the everyday stress of trying to fix a stupid inflatable Santa, for instance?"

"Santa's not stupid," the older of her nieces said with an alarmed look. "You better not say that or he might put you on the naughty list."

"He's not. But these decorations definitely are."

"You know, one of my best tips for living your best life is to accept help when people offer it."

She huffed out a breath and rose, mallet outstretched. "Have at it, Dr. Taylor."

He looked at her and then at the deflated Santa, as well as the stakes she was trying to drive into frozen ground. Maybe he should have offered to help her with something at which he could actually claim some small level of expertise. Inflatable Santas definitely were not on that list.

But he had pitched plenty of tents in his day. How different could this be?

He grabbed the mallet and bent down to drive in the four stakes securing the inflatable with several sharp blows.

When he was certain it wasn't going anywhere, no matter how stiff the wind, he turned back to Natalie and her nieces.

"Okay. Want to plug it in?"

"Desperately," she said dryly.

"I can do it," her older niece said.

"I will," she answered firmly. "You two stand back and watch the Santa come to life."

She grabbed the cord and inserted the plug into an outlet by the front door. A moment later, the Santa rose from the ground as if by magic.

"It's Santa! You did it!" The older girl clapped her hands together. Her sister joined in, both of them beaming, and Griffin felt quite accomplished.

"I love it!" Nora exclaimed.

"His belly looks like Mommy's." The other girl—Hazel, he remembered—giggled. "Does he have a baby inside too?"

Natalie hid her smile. "No. Maybe he just needs to hear Dr. Taylor talk about healthy habits."

"Maybe he ate too many of Birdie's cookies," Nora said.

Griffin tried not to wince, since he knew he was guilty of that particular habit. "That is a distinct possibility," he said.

"We love Birdie's cookies. Don't we?" To his surprise, Nora came up to him and slipped her little mittened hand into his.

"We definitely do."

"You should try them," Hazel said to her aunt. "They're delicious."

"I don't really need another vice. I have a serious chocolate addiction. I got hooked on Belgian chocolate when I lived there for a few months last year. Now I have to look for it everywhere I go."

He raised an eyebrow. "Sounds like you need to come hear me talk to the book group."

"I wish I could, but I have a little work to do tonight." She gestured to the boxes, which he could now see contained Christmas decorations. Lots and lots of Christmas decorations, mostly of the inflatable variety.

"Seriously? You're putting up all of these?"

She sighed. "I'm afraid so. Some of the residents casually mentioned this afternoon that they were disappointed about the lack of decorations this year. Apparently in years past, the building has had quite a display, mainly put up by my sister and aunt, with a little help from Travis, McKenna's husband."

"The building doesn't seem very festive."

"Right. Well, obviously with Liz on crutches and McKenna in bed—and Travis working until all hours of the day and night—someone had to step up. The girls and I decided to try. This is my first time with inflatables, though. I'm trying to figure it out as I go."

He looked at the boxes, then back at Natalie, his thoughts of going home and crashing after the book group melting away like a snowman in July.

"I can help, if you want."

She pursed her lips. "That's incredibly kind of you, but you have another obligation. You're on your way to Birdie's book group."

"That should only take an hour or so. Maybe ninety minutes. I can sneak out while they're having refreshments and meet you back here. It shouldn't take us long, if we're working together."

She pushed a wayward strand of hair from her face, her expression undecided for a long moment then softening into gratitude.

"I should refuse and assure you I am a strong, confident woman and can handle things on my own."

"I have no doubt about that. But why not take a little help when it's offered?"

"By my count, this would be the third time you've come to my rescue. First the night I crashed my car, then the other day with Nora's jingle bell emergency, then tonight."

"Who's counting?" he teased.

"Me. I'm counting. I'll figure out a way to pay you back."

"You don't owe me anything, Natalie. I would be happy to help. Give me an hour or so, and then I'll be at your disposal."

Something flashed in her gaze, something hot and glittery,

but she lowered her eyes and he was certain he must have been mistaken.

"Thank you. It's actually almost the girls' bedtime. We were about to go in and warm up with a hot bath and then settle down for the night. If you're sure about this, I can meet you at the book club when they're down."

"Perfect."

He headed into the building, trying his best not to grin. He wasn't sure how his mood had shifted so quickly from resignation to excitement, but he had a strong feeling Natalie Shepherd was responsible.

He was still a little early for the book club. He figured he would head to Birdie's apartment first and turned in that direction just as his grandmother came down the hall with her arms full of boxes and her dog, Dash, at her side.

Alarmed, he hurried forward, envisioning her stumbling because of her compromised eyesight.

"Grandma!" he exclaimed, taking the boxes from her. "Be careful. You could have waited until I was here to help you."

"Why would I do that? I can still manage for now, especially with Dash's help."

He worried that someday the dog would actually be the thing that tripped her up, but he wasn't going to argue with her tonight.

"I'm assuming I'm taking this to the recreation room."

"That's right. I booked it weeks ago for the whole night. I knew my apartment wouldn't be big enough. I'm expecting a good crowd. You know how much all the ladies here love you."

Griffin might have been flattered by that, except all the ladies in question were over seventy and he suspected they mostly liked him because he could dispense a steady source of medical information.

"I'm not sure how much I'll be able to contribute to your book club. I haven't had time to finish the book, to tell you the truth."

"Don't worry about that," she said, eyes twinkling. "Neither has most of the group. They're all a bunch of slackers. You'll be fine, I'm sure. You only have to give that charming smile of yours and talk about some of the ways we can all live our best lives."

He really wished he had the answer to that. Lately, he definitely didn't feel like he was living his own best life, whatever that meant.

For so long, he had been focused on the next thing. Finishing med school. Wrapping up his residency and internship. Opening his practice.

Now that he had checked off all those things from his list and was back here in Shelter Springs, where he had always planned to practice, he still felt as if something was missing.

He worked hard to help his patients, to offer treatments and advice that healed ailments and improved lives. He wanted to think he was making a difference. Yet no matter how hard he tried, he sometimes felt as if he could never escape the stain of being Dennis Taylor's son.

Griffin wasn't sure he could ever atone for the harm his father had wrought among the people of Shelter Springs. Four lives, four futures, untold promise, gone in a blink.

He carried the weight of his father's actions with him everywhere he went in Shelter Springs.

The room began to fill with residents of the apartment building and Griffin did his best to put away the restlessness, to be polite and friendly.

Finally, Birdie stood to welcome the group, now a dozen women and three men. In years past, Griffin might have seen only a sea of gray and white hair, but at least three of the women sported vibrantly colored locks, one lavender, one pink and Birdie, with her bright turquoise hair.

For the first part of the evening, his grandmother led the group in a general discussion about the book they had read.

Finally, she introduced him.

"I believe you all know my wonderful grandson, Griffin. Dr. Griffin Taylor, actually. He has agreed to join us tonight to talk about some ways we can all have a healthier new year."

Griffin stood to a round of enthusiastic applause. After talking about some of the most common avoidable health conditions he saw most among his older patients, he went on to detail some of the small behavior changes that could lead to big results, like incorporating even a few moments of daily exercise into their routine, reducing sugar and salt intake and opting to fill their diets mostly with vegetables, fruits and lean meats.

None of what he said had to be new information, but Griffin knew a refresher could sometimes be helpful. Nobody fell asleep, anyway, though he thought a couple of the men might have come close.

When he finished to another round of applause, Birdie rose again.

"Now, before we get to the refreshments—which do include brownies, I have to admit, along with a couple of fruit and relish trays—Griffin has agreed to answer some of our questions."

"I should add the disclaimer that unless I am your personal physician and know your complete medical history and medication you might have been prescribed, you should take everything I say as only suggestions, not strictly medical advice. Your mileage may vary. Please discuss any concerns in-depth with your own personal physician."

For the next half hour, he answered a wide variety of questions, everything from exercise recommendations for people with bad knees to what kind of salt substitute he would recommend for someone who hated bland food to how much pickleball was too much pickleball.

He managed to answer everything with some semblance of expertise, until a woman in the back whom he didn't know raised her hand.

"I want to know how a woman of a certain age on hormone replacement medicine still has such a harder time having an orgasm than she did even a decade ago."

The crowd snickered, and he saw Mabel Mulcahy compress her lips tightly together. He was a physician, Griffin reminded himself. There was absolutely no reason he should be embarrassed to talk about a completely natural and wonderful part of life, even with his grandmother and a dozen of her closest friends.

It didn't help his discomfort, though, when he saw a newcomer slip into the room and take a seat in a chair at the back.

Natalie.

The girls must have gone to sleep and now she was ready to work on the decorations. He had an overwhelming urge to make his excuses and stop the conversation there.

That was a cop-out, though, in response to an earnest question.

He cleared his throat. "Needs can change as people age and their bodies change as well. That's completely normal. Sometimes the usual, um, stimulation doesn't work as it used to. Sometimes a person might have health conditions that can impact their love live. There's nothing wrong with any of that. It only requires a little more creativity and adaptation. The first thing you should do is talk to your partner about how your needs have changed. Let him or her know if you need more foreplay or a different kind of approach in the bedroom. Second, you should definitely speak with your primary care physician to see if there's a medical reason for your changing needs. Perhaps your hormone replacement regimen needs an adjustment or you could possibly need a prescription oral medication or ointment that might help."

"I want to know why most of the noise and attention is about helping men with erectile dysfunction when women go through a lot of the same changes," Barbara Wiggins muttered. "Where are our bathtub commercials?"

The women all laughed. The men, he saw, looked more than a little uncomfortable.

"It's a good question. There have been a lot of advances in that area over the past decade or so as the medical field increasingly recognizes the changing sexual needs of an aging population. I would advise you all to speak with your primary care physician or gynecologist about this. He or she can provide you much more advice for your specific concerns than I can in this kind of setting. And certainly talk to your partner. That's a great place to start."

"On that note," Birdie said, "let's give our guest a big round of applause and have dessert. The direction this discussion has taken kind of makes me wish I'd fixed my mom's old recipe for Spotted Dick, but instead it's just plain old peppermint brownies and gingerbread cookies."

Griffin let out an exasperated laugh at his grandmother's sometimes sly sense of humor.

"I've got two kinds of brownies, one made the traditional way with all the sugar and oil, and the other, for those trying to cut down on carbs, with black beans and unsweetened applesauce."

As soon as the formal part of the program was over, Griffin was inundated with more questions, as he fully expected.

He was aware of Natalie chatting easily with some of the other residents, holding a plate with a brownie and some strawberries.

Finally, he was able to extricate himself from a conversation about whether red wine or white wine was healthier and made his way over to Natalie, now talking with Barbara Wiggins and her husband, Calvin.

She looked up when he approached and for an instant, her gaze warmed, leaving him with a curious ache in his chest.

"Sorry. The discussion went a little longer than I planned."

"Please don't worry. You seem to have your hands full here.

I can handle the decorations on my own. Maybe I can enlist a couple of the residents to help me tomorrow."

"No. I want to help," he assured her. "As long as this is not too late for you."

"Not at all. If you want the truth, I'm still struggling with the time change, even though I've been here several days."

She gestured to her plate. "You should have one of Birdie's fantastic brownies first. You've earned it, especially with those questions I caught toward the end."

While Griffin had eaten a late lunch in his office, he hadn't found time for dinner yet and his mouth watered a little at the delicious-looking brownie.

"Just one," he said.

He grabbed a plate from the refreshment table he had helped his grandmother set up earlier and swiped a regular brownie and one of the black bean brownies that had been cut in half. As he and Natalie chatted about the relative differences between them, he happened to catch sight of his grandmother. She was turned toward them, head cocked as if listening to their conversation.

He knew she couldn't see them from this distance, since her AMD limited her distance vision, but he was almost certain he saw a speculative edge to her expression.

He really didn't need Birdie getting any strange ideas about him and Natalie Shepherd. As soon as her sister had the baby, Nat would be taking off again. She was not the sticking-around kind.

He had a feeling it was too late, especially when Birdie nudged her friend Florence Johnson, angled her turquoise-topped head toward him and then to Natalie and whispered something. Florence immediately grinned, looked closely at them both and whispered something back that had Birdie giggling.

Griffin swallowed a groan. He would have to set her straight, let Birdie know that any matchmaking ideas she might have toward him and Natalie were doomed to disappointment.

They were only friends. Given the history between them, he felt fortunate to have that much with her.

The familiar pain he always felt when he remembered her brother's last moments burned under Griffin's skin, sharp and painful.

Birdie's brownies suddenly tasted acrid, but he didn't know if that was from the different ingredients or from his own guilt.

"What do you think?" his grandmother said as she approached them, her expression bright.

"Delicious," he said, doing his best to disguise the effort it was taking him to chew and swallow.

"I love them," Natalie said. "I tried both, and you can't even tell which one is relatively healthy."

"Oh good. That's what I was hoping. I almost like the black bean brownies better. They're creamier."

"They are," Natalie agreed.

"I'll be sure to bake a batch just for you before you leave again. You'll have earned it, watching out for those two girls. How is that going, anyway?"

"Not bad, though I've already had to visit urgent care with Nora. Did Griffin tell you?"

Birdie looked intrigued. "He doesn't talk about his patients, unfortunately. I wish he would spill the tea once in a while."

"Ever heard of a little thing called patient privacy, Gram?"

She made a sound of dismissal. "I've heard of it. That doesn't mean I have to like it. I want all the gory details. What happened to Nora? You're not a doctor. You can tell me," she said to Natalie.

She told them the story, relating it in a funny, self-deprecating way that made those around them chuckle.

"It might seem funny now, but I can assure you, neither Nora nor I was laughing at the time. I was certain she was going to need brain surgery to extricate it."

"Poor little lamb," Florence said. "I would bet anything her older sister had something to do with it. If there's mischief to be had, that Hazel always seems right in the middle of it."

"Do you remember that time she and Nora added a whole bottle of dish soap to the hot tub because they wanted to make bubbles?" Arlene Gallegos chuckled. "Or at Halloween, when they would sneak out of their apartment and try to go trick-or-treating through the building for two weeks straight before the actual holiday?"

Natalie smiled at the antics of her nieces. "Somebody should have warned me what I was facing when I agreed to help McKenna."

"Don't listen to them," Birdie said, shaking her head. "They're adorable girls. Just a little...high-spirited. They bring life and spark to this old place and to all us crusty old folks who live here, that's what I think."

Natalie smiled, her features soft, and squeezed Birdie's hand. "I adore them, high jinks and all."

She looked so lovely that Griffin had to shift his gaze away so she didn't catch him staring at her.

"Is there anything else you need from me tonight?" he asked his grandmother.

"Oh no. Florence and James can help me carry all the things back to my apartment. After everything you've done tonight, you should go home and go straight to bed."

"You should," Natalie said.

He shook his head. "I told you I would help you."

"Help her do what?" Birdie asked, looking intrigued.

"He offered to help me put up the rest of the outside decorations," Natalie answered.

"Oh, that's sweet of you." His grandmother beamed at him.

"It's about time we got into the holiday spirit around here," Bud Roundy said.

"You could have put up the decorations," his wife, Linda, said tartly. "We all know what a hard time Liz and McKenna are having right now. I'm sorry we didn't already think about decking all the halls so they didn't have to worry about it."

"Do you need our help?" Bud asked.

Natalie sent Griffin a sidelong look, as if silently asking his opinion. Griffin was a jumble of conflicting instincts. He wasn't sure it was a great idea to spend much more time alone in her company, when he was already beginning to have inappropriate thoughts about her.

On the other hand, he had been looking forward to spending the evening with her.

He shrugged, as if to tell her the decision was hers.

"There's not that much to do outside," Natalie assured them all after a moment. "I *could* use some help decorating the tree that Hazel tells me should be here in the rec room. That can wait until tomorrow, though. I have to take the tree and ornaments out of storage first."

"We can certainly help you with that tomorrow," James Johnson, Florence's husband, assured her.

"Definitely," Bud said. "I've got a haircut appointment in the morning, but I'm free all afternoon."

This was a warm, caring community. After helping Birdie make the decision to leave her house, he had worried she would hate living in a senior apartment facility.

He needn't have been at all concerned. The Shelter Inn was filled with kind people who reached out to help each other when needed. He found great comfort in knowing his grandmother wasn't alone, even when he and Amanda or their other relatives couldn't always spend time with her.

"Should we get started?" Natalie asked him.

"Bring on the inflatables."

She rolled her eyes and led the way outside, into the December night that smelled of pine trees and snow.

He inhaled a deep breath, knowing full well he shouldn't be

so excited about the prospect of putting up about a hundred inflatables.

It wasn't the work ahead of them, he knew, that made him buzz with anticipation. It was knowing he would be doing the job with Natalie Shepherd.

eight

Was it the cold or the company that sent that little zing of adrenaline through her?

Natalie walked out into the December evening, aware with every step of Griffin moving beside her.

Snow was lightly falling, tiny crystals that seemed to hover in the air then disappear before they could hit the ground.

The moon was about half-full, peeking in and out of the dark clouds that drifted past.

The evening seemed surreal somehow, not only because it was lovely, but because she was here in Shelter Springs with Griffin Taylor, of all people.

She didn't want to be attracted to him, especially knowing absolutely nothing could ever come of it. Still, somehow, she couldn't help wondering what Dr. Taylor would do if she suddenly grabbed him by the lapels of his expensive-looking jacket and kissed him there in the moonlight with the gentle snowflakes fluttering down around them…

"Where would you like to start?"

She blinked at his question, horrified that he might have read her thoughts, then reality returned. He was talking about putting up the blasted Christmas decorations, not living the fantasy conjured up by her overactive imagination.

"I would like to start by putting all the inflatables away and forgetting about them, if you want the truth."

He laughed. "You don't like them?"

"They're fine. I'm not inflatist. The residents love them, according to Aunt Liz. We just have so many of them. I think a Christmas inflatable collection ought to be no more than three. Four at the outside."

"And the Shelter Inn has...?"

"Twelve in total."

"Wow. So we've got eleven more to go. That's not so bad," he said, though he looked more than a little overwhelmed at the prospect.

"It's fairly ridiculous, isn't it? Apparently, the collection has grown over the years as more residents have contributed their own Christmas decorations after they downsize and move from their homes to one of the apartments here. McKenna said she and Liz talked about rotating the collection and only putting up two or three each year, but they don't want to disappoint anyone."

"That makes sense. I know how tough it was for Birdie to get rid of all the holiday decorations she had collected over a lifetime after she moved to her apartment here. My sister got a few of the most cherished items, and the rest ended up at Goodwill. She did hang on to her collection of outhouse Santas as well as the toilet seat cover of Santa's face."

"That must be a great comfort to your family."

Her dry tone sparked a laugh from him, warming her to her toes.

"Yes," he answered. "We all sleep better at night now."

He turned to the various boxes. "Any idea where to put everything? Do you want one big collection of inflatables or to, er, spread the wealth?"

"I tried to grill my sister about this. She said she and Liz always tried to spread them out, not only because of the load on the electrical system, but also in an effort to place the inflatables on whatever side of the apartment building where the donor lives. That way they can see it from the window of their apartment and enjoy it. She drew a quick diagram for us about which one should go where. It's pretty evenly split, actually, with three on each side of the building."

"That should make things easier."

"I hope so. The girls and I sorted them earlier into four piles. It might look haphazard, but we did create a system."

"If you can explain your system to me, I can carry the boxes to their final destination, and then you can do the grand unboxings."

She directed him to which box went on which side of the apartment building, then tried not to stare when he picked up three boxes at a time and made his way around the Shelter Inn.

She picked up one of the boxes that went on the side closest to them. By the time she returned for the second one, he had taken the other pile to the side opposite them.

He returned in time to take the final box for her.

"Want to start here in the front?"

"That's as good a place as any, I guess."

They developed a good system as they worked together, spreading out each decoration into its designated spot and untangling the guylines. He used the mallet to drive the supports into the frozen ground while she moved on to position the next inflatable.

"Good thing we had a warm weekend or we would be working our way through at least a foot of snow," he said.

While three or four inches still covered the ground, most of the snow from the storm that had caused her so much trouble when she first arrived in Shelter Springs had melted over the past few days.

As they worked their way around the building, Natalie slightly revised her initial opinion of the inflatables. Sure, they were big and somewhat gaudy, but as she plugged in each one, she knew the girls would love them. If the decorations brought a little enjoyment to Nora and Hazel as well as the residents of the Shelter Inn, who was she to judge?

"Look at you. You're a pro at this now," she said as he was anchoring the guylines for the final inflatable. "Next thing you know, you'll be buying an inflatable dragon in a Santa hat for your own place."

His laugh was low and rich and entirely too sexy for her peace of mind. "I'm not sure my condo association would agree."

"I would have thought a successful young doctor would have a big, fancy house in the Lakefront Estates," she said, mentioning the most exclusive neighborhood in Shelter Springs.

"Not interested, thanks."

She gave him a quizzical look. "You're not?"

"The lakefront is nice, don't get me wrong, but I prefer the mountains, where I have a little space to breathe. I bought some property when I first moved to town on Heartbreak Mountain."

"Oh, how nice." Despite its sad name, that was one of Natalie's favorite areas, in the forested foothills overlooking town.

"Maybe someday I'll build a house there, but for now I'm too busy trying to convince people in town I'm not my father."

She frowned, startled by his words.

"Has that been an issue for you?"

Griffin paused, as if regretting his words. "Let's just say the previous Dr. Taylor didn't exactly leave what anyone would call a positive impression."

"He wasn't a bad doctor." She remembered his father being incredibly kind to her mother during her cancer fight.

"No. Just not so great in the human being department."

His father had died after a fiery crash where he had been behind the wheel while heavily intoxicated, she knew. Worse than that, four teenagers had died as well, innocent victims in the car he had hit head-on. Dennis Taylor had left a horrible legacy of pain and loss.

"Surely people don't blame you for what your father did."

He pounded the mallet into the last stake with more force than he had used before. "Most people don't, but there are always a few exceptions. People who believe Dennis Taylor's son has to be cut from the same cloth. I can't go to the Saddle and Spur for a single drink without people whispering about me. And heaven forbid I should add a case of beer to my shopping cart at the grocery store."

She frowned. "So why did you come back here? You could have gone anywhere to start your practice when you finished med school. Wouldn't you rather practice near a beach somewhere?"

"We have a beach. Several of them." He gestured to the vast expanse of lake gleaming silver in the uncertain moonlight.

She made a face. "Sure. Where the temperatures are supposed to drop down into the teens by morning. Not exactly sunbathing weather."

"Maybe not. But Lake Haven has plenty going for it."

"Enough to put up with the whispers and stares? I would have thought you would prefer to be anywhere else but here."

He continued looking out at the lake, so deep and wide and fed by various hot springs that it never quite froze completely, only sometimes around the shore. She couldn't read his expression in the glow from the exterior landscaping lights or from the other two inflatables she had plugged in on this side of the building, though she could see his jaw was set.

He looked rugged, gorgeous, distant.

"I know it probably seems irrational, but I never considered practicing anywhere else. I had some good offers, especially at the hospital where I did my residency in Los Angeles County. But since the day I started med school, I knew I would move back one day."

"You love it here that much?"

The concept seemed so foreign to her. Yes, Shelter Springs offered limitless recreational opportunities, stunning scenery and people who were decent and hardworking, for the most part.

But for her, it was a place that held so much pain. She struggled to associate her hometown with anything but loss.

"I do love it." He gestured to the lake and the lights of downtown they could see from here. "Look around. You have to admit, you won't find a prettier town anywhere."

She wanted to tell him about the small villa she had stayed in for a month in a village on the shores of Lake Como, with picturesque gardens and porticos and old stone steps, worn smooth by hundreds of years of foot traffic. Or the apartment in the Spanish medieval town of Toledo, with its beautiful architecture, history-steeped buildings and churches containing priceless artwork.

"It is a pretty town," she finally said. She couldn't argue with that.

"Even if Shelter Springs was a tiny, dusty little hole-in-the-wall town in the middle of the desert with nothing for miles around but cactus and rattlesnakes, I would still have come back."

She narrowed her gaze, trying to make sense of why he was so compelled to practice medicine here, of all places.

"You think you owe the town something, don't you?" she said suddenly as the realization came to her. "You're trying to make up for what your father did."

The line of his jaw tightened. "That's impossible. I know that I can't fix the past. I can't bring back the four teenagers he killed. I can't go back in time and snatch the keys to the car from him or keep him from taking those pills, drinking that entire bottle of Johnnie Walker. I wish to hell I could."

She remembered that awful time, shortly after her mother died of cancer, when his impaired father had taken a curve too fast and had driven straight into the oncoming path of a group of teenagers in a Jeep, returning home after a fun day on the lake.

While the young people had been a few years older than she was, Natalie had known them all. She remembered how the town had grieved the loss of all that promise and how his mother had been unable to face the fallout and ultimately had moved away from Idaho, even though she and Dennis Taylor had been divorced at the time of the accident.

She had heard from Liz that Lena Taylor had remarried and now lived in Florida with her new husband.

Lena had always been nervous and fussy. As Nat remembered, Birdie, Lena's mother, had been much more of a supportive maternal figure to Amanda and Griffin.

"I'm sorry," she murmured.

His gaze met hers. "Why? None of it was your fault."

"Or yours," she pointed out.

"I know I can never atone for what my father did. The pain he caused, the four bright futures he destroyed in one terrible night."

"Exactly. You can't. Nor should you feel like you have to try."

"My father was an addict. Alcohol, opioids, whatever he could find toward the end. He had lost his medical license the day of the accident, did you know that?"

"I didn't."

"He lost everything he loved. He lost his career and was likely headed for prison because of earlier infractions. He had nothing left. The teenagers he killed had *everything*. What a waste."

"Oh, Griffin. I'm so sorry."

Her own father had walked away from his family, but at least he hadn't done so in a brutal, tragic way that left so many repercussions.

"He made his own choices, just like I made one a long time ago that I will do what I can for the people of this area, whether they were impacted by his actions that night or not."

Touched by his words and the passion behind them, she fought the urge to wrap her arms around him. "You're a good man,

Griffin Taylor," she said softly. "If the people of Shelter Springs can't recognize that, they don't deserve to have you here."

He looked down at her, his blue eyes suddenly warm. For one glittery, breathless moment, he looked as if he wanted to kiss her. He might have even leaned down slightly before he seemed to check the movement and step away.

"Thank you for saying that," he said after a moment. "Now, should we plug this last inflatable in and see how everything looks?"

She nodded, hurrying to the outlet while she tried to ignore the sharp disappointment she knew she had no right to feel.

nine

Natalie Shepherd was a dangerous woman.

Griffin picked up the empty cardboard boxes that had once held the Christmas decorations in storage, aware of a deep ache of yearning he knew he had no right to.

Oh, Natalie might look all sweet and innocent, but that soft smile and those big green eyes could lead a man into all kinds of hazardous territory, into revealing far more about himself than he ever intended.

If she wanted to, she could make a pretty good career for herself as a police interrogator. Five minutes with her and a man was willing to spill all his secrets.

Not only had he told her far more than he ever intended—or than he had shared with anyone else—about his motives for opening his practice here in Shelter Springs, but for one breathtaking moment, he had almost kissed her. In full view of anyone in town who might have been driving by or any residents of the Shelter Inn, including his own grandmother, who might look out their windows at that particular moment.

Okay, his grandmother couldn't see them, but someone else might and they would be sure to report back to Birdie.

He had come within a heartbeat of pulling her against him, warming her body with his, tasting that lush mouth.

He had stopped in time, though he really, really hadn't wanted to. What if he hadn't?

He had no real compelling reason to stop. They were two unattached adults, working together on a lovely December evening. It was rather magical, actually, with wispy snowflakes still swirling gently through the air and the moon peeking in and out of the clouds.

Would it have been a big deal if he had taken that last step and lowered his mouth to hers?

Yes. He answered his own question. Unequivocally yes.

They were completely wrong for each other.

As he had just explained to her, Griffin felt a fierce obligation to stay here and care for the people of Shelter Springs who had been hurt by his father's actions. He was compelled to do his best to make a difference here.

Natalie, on the other hand, was a wanderer always looking at what was beyond the next curve in the road.

Even if she were a different sort of woman, the kind who might be willing to stay here and pick up the life she had once walked away from, Griffin had secrets, things he could never tell her.

Things that would devastate her and McKenna. Somehow, Nat had persuaded him to talk about his father and his sense of obligation to this town. What else might she wriggle out of him?

"What's in these last few boxes?" he asked as he carried the empty boxes around to the front entrance.

"A few lights to put around the potted fir trees near the entrance. I can do those tomorrow."

"I'm here now. I don't mind helping. And unlike you, I can reach the top without a ladder."

"Well, there is that," she said ruefully. "You've done so much already. Are you sure you don't mind?"

If he were a wiser sort of man, he would make some excuse and head home. He told himself he was only staying a little longer so he could help her finish the job, not because he found her company entirely too appealing.

"It shouldn't take us long. I'll do the top branches here then let you finish while I do the top branches of the other one."

"Good plan."

He pulled out a string of lights from the box, grateful that whomever had stored them had organized the strands so they didn't have to be untangled. She waited while he twisted the lights through one of the two seven-foot-tall trees at the entrance to the building.

"The night you came to town you said you were coming from Tenerife," he said as he worked, mainly to make conversation. If he were the one asking questions, she wouldn't be able to extract more information from him that he didn't intend to share. "Off the coast of Africa, right? That's what you said. How long were you there?"

"Right. Tenerife, in the Canary Islands. I was there less than a week, actually. I was supposed to be house-sitting and dog-sitting while the homeowners spent six weeks skiing in Switzerland. After McKenna reached out to me, I had to hand over the job to someone else. It was a bit of a last-minute scramble. Fortunately, the agency I work for was able to find a person willing to come out on short notice."

She was a good sister to drop everything so she could return to Shelter Springs and help while McKenna was on bed rest, he thought. Not every woman would be willing to do the same.

"I don't know how things work in the pet care and house-sitting world. Will this affect future bookings for you?"

"I hope not. I wouldn't think so. I've worked with the same agency since I graduated from college. They know me and know I'm generally trustworthy. Everyone has emergencies, right?"

He handed the string to her once the top third of the tree was done, then headed for the other fir.

"Does it pay enough to survive? Caring for other people's homes and animals while they're gone?"

She looked up from the branch she was decorating to give him a rueful look. "It's not physician wages, that's for sure. My accommodations are always covered, obviously, and sometimes I receive a small stipend if there's more than one animal to care for. Often the job includes the use of a vehicle, which is nice for sightseeing. It doesn't include gas or food or the plane ticket to the country, so I pay the bills with my freelance work."

"That's right. You said you work as an editor and freelance writer?"

"Yes. I write travel articles for several different websites, and I'm a freelance copy editor for a couple of publishing houses. Guess that English degree came in handy after all."

"Did you have other jobs lined up after Tenerife?"

"I was supposed to be there through most of January. I'm not sure what I'll do after that. Starting in April, I'm booked for a few different jobs throughout the UK and Ireland. One in Ireland, one in Scotland and two in England. I won't be house-sitting every single day of that time as jobs don't usually overlap perfectly, so I plan to do a little traveling while I'm there, staying in B and Bs and with friends."

"Don't you get tired of living out of a suitcase? Or duffel, as the case may be?"

He could see her better here in the front lights of the building, as well as from the sparkly white lights they were stringing around the trees. Her expression was pensive, thoughtful.

"Not really. If I can, I like to schedule jobs that last at least a month, so I have time to settle into an area and really explore my surroundings. I love it, actually. I'm usually caring for beloved pets at a comfortable home in interesting surroundings. What's not to love?"

"Aren't you ever...lonely?"

For a moment, she stopped twisting the lights around one of

the lower boughs and seemed to stare off into space, as if trying to figure out how to answer him.

Finally, she flashed a smile that struck him as not completely genuine. "How can anyone possibly be lonely with a dog or cat snuggled up beside them on the sofa while they work?"

He wanted to ask about romantic relationships, how she could ever establish anything long-term when she moved from country to country, but he couldn't figure out a good way to casually slip the question into the conversation.

"On those rare occasions when I feel I need human companionship," she went on, "I reach out to McKenna or the friends I've made in my travels around the world, and we have a video chat. Pubs are also great places to make friends so I try to stop in at the local hot spot soon after I arrive in a new place. I can usually find plenty of people who are thrilled to tell me about all the great things to do and see in their area."

She made it sound as if her world was perfect, but was that a subtle thread of discontent he sensed weaving through her words? He couldn't be certain.

"You couldn't wait to leave Shelter Springs, could you?"

She looked up at the solid, graceful building beside them.

"I don't hate it here. McKenna thinks I do, but it's not true. I never hated it, but when I was a kid living at the inn, back when it was truly a hotel, I felt like the rest of the world was out there having all these exciting adventures while we were stuck here cleaning their rooms and changing their sheets."

"I could see where that could be tough on a kid."

"After my mom died and my dad took off for Alaska, I decided I would leave as soon as I could."

"You still had a few years left of high school, didn't you?"

"One. My mom left me a little money for college, and I earned a couple of scholarships out of state. As soon as I knew Kenna would be okay with Liz while she finished school, I decided to head to Portland."

"Did you like it there?"

"It was different. I saw college as a means to an end, really. I graduated as soon as I could, taking classes over the summer and staying on campus. I did one study abroad semester in England, where I was able to take the Eurostar over to the continent. That's when I became completely hooked on travel."

"Is there somewhere you would like to travel that you haven't had the chance yet?" he asked as he used the last string of lights on his fir tree.

She looked intrigued by the question. "At this point, I've ticked off just about everything on my bucket list. I haven't seen as much of Asia as I would like, but I'm sure I'll still get the chance someday."

Her voice trailed off as an older model white pickup truck pulled into the parking lot. Natalie's gaze narrowed as her brother-in-law walked toward them, shoulders sagging. He stopped when he reached them, looking a little disconcerted to find Natalie and Griffin working outside the building.

"Travis," Natalie said, her voice tight. "You're home late."

"I know. It's been a day. Um, thanks for putting up the decorations. I've been meaning to get to it, but life has been a little crazy since we barreled into the holidays."

"You're welcome," she said, though her tone conveyed the exact opposite.

"How are things?" Travis asked, gesturing vaguely toward the building.

"Fine. We haven't had any more jingle bell incidents for a few days, anyway."

"Thanks for holding down the fort while Kenna has to stay in bed."

"That's what family is all about, right?" she said, her tone pointed.

"Right," Travis said, though he seemed not to have even heard her.

"Well, good night."

She didn't answer as the man headed for the front door, where he seemed to pause, head bowed, before he punched in the key code and opened the door.

Natalie's mouth tightened as she watched him go inside, though she didn't say anything.

"He's a hardworking guy," Griffin finally said.

"Is that what he is?" She shifted her gaze to his, and he was startled by the spark of anger there.

"You don't think so?"

"Unless his company has started handing out six-packs for those working double shifts, he hasn't been at work this whole time. Didn't you smell the beer on his breath?"

He tensed, as he always did when memories of his father rushed in. All those times he had come home late, smelling more like scotch than beer.

"Maybe he stopped after work for a drink with his buddies to let off a little steam before he came home."

His father used to do that after working in a busy clinic all day, but he would end up staying until closing time. He could still remember the times his mother would tell him to watch Amanda while she went in search of Dennis.

"His wife is in bed doing her best to keep their baby as healthy as possible," Natalie said with a frown. "His little girls are stuck with their clueless aunt who doesn't know the first thing about caring for them and a great-aunt on crutches who can't chase after them. I'm sorry if Travis has steam to let off, but his family needs him here."

He couldn't argue with that. Griffin wished he had magic words to say that would make the situation better, but he knew this was among the many things he couldn't fix.

He could help her finish the decorations, though. He finished hanging the lights on the tree, then stood back to admire their work.

He wasn't a huge fan of the inflatables, but had to admit they brought a festive touch to the Shelter Inn.

"Thank you so much for helping," she said as they put away the boxes in the storage shed at the end of the parking lot. "I know this was weighing heavily on my sister's mind."

"It was my pleasure."

He meant the words. He enjoyed spending time with Natalie, even if she was uncannily gifted at wresting out his inner thoughts.

"I know Liz and McKenna wanted the place decorated before the holiday giving market kicks off."

"That's right around the corner, isn't it? My sister has been even busier than normal trying to get ready. Does it start next week?"

"Yes. A week from today. Everyone in the building has apparently been working hard to make items to sell at the Shelter Inn kiosk. Everything from painting wooden toys to sewing reusable shopping bags to making holiday ornaments."

"I know Birdie has been tatting a bunch of snowflake ornaments. They're still determined to do it this year, even with McKenna laid up and Liz still in recovery from surgery?"

"Apparently. Liz is still planning to work at the kiosk, but since McKenna is out of commission, I said I would try to help where I can. I keep reminding myself it's for a good cause."

"If I can help with anything, let me know."

"I think you've done enough tonight. But thank you."

To his astonishment, she reached out and gave him a quick hug.

"Seriously, thank you. You've taken a huge weight from me."

"I'm glad I could help."

She smiled up at him, her eyes bright and her cheeks and nose flushed with the cold. Griffin again had to fight the urge to pull her into his arms. He could almost taste the chocolate and peppermint brownie taste of her kiss.

Big mistake, he reminded himself. Something told him that if he kissed her now, here in the snowy moonlight, he would never be able to enjoy that particular combination of flavors again without remembering this moment.

"Good night," he said, somewhat abruptly, then hurried to his pickup truck before he could act on the impulse and do something he wouldn't be able to forget.

ten

They were heading for a meltdown. Natalie could see it coming a mile away and felt like she was teetering on a rickety old rail bridge, staring at the lights of an oncoming train she had no way to avoid.

Hazel stomped her little pink boot into the snow, her forehead furrowed beneath her hat with the two pom-poms that looked like Mickey ears.

"I don't want to go home," she said. "We just got here and I'm having fun. Why do we have to?"

She forced a patient tone. "Because your sister's feet are cold, and she can't walk up the hill anymore."

"They're not, are they, Nora? Say they're not."

Her mother would have called Hazel a bossy little bag of bones. Or at least that was what Jeanette always used to call *Natalie* on the frequent occasions when she would try to tell McKenna what to do.

Hazel was unfortunately just like her, which might be the reason Natalie was always more inclined to hide her smile at the girl than to chastise her.

She had to do something now, especially when Nora's chin quivered and she looked indecisive, clearly torn between the reality of her discomfort and the potential consequences of disappointing her sister.

"I don't know," she said, tears welling up in her eyes.

"Your feet aren't too cold, are they?" Hazel pressed.

Time for Auntie Nat to step in. "We've already been here an hour, sweetheart. You can sled down one more time, then we have to pack it in."

Hazel huffed out a resigned breath, clearly unhappy with the decision, but at least she stopped haranguing her sister. "Will you watch me?"

She really wanted to be back at the Shelter Inn with cups of hot cocoa all around. Short of dragging Hazel away from the park kicking and screaming, she didn't know how to reach that goal without letting her have one more run.

"We'll watch from the sidewalk, where Nora's feet can be a little more warm."

"Okay. I can go fast."

She and Nora trudged through the snow toward the sidewalk that would take them a block north toward home.

"Stomp your boots. Like this," she said, demonstrating to the girl. "That will knock some of the snow off and the movement will help keep your feet warm."

Nora rotated her weight from foot to foot with a determined, dutiful look on her little features. "I'm still cold," she said, a wobble in her voice.

"I know, honey. Think about something warm. Chicken noodle soup. Or a warm bath. Or wrapping up in a blanket by the fire."

Her forehead screwed up as she apparently put all her energy toward imagining a different circumstance. "Now I have to go potty," she said with a slightly worried expression.

Great. What was she supposed to do about that? She couldn't leave Hazel alone on the sledding hill, and the small building housing park restrooms was locked up for the season, as they had already determined.

"Can you hold it for a few more moments? It looks like Hazel is almost ready to sled down."

"I don't know. I can try." She bounced again from foot to foot, and Natalie didn't know whether she was trying to keep warm or performing the universal hold-it-in dance.

It made her smile a little, remembering a time she had stayed in a riad in Fes, Morocco, where the children had played soccer in the narrow alleyways between the ancient buildings. One boy had danced just like this, until he had finally given in and hurried around the corner and through one of the elaborately designed doors.

They watched Hazel reach the top of the gentle slope, pulling her plastic saucer behind her. A couple of school-aged boys helped her onto it, then gave her a little push. Hazel's shriek of delight rang out across the December afternoon as she bounced down the hill, landing near them in a heap.

"Did you see me?" she exclaimed as she struggled to her feet in the snow.

"I did. You were amazing." A soft, sweet warmth filled her as she and Nora went to the older girl and helped her up.

She adored these girls.

She had spent time with them before. Two summers ago, she had come for a week, but they had both seemed so young. They had been precious—Nora, still a baby with those big, emotive eyes, and Hazel with round cheeks and a laugh that could brighten even the hardest heart. At the time, Hazel had been only beginning to talk, or at least to speak in understandable sentences.

Travis had been an active, engaged part of their lives then, taking them on walks, picnics at the park, even an outing to Boise to the zoo. He had been attentive and adoring to his daughters and his wife.

McKenna had confided that they were trying for another child, though Nora was barely a year. Two months later, when Natalie had been in Denmark, her sister had suffered her first miscarriage. The second miscarriage was mere months later.

Through those miscarriages, McKenna had told her how loving and supportive Travis had been. So what was his problem now?

She hadn't even seen him since two nights earlier when she had talked to him while she and Griffin were decorating the grounds of the apartment building.

She hadn't seen Griffin, either.

That hadn't stopped her from thinking about him, far more than she should.

"I love sledding!" Hazel exclaimed. "Can we come back tomorrow?"

"We'll have to see. I think you have dance practice tomorrow."

"Oh yeah!"

As Natalie herded them back toward the Shelter Inn, Hazel did a few little dance moves awkwardly in her snow boots.

Nora, she saw, moved along with a determined, rather pained expression and Natalie tried to pick up her pace.

"I love dance practice. Do you know I get to be a kitten in a Christmas show? I have kitten ears and a kitten tail and kitten whiskers."

"I can't wait to see it."

"Nora doesn't get to be a kitten. That's for the older class. She's a dumb candlestick."

"It's not dumb. It's pretty. Mommy said don't say dumb."

Hazel stuck out her tongue. "Dumb. Dumb, dumb, dumb."

"That's enough," Natalie said sternly. "I'm sure both of you will look wonderful. I can't wait to see your show."

"Will you still be here for our show?" Hazel looked as if she didn't quite believe it. "I thought you wouldn't. Mommy says you have itchy feet and then you have to go. Where do you go? Do you have to go to an itchy feet doctor?"

Was that how her sister saw her, as a wanderer who couldn't stay put?

"Someone with itchy feet just means somebody who likes to travel. They don't like to stay in one place for very long."

"Don't you like staying with us?" Nora asked, looking stricken.

"Oh, honey. I love hanging out with you. I've had so much fun this week. But I also like to see new things and meet new people. There's always new adventures to have and new friends to make."

"I like having you here," Nora said, slipping her mittened hand into Natalie's and completely melting her heart.

When she let them into the apartment, she heard a male voice coming from Kenna's bedroom and felt some relief. Travis must have squeezed out a few hours of leave, she thought, but she was too busy rushing to get Nora out of her winter clothes to check for herself.

She had just helped Nora step out of the snow pants and ushered her into the bathroom when she heard Hazel give a shriek of excitement.

"Grandpa!"

She jerked her head up to see a tall, lanky man with graying hair and a neatly trimmed beard standing in the hallway.

"Dad!" she exclaimed, feeling as if Nora had headbutted her in the stomach on the way into the bathroom.

Her father gave her a nervous-looking smile. "Nat. Hey there."

She couldn't seem to suck in a breath, and wondered if she was about to hyperventilate for the first time in her life. She turned slowly to face the man she loved and despised in equal measures.

Hazel had rushed to him and now Steve picked her up, hugging her close. A moment later, the toilet flushed, the sink ran with water for much too short a time for an adequate handwash, and Nora came running out to leap into his arms as well.

Natalie finally was able to make her lungs cooperate and took in a sharp, steadying breath.

"What are you doing here?"

Her father hugged the girls closer. "I decided to come and spend Christmas with my family. I also thought it would be nice to be here for the birth of my grandson, since I missed when these two were born."

"Did you bring me something, Grandpa Steve?" Hazel demanded.

"I might have. We'll have to take a look in my suitcase later and see if I can find it."

"Yay!"

"And for me?" Nora asked.

"Of course. I wouldn't forget my little Nora-bunny."

"Guess what, Grandpa Steve? We went sledding and I went down so fast. I love sledding."

"It is pretty fun."

The girls chattered away to him about a hundred different things. Their upcoming dance program, their favorite Disney princess, what they wanted Santa to bring them.

All while Natalie tried to adjust her thoughts to finding the last man she expected to see in her sister's apartment.

She hadn't seen her father since Travis and McKenna's wedding nearly seven years earlier. Hadn't *wanted* to see him. If she could have gone another seven years—or forever—without seeing Steve Shepherd again, she would have been completely fine.

"Where are you staying? There's no room here." She knew she sounded rude, especially since it wasn't her house anyway, but she couldn't seem to help it.

"Your uncle Dave offered to let me crash at their place while he and Marie are visiting their kids in Washington State for the holidays."

Her father's brother, his only living relation, lived outside of town, between Shelter Springs and Haven Point.

Dave and Marie had been a steady source of love and encouragement to her and McKenna after their mother died, especially after things had turned so ugly with Steve.

Dave and Marie—and Liz, of course, her mother's sister—had come to her high school graduation, had helped her pick out her first thirdhand car and shop for the things she would need for her college dorm.

She remembered Uncle Dave once driving halfway between Shelter Springs and Portland to rescue her when that piece-of-crap car had suddenly lost power on the interstate while she had been driving home for a July Fourth weekend. He had towed her to a shop and brought her back here, then drove her all the way back to pick up her repaired vehicle after the weekend.

He had been far more of a father to her for the past decade than Steve had been, and she had been sorry she hadn't had the chance to see them, as they left town the day she arrived.

"That's nice of them," she said, her voice tight.

What the hell was he doing here?

She knew McKenna and Steve were in contact and that he had visited her here several times over the past few years.

Her sister had waited nearly a year to finally confide in her that she had reestablished a closer relationship with their father and he had become a regular part of her daughters' lives.

When McKenna finally told her, they had fought bitterly, their first real disagreement as adults that couldn't be resolved with a hug and an apology.

Steve had become a subject they both decided not to talk about.

Natalie couldn't control what her sister did, much to her frustration. She still couldn't quite believe her sister had him walk her down the aisle and then to be part of her children's lives, as if nothing had happened. How could Kenna so easily forgive and forget the past?

And why hadn't her sister told her he was coming, when she knew how hard Nat worked to keep him at arm's length all these years?

Her father gave her a tentative smile as the girls chattered away, and it seemed to strike her like a physical blow.

They had once been a happy family. Once she had adored him as much as the girls clearly did. She could remember how happy she used to be on the days she could spend with him running errands or working around the hotel.

And sledding. He had taken all of them sledding on that very same hill where she had taken the girls, she remembered. Her and McKenna and Jake.

The son and daughters he had abandoned as if they meant nothing to him.

She swallowed down a hard lump in her throat, her hands still squeezed around Nora's coat.

"Do you go sledding at your house in Alaska?" Hazel asked him.

He set her and Nora down. "All the time. Sometimes when you don't mean to. Once I was out below my cabin trying to take pictures of a moose and my boots slipped on a patch of ice. I slid clean down the hill. Believe it or not, I managed to stay on my feet like I was skiing the whole way down until I hit the bottom, when I fell right on my behind. Scared the moose, I'll tell you that much."

Both girls laughed at the mental picture he painted, though Natalie was quite certain Nora was only laughing to join in the fun with her sister.

He listened to the girls talk about times *they* had fallen on their respective bottoms, then turned to Natalie, who felt as if she had turned to ice in the past ten minutes since encountering her father.

"I thought I would take the girls out to dinner. Their favorite gourmet restaurant. The one with the golden arches."

"Yay!" Both girls exclaimed, eyes bright at the prospect, as if she hadn't taken them there three days earlier.

"Can we get a toy and play in the playland?" Hazel asked. "I won't push Nora down the slide this time, I promise."

She had planned dinner already. Chicken enchiladas, one of her few specialties. Hazel and Nora had helped her put it together earlier that day, rolling up the filled tortillas and preparing the casserole dish. She supposed she could always cook it for her and McKenna and heat it up for the girls another day. Warmed-up enchiladas were sometimes better than first-day enchiladas, in her experience.

"Would you…like to come with us?"

At Steve's tentative question, she stared at him, her mind filled with images of watching him drive out of town with his pickup truck loaded with camping and survival gear.

I don't know when I'll be back, girls. This is something I have to do. You'll be fine with Aunt Liz and Jake. Don't worry about me.

She had been sixteen, still grieving for her mother and now without a father as well. She had gone inside the hotel feeling numb, broken.

Sometimes she thought she was still that dazed teenager watching her father drive away. His abandonment—and she could think of it as nothing but that—had led her to make all kinds of stupid decisions in her late teens and early twenties.

She didn't want anything to do with him now. She certainly didn't want to go to a fast-food restaurant and share a meal with him.

"I should stay here in case McKenna needs something."

He opened his mouth as if to argue, then closed it again and nodded. "No problem. Um, Kenna told me to drive her car since the girls' car seats are there. She said you have the spare key."

Right. She had to think for a moment to remember where it

was. In the tiny guest bedroom, in the bag she had bought at a market stall outside Medellín.

"Yes. I'll grab it."

She walked to her room, rooted through the bag until she found the key and returned to where her father was now sitting on the sofa with a girl on either side.

She still had Nora's coat, she realized. She had shoved it under her arm when she was looking through her bag and now she pulled it out.

"You don't have to wear the snow pants, but you do have to put your coat back on," she told the girl.

"I still have my snow pants on," Hazel said. "Should I take them off?"

"That's probably a good idea."

For a few moments, she was busy helping the girls get ready to leave with their grandfather. She could only imagine how much easier leaving the house must be for her sister when she didn't have to suit up the girls with coats and mittens and beanies.

When they were ready, Steve took each excited girl by the hand. He paused by the doorway. "It's good to see you, Nat. You look great."

"Thanks." She didn't return the sentiment. What was the point in lying? While her father did look as handsome and rugged as ever, she could never again say it was good to see him.

eleven

As soon as they left, the spacious apartment seemed to echo with silence. The girls filled up so much of the space with their giggles and conversation. She picked up the snow pants they had discarded on the floor and put them away in the hall closet so they could find them again. Her sister's door was ajar and she could see McKenna sitting up in bed, thumbing through one of several magazines Natalie had picked up for her the day before at the grocery store.

She rapped on the door, then pushed it open when McKenna looked up expectantly, though Natalie didn't miss the edge of apprehension in her gaze.

She had to know perfectly well that Natalie would be furious to find their father at the apartment.

McKenna needed peace and calm right now. She didn't need Natalie to come in hot, she reminded herself. She breathed deeply, doing her best to rein in the wild stampede of emotions.

"How long have you known Dad was coming for Christmas?" she finally asked, relieved that she managed to keep her tone even, measured.

McKenna looked down at her red-and-white quilt, her features a picture of guilt. She never had been able to show much of a poker face.

"I didn't know for certain until he showed up an hour ago. I told him the same time I told you that I had been put on strict bed rest. He said maybe he would try to come down for the holidays, to be here when the baby was born. He said maybe. I wasn't sure he would actually do it. Book the plane ticket, I mean. You know how Steve can be."

"Yes. Yes, I do. Which is exactly why I have chosen not to let him be a part of my life." She still maintained that cool voice, but she could see McKenna wasn't fooled. She looked even more miserable, close to tears.

Natalie sat down on the edge of the bed and took her sister's hand. "I'm sorry. I don't want to fight with you."

"I don't want to fight, either. I hate feeling like I'm stuck in the middle."

There should be no *middle*. Natalie simply couldn't understand how McKenna still wanted a relationship with their father.

"He left us, Kenna. You and me and Jake. After Mom died, we were all lost and grieving and he couldn't cope with any of it."

"I know."

"Instead of maybe taking us to counseling and helping us deal with our loss in some healthy way, he chose a different path. He decided to completely turn his back on our family, to walk out and go live off the grid in Alaska, where we couldn't reach him even if we had wanted to. Can you imagine Travis doing that to your kids if something happened to you, God forbid?"

McKenna's fingers trembled in hers and Natalie wanted to stop talking, but couldn't seem to halt the words, as if they had been dammed up for a long time inside her and now were fighting to break free.

"We couldn't even reach him until a week after Jake died because he was apparently even further off the grid than usual on a backcountry fishing trip."

"I remember."

"Do you remember how we had to make all those funeral

decisions for Jake by ourselves, with only Aunt Liz and Uncle Dave and Aunt Marie to help us? How Uncle Dave spent days trying to track him down and finally flew up there himself to let him know his only son had died at twenty years old?"

McKenna let out a sob of a breath. "Yes, of course I remember. How could I forget? It was horrible. But Dad has changed. I know you don't believe that, but he has. I think he finally came to terms with his own grief over Mom and then Jake only a year later and realized how much he had hurt us by leaving when he did."

"We needed him. So much." Old sadness edged her voice, but she swallowed down the tears. "As much as he might have been grieving, he had responsibilities. He chose to ignore those and focus on himself, on his own needs. As far as I'm concerned, he tore up his Dad card."

"You've never loved someone so much, they become part of every breath, every heartbeat. If you had, you might be a little more understanding about how deeply Mom's death impacted him."

Natalie gazed into her sister's eyes, so much like her own. "Do you know why I haven't? Why I don't date anybody longer than a few weeks? Partly because of Dad leaving when he did. I was sixteen years old, at the most vulnerable of ages, and the man I loved and respected more than any other chose to wallow in his own pain rather than be here when his grieving children needed him most."

McKenna made a small sound of distress, and Natalie immediately wished she hadn't said anything. She should have just gone into her own room and not come here to vent all her jumble of emotions.

"I'm sorry. I'm so sorry," McKenna said, sounding miserable.

Natalie hugged her sister. "It's not your fault. It's mine. I know I should be able to get over it but... I can't. I'm not like you, generous and loving and kind. My heart is small and shriveled. Me and the Grinch."

"It is not," McKenna protested.

Natalie didn't argue. She was overwhelmed with an instinctive need to pack her bag and flee, even as she knew it was impossible.

That was her answer to anything. And why not? She had learned from a master.

"I've invited him to spend Christmas with us," McKenna said. "The girls love him. Whatever kind of dad you might think he was to us, he's a wonderful grandfather to them."

"That's nice," she said.

"If I had truly expected him to come, I would have said something to you, I swear," McKenna went on. "I wouldn't have sprung him on you like that. I was just trying to text you and warn you he was here when you came back from the park early."

"I left my phone here, so I wouldn't have gotten your text anyway," she answered.

"You've been amazing this week and I'm so grateful. But if you feel like you need to leave now that Dad is back in town, I totally understand."

"I'm not leaving," she said, her voice more clipped than she intended.

As much as she wanted to flee, Natalie was *not* her father. She wasn't about to abandon her sister when McKenna needed her most, no matter how hard it might be to stay and be forced to interact with the man she would have preferred to avoid for the rest of her life.

twelve

As Griffin parked in his grandmother's assigned spot in the Shelter Inn parking lot, greeted cheerfully by the three large inflatables on this side of the building that he and Natalie had put up a few days earlier, anticipation swirled through him like the softly falling snow.

He did his best to tamp it down. He didn't even know if he would see Natalie that afternoon. If he did, it would be the first time since the night they had put up those decorations outside the apartment building, though he was honest enough with himself to admit that she hadn't been far from his thoughts during the past five days.

He would be in the middle of reading over a chart and would suddenly remember the rosy glow of her skin and her green eyes glittering in the cold air and that heady moment when he had almost kissed her.

He had tried to stay away from her as long as he could. He had managed to keep from dropping everything and running to the Shelter Inn until Birdie had called him the night before to ask if he would come over that night. It was the first night of Hanukkah, and she wanted him to help her light the candle in the menorah she put in her window in honor of her best friend Dorothy Friedman, who had died after a stroke the year before.

He wasn't sure a lit menorah was the safest thing for a woman who didn't have the greatest vision, but he could never say no to his grandmother.

Unfortunately, he had been working a shift in the emergency department of the hospital the night before and couldn't make it for the first night so he had offered to come on Saturday, when he wasn't working.

All day, he had been aware of the glow of anticipation, even as he spent the morning cross-country skiing with friends in the mountains west of town.

He was hoping a few hours of hard exercise would ease some of his restlessness. No such luck. He still felt on edge, as if waiting for something unknown.

He had to get over this. He was perfectly content in his life. It was the one he wanted, the one he had created for himself. He didn't need Natalie Shepherd to blow into town and make him wonder if there might be something more out there for him.

He climbed out of his pickup truck and walked into the apartment building. Immediately, he could see the recreation room lobby had undergone a transformation since he'd been here five days earlier. A big Christmas tree dominated the space, sparkling with white lights and colorful ornaments. The gas fireplace glowed in the hearth, and the room was crowded with people working at tables.

His gaze immediately found Natalie. She hadn't noticed him yet as she worked with several of the apartment residents on something, her head bent over the table.

He was trying not to stare when her niece Nora raced over to him. "Dr. Jingle!" she exclaimed. "Hi, Dr. Jingle."

He wasn't sure he was a huge fan of the nickname, but had to admit it was cute of her to give it to him.

"Hey there, Nora. Looks like you're having a party out here."

"Not a party. We're working," she informed him. She was adorable, with all those dark curls and her big eyes.

"Working on what?"

"Come see."

He was startled when she reached up and gripped his hand with her little soft fingers. Somewhere deep inside, regret and loss he thought long dormant seemed to awaken like some kind of hibernating creature that now reached out and clutched at his heart with sharp talons.

Leaving him little choice but to follow her, Nora pulled him over to the tables. As they drew closer, he was assaulted by the noise of random hammering and a dozen voices chattering at once, along with some rollicking Christmas music with a country vibe playing on the sound system.

Much to his surprise, his grandmother was there, Dash at her feet. Birdie sat at one of the tables, her turquoise hair gleaming in the Christmas tree lights as she worked on something he couldn't see.

Next to her, looking bright and cheerful in a red sweater and dangly earrings, Natalie said something to Birdie that made his grandmother's shoulders shake.

Nora tugged his hand harder and he realized he had stopped abruptly, as if wary to go closer.

"Come see," she said again.

He took a few more steps closer until he could see thick brown, red and cream yarn strewn across the table.

Not yarn, he realized. Wool.

Two other women besides Birdie and Natalie were at the table as well, neighbors and friends of his grandmother. They all appeared to be stabbing with relish at balls of wool, using long silver needles that reminded him of his surgical rotation.

Hazel, Nora's older sister, was squeezed in between Arlene Gallegos and Florence Johnson, coloring studiously with markers on a rectangle of thin balsa wood.

"You're all doing great," Natalie was saying. "At this rate, we'll have at least a dozen more ornaments to sell by the end of the night."

Ornaments. They were making ornaments.

"These are so cute. And so fun to make too. I'm pretending this little ball of wool is the heart of every one of my enemies," Florence said.

Natalie's eyes widened, though she smiled. "I wouldn't want to be on your bad side," she said.

"Smart girl." Florence beamed, her dark eyes sparkling with mischief.

"I predict these will sell out on the first day of the market," Birdie said. "Don't you think?"

"Yes," Florence answered. "It's too bad we only learned how to make them today, but we can always make four or five more each day to sell. New stock never hurts."

"Everyone has been working so hard," Natalie said, still not noticing him. "Liz showed me all the boxes of wooden toys plus the knitted mittens and scarves you've all been working on. These felted owl ornaments are just extra."

"So extra," Arlene said. "They're darling. I just love their little heart-shaped faces. I might have to whip up a few for my tree, now that I know how to make them."

"And soft too," Birdie added. "I've always wanted to learn to felt. Thank you so much for teaching us."

Natalie smiled at his grandmother, and Griffin couldn't seem to look away. As if she felt his gaze, she looked up and her eyes widened with shock.

"Griffin!" she exclaimed.

"I found Dr. Jingle," Nora announced happily. She released his hand and slid into a chair next to Florence, where crayons and a Disney Princess coloring book hinted at her earlier activity.

"Dr. Jingle?" Birdie asked with a laugh, lifting her face and pointing at her cheek. He complied with her unspoken order and leaned down to kiss her cheek, which smelled of face cream and lavender.

To his amusement, Arlene and Florence both pointed to their own cheeks and gave him expectant looks. Griffin made his way around the table obediently. When he reached Natalie, he paused for only a moment, then brushed his mouth quickly against her skin.

She didn't smell like face cream and old-fashioned perfume, as the older women did. She smelled of vanilla pods and jasmine. He wanted to lick every inch of her.

Her chest rose with a quick intake of breath and when he eased away, he saw color rise in her cheeks.

She turned back to her work, stabbing hard at the ball of wool in front of her.

"Dr. Jingle, sit by me," Nora ordered.

"Are you going to explain the Dr. Jingle?" Florence looked confused.

He shrugged. "Apparently, I have a new nickname, after I rescued a jingle bell from a certain young lady's nasal passage."

"Nora stuck a bell up her nose," Hazel informed the group. "And I didn't even tell her to."

He strongly suspected that wasn't necessarily true but now didn't seem the time to argue with her, even if he thought he had the smallest chance of winning against a five-year-old.

Birdie reached for his hand. "I wasn't expecting you until closer to sunset. We can't light the menorah until then."

"Better too early than too late, right? I went skiing this morning and then finished some paperwork this afternoon and since I was done earlier than I expected, I decided to head here."

He took in the chaotic recreation room. "What's with all the frenzied activity in here?"

"We're in the middle of trying to finish things for our stall at the market."

"Some last-minute additions to your offerings?"

"That's right. The men are finishing painting a few more toys, and Natalie has taught us how to make these cute ornaments."

She held up a finished ball-shaped creature that really did look like a round, woolly owl.

"How does this work? You look like you're mad at someone and stabbing at voodoo dolls."

"It is very cathartic," Birdie said. "Even I can manage it, and I can hardly see what I'm doing. You should try it as a way to take out your frustrations when you're mad at some insurance company for refusing to pay a claim."

"What is it?"

"It's called needle felting," Birdie said. "Our Natalie can explain it better than I can."

She looked uncomfortable at being in the spotlight. "It's quite easy. You start with wool or wool roving, which is wool that has been processed but not yet spun into yarn." She gestured to one of the thick balls in front of her. "You take a wad of it and form it in approximately the shape you want."

She demonstrated by taking a few feet of the tan roving and winding it into a ball.

"Then you repeatedly stick either a special needle or felting tool into it, which binds the wool fibers tightly together. When you're done, you've turned your soft wool into a solid object. You can make whatever you want. Small animals, ornaments, little toys."

"Feel how soft it is," Birdie said, holding out what looked like one of the finished ornaments. He rubbed his thumb over it and had to agree.

"Nice," he said.

"I've always wanted to learn how to needle felt," Arlene said. "It's surprisingly easy."

"Do you want to try?" Birdie asked. "You have strong surgeon hands."

"Except I'm not a surgeon."

"But you could do surgery, if you wanted to."

That was true. He had the skills, he just didn't necessarily want to use them. He hadn't enjoyed the surgical rotation, though he had great respect for his colleagues who excelled in that arena.

Griffin had always been drawn to the idea of being a primary care physician, establishing relationships with patients and their families and helping with their everyday health problems.

Flus, colds, ear infections.

Removing jingle bells.

"You really don't have to help," Natalie assured him.

"You don't," his grandmother agreed. "But you might as well do *something*, since you're here. Maybe you could help the team over there painting the wooden cars and block sets they've been making."

"Or our knitting club, on the couches over there."

He followed the direction his grandmother pointed and saw a group of about six people, men and women, on the sofa, knitting needles moving quickly as they chatted away.

He was again grateful for the warm, supportive community McKenna and Liz had created here at the Shelter Inn, giving purpose and companionship to the senior citizens who had moved here.

Birdie hadn't wanted to leave the home she had lived in for six decades. He certainly couldn't blame her for that. It was bred into her and so many others of her generation to be self-sufficient and not have to lean on anyone else. He expected he would fight hard for his own independence, when that time came.

This was a good place for her, where she could still live on her own but also had friends and activities and stimulation.

"Stay," his grandmother said. "We have an hour until sunset. I would rather not stop until I've finished this ornament and maybe started a few more while the supplies are here so I can work on them this weekend as I'm listening to my audiobook."

Birdie had always been an avid reader, serving on the town's library board for years and hosting numerous book clubs. Of all the things she grieved over when her sight began to deteriorate, the pleasure of curling up with a book in her hands was one Griffin knew his grandmother missed most.

"I don't mind waiting," he said.

"You can color a bookmark with me, if you want," Hazel offered.

He caught Natalie's gaze and saw her cheeks were still a little pink.

"Those are very nice," he replied. She seemed to be very good at coloring, studiously trying to keep within the lines. Nora, on the other hand, was all over the place with her picture, scribbling away with joyous abandon.

He wanted to ask if he could just watch, but he didn't want his grandmother to call him a slacker too.

"It's really quite simple," Florence assured him.

"Even I can do it, and I am the most uncrafty person you'll ever meet," Arlene added.

"In that, we are kindred spirits, then," he assured her. Arlene chuckled with an affection that touched him.

She was not one of the people in town who held a grudge against him because of his family. She and her partner, Caro, had been their neighbors when he was growing up, and he had never known them to be anything but kind.

Caro, who had run a small café in town, had died four years earlier after a long fight with uterine cancer, which Arlene had nursed her through with grace and courage.

Arlene had her own health challenges, suffering a stroke a year after her partner died, he knew, which had led her to moving into the senior apartment complex.

He didn't know Florence well, as she and her husband, James, had moved to town from California while he had been away at med school.

From what Birdie had told him, Florence and James had

come to Shelter Springs to retire near their grandchildren after their son took a job teaching at the high school and coaching the football team.

He liked them both very much. She always treated him with cheerful warmth.

He took the only empty seat, which happened to be next to Natalie.

"What do I do?" he asked.

"Do you know how to make a yarn ball like I did a minute ago? You do the same thing with the roving," Natalie said, handing over a length of the wool.

"No. But I can probably figure it out."

"It's easy, son," Florence said. "I'll show you."

She picked up the wool and roving and started wrapping it around and around, as Natalie had done, until it made a ball about the size of his palm.

Natalie handed him another length of wool. "Now you want to make a smaller one for the head."

This time he wrapped the ball himself. It was misshapen and in danger of falling apart until he wrapped more of the wool around it. He hadn't felt this inept since the first time he had to draw blood in medical school.

"Here's a needle you can use."

Natalie held one out to him. When he took it from her, their fingers brushed and he knew he wasn't the only one who felt the sparks. Her hand trembled, and she hitched in a little breath he was quite certain nobody else noticed but him.

"Take the needle and start poking it in to push the fibers together so they can tangle together. Like this."

She stabbed at her project, which looked far more like an owl than his.

He followed her lead and was astonished after a few moments to feel the fluffy wool ball growing harder and more compact.

His hands felt big and awkward. He had never been one for

arts and crafts, but the approving looks from all the women definitely went a long way to make him feel more comfortable.

After several more moments, Griffin could feel some of the tension leave his shoulders. The activity was oddly restful, especially listening to the little girls chatter and the older women share jokes and anecdotes.

He had always given his patients who suffered from anxiety the advice to incorporate plenty of sleep and regular exercise into their routines. He might have to advise that they should also pick up some kind of handicraft.

"Where did you learn how to do this?" he asked Natalie, while the three women were occupied discussing a movie they had watched together the night before.

"A few years ago, I spent a month in a small town in Norway, staying at the house of a couple who were visiting a new grandbaby in the UK. They had two cats and a really adorable dog named Rufus. I happened to wander into a yarn shop there where a woman was teaching a needle felting class. I watched for a moment and was fascinated."

She smiled softly at the memory. It was hard to look away from her when she looked so lovely, but if he didn't, he was going to poke the needle through his finger.

"I loved it immediately," she went on. "I always find it restful, shaping and needling, without the mental gymnastics I have to go through of counting stitches when I knit or crochet."

"I was thinking the same thing. About it being restful, I mean. I might have to advocate this for some of my patients."

She flashed that smile again and this time his needle completely missed the ball of wool and hit the table, which fortunately had been covered with some kind of protective surface.

"You must have picked up all kinds of fun skills in your travels," he said, hoping she didn't notice.

"Oh, definitely. I know how to decipher train schedules across the world. I can haggle without even saying a word. I can cook a few excellent pasta dishes I learned from a couple of elderly sisters in Naples. Oh, and I know how to tell a guy I'm not interested in about eight different languages."

Griffin laughed, then happened to catch his grandmother looking at the two of them. Too late, he remembered he was planning to do all he could to convince Birdie that he was only friends with Natalie Shepherd, who would be leaving town as soon as her sister gave birth.

The reminder suddenly felt like the needle was poking under his skin instead of into the wool.

He did his best not to pay too much attention directly to Natalie for the rest of the time it took him to shape his wad of wool into something that sort of resembled a lopsided owl.

She offered him a few pointers on making the face by felting in more wool in a contrasting color to outline it, but in the same casually helpful tone she used with everyone else, including her nieces.

"That looks great," Florence told him when he held up the finished ornament.

"I wouldn't go that far. I'm not sure anyone would be willing to shell out money for this, even if it is for a good cause."

"Sure they will." Natalie picked it up and turned it in her hands. "You're a fast learner. We can definitely sell that one at the market. Unless, of course, you would rather keep it for yourself to hang on your own tree."

He didn't want to forget the cozy warmth of the afternoon, but was quite certain he wouldn't need any ornament to remind him. "If you think you could sell it, I am fine with donating it to the cause."

"That's great."

"Well, that's probably it for me today," Arlene said. "My arthritic hands are complaining at me again."

"Um, hands can't talk. They don't have mouths," Hazel informed her in a tone that clearly implied the girl thought Arlene might be in need of a reality check.

"Sweetie, when you get to be my age, every part of your body talks to you all day long," the woman answered.

"True enough," Birdie said. "Right now, my knee is telling me it's time to get up and move around. Can't you hear it?"

Hazel cupped her hand to her ear and leaned closer to her. "I can only hear Dash snoring."

At the sound of his name, the dog opened one eye and flapped his tail on the ground, which made both little girls giggle.

"It's getting close to sunset," Griffin said. "Should we go light the menorah?"

"Good idea. Help me up."

"I didn't know you were Jewish." Natalie looked startled and intrigued.

"Oh, I'm not. I'm afraid we're as gentile as they come. But my dear friend Dorothy and her husband, Sam, were. Since the Jewish community around here is fairly small, I always tried to celebrate important holidays with her. She's gone now and Sam's moved closer to their daughter in Arizona. Lighting the menorah in Dorothy's memory is one way I try to keep her in my heart."

"That's lovely." Arlene's pale blue eyes wrinkled at the corners with her smile.

"I always think of my mother as well when we light our Kimora candles during our Kwanzaa celebration," Florence said. "She was what they call an early adopter of the tradition. We were the first ones in our neighborhood in Los Angeles to celebrate."

"What's Kwanzaa?" Hazel asked.

Florence gave her a short but lovely summary about the celebration of African culture and values and how important the tradition had become to her and her family, in addition to their Christmas celebrations.

"Isn't this a magical season, when everyone focuses on faith, tradition and caring, no matter what they celebrate?" Birdie said. "Would any of you like to come and help my handsome grandson light Dorothy's menorah?"

"I would love to," Florence said.

"So would I," Arlene said.

The women got up from the table with an assortment of joint pops and muffled groans at the aches and pains of movement again after sitting too long in one place.

"Where are you all going?" Florence's husband, James, asked from one of the other tables, where he had been chatting with a couple of the other residents while they sanded wooden blocks to be painted.

"We're lighting a menorah at Birdie's place," his wife told him. "We shouldn't be long."

"May we come along?" he asked in the deep, resonant voice that must have served him wonderfully well as a minister before he retired.

"Sure," Birdie said. "The more the merrier."

She hooked one arm through Griffin's and held her dog's leash in the other, then led the way to her apartment.

thirteen

When she had agreed to come back to Shelter Springs to help her sister with the girls over the holidays, Natalie had never expected to find herself attending a menorah-lighting ceremony with a dozen senior citizens of various backgrounds, faiths and ethnicities. Or that Griffin Taylor would be the one holding the shammes, the middle candle that was used to light the others.

"Grandma, would you like to say a few words or should I just light two candles?" he asked Birdie.

His grandmother looked surprised. "I could say a few words. I know there are traditions and prescribed prayers. If I were truly Jewish, I would know those things more. I wish I did. I mostly remember my friend Dorothy. Her kindness and goodness. She was a light to the world around her, full of humor and wisdom and grit. I learned so much from her and miss her every day."

"What happens now?" Hazel asked in a loud whisper. "Do we blow out the candles and make a wish, like a birthday cake?"

Birdie smiled. "No, my dear. These candles should stay lit. They represent a moment when a group of people dearly needed a miracle to survive and found one."

"They're pretty," Nora said, her little face lifted to the glow of the candles and the small tabletop Christmas tree next to it.

Natalie again felt the wistful ache in her chest that had hit her at random moments over the past week since she had come to help McKenna with the girls.

Was it her heart or her ovaries? She wasn't sure. For the first time in her life, she had begun to wonder what it might be like to have a child of her own.

She had always told herself she didn't want children. She had designed her life exactly as she wanted, with no room for a family. She loved being a wanderer. She had the opportunity to make friends around the world, to learn new traditions and experience unique places.

She would never again be the girl stuck in this hotel, watching the world move along without her.

Over the years, she had experienced major holidays all over the world. Rosh Hashanah in Israel, Eid al-Fitr in Morocco, Holy Week and Easter in Italy, Epiphany in Greece and Christmas traditions in several countries throughout Europe and the Americas.

But sometimes, when Nora was cuddled up on her lap listening to a story or Hazel was chattering away about something, Natalie felt this same tug of longing that must have been buried so deeply inside that she thought it had shriveled and died.

She would never regret the choices she had made or the rich and interesting life she had designed for herself. This time in Shelter Springs had made her question, though, if her lifestyle was truly sustainable. How much longer would she be content living a month at a time in someone else's home, taking care of someone else's pets?

She pushed the worry away for another day.

"We probably need to go, girls. We should go find some dinner."

"You don't have to worry about that," Birdie said. "I knew everyone would be hungry after working so hard all afternoon so I arranged a delivery of sandwiches and soup from the Trestle Top Café."

"Oh, we love that place, don't we, James?" Florence nudged her husband.

"Oh yes," he answered. "They have the most marvelous cream of mushroom soup I have ever tasted in my life."

Hazel made a disgusted face. "Ew. I hate mushrooms. They taste like slugs."

"How do you know what slugs taste like?" Natalie had to ask. "Have you ever had one?"

"No. But I bet they taste gross. They look gross."

"Well, mushrooms aren't gross, but it's fine if you don't like them," Birdie said. "I also ordered chicken noodle soup and those delicious croissant sandwiches they make there. You'll have to make sure you take some to our McKenna."

As they walked back to the recreation room, Natalie was not surprised to see that Nora migrated to Griffin. Her youngest niece seemed fascinated by the man and couldn't resist the chance to spend more time with him.

Natalie walked with Arlene, a woman she had always found to be warm and kind.

When this odd assortment of people arrived back to the community recreation room, the smell of delicious food wafted toward them.

The counter area around the kitchen was filled with trays of food and bowls and silverware. A man was taking the lid off a gallon bucket of soup and Natalie's spine stiffened.

Her father.

Somehow, she had managed to avoid him since his arrival in town, though it hadn't been easy.

He had visited McKenna and the girls twice. Once, she had used grocery shopping as an excuse to conveniently disappear ten minutes before he was due to arrive. The second time, she had stayed in her own room, feeling like an immature teenager being pouty and petty.

She couldn't hope to avoid him now, especially when he stood beside her aunt Liz, arranging sandwiches on trays.

The girls spotted him at the same instant.

"Grandpa Steve!" they shouted together. They rushed over for his embrace. He laughed and picked them up, burying his well-trimmed beard into their necks, much to their squeals of delight.

"Your dad's back in town," Griffin said from behind her, his low, surprised voice sending shivers ripping through her. "When did that happen?"

"Earlier this week. It's temporary, of course. He won't be here long, but apparently he wants to spend Christmas with the girls and plans to stay until after the baby is born."

"That will be nice for McKenna."

Yes. She had been trying to focus on that. Her sister wanted their father here. If it brought McKenna some comfort and peace during her difficult pregnancy, especially with Travis playing his disappearing act during these final days, how could Natalie object?

"I'm sure McKenna will enjoy having him home for however long he chooses to stay this time."

He gave her a careful look, which clearly told her she hadn't been very successful in hiding her feelings toward her father.

"You don't expect that to be long."

"Sorry. My cynicism is flaring. Much like Arlene's arthritis."

"I take it you and your father don't get along."

"I've seen him exactly twice in thirteen years. Three times now, I suppose, counting today."

"Seriously?"

She watched her father help the girls get plates of sandwiches and chips, then settle them at one of the tables. His solicitous care made her throat ache.

"We haven't kept in touch. I'm bitter, if you want the truth. He has tried to reach out over the years, but I'm not interested, thank you very much."

"You must have your reasons."

She let out a breath. Those reasons were huge to her, but somehow McKenna didn't share her opinion.

"He wasn't here when we needed him most after we lost our mom and then Jake within a year. I'm not as good as McKenna at pretending everything is rosy and bright."

"Is that what you think she's doing?"

She had come to see during the time she had been here that McKenna always tried to see the best in people. Her husband. Their father. Natalie.

That wasn't necessarily a bad trait. She admired her sister for her generous heart. At the same time, she worried it put McKenna in a terribly vulnerable position.

If her marriage to Travis failed, what would McKenna do on her own with three young children?

"Sometimes it's easier to pretend everything is okay, like wrapping a rotten apple up and then tying a pretty ribbon around it and hoping nobody notices what's beneath the paper."

His features softened with compassion, and he reached for her hand. "Something tells me you're not a woman who is very good at pretending."

She was. She had been pretending since she came back to town that she wasn't fiercely attracted to Griffin.

It was more than that. She liked him. How many other men she knew would be willing to hang out crafting all afternoon with a bunch of senior citizens, simply because it made his grandmother happy?

She thought of how sweet he was with Nora during their emergency trip to urgent care and how kind he had been the night he helped her put up the inflatables.

If she wasn't careful, she might find herself falling head over heels for Griffin.

She let out a shaky breath and lifted her gaze. To her aston-

ishment, his attention was focused on her mouth, almost as if...
as if he wanted to kiss her.

Her lips parted, and she thought she might have made a sound.

She must be mistaken. She blinked, but when she opened her
eyes she found him still wearing that almost pained expression.

No one could see them where they stood out here in the hall.
Everyone was busy inside the common room, grabbing food and
finding somewhere to sit.

She had been aware of him sitting next to her all afternoon,
his head bent over the tiny owl ornament and a small smile on
his face as he listened to the conversation flow around him.

She had wanted to kiss him then, with a ferocity that startled
her. The urge had only grown stronger as the afternoon went
on, shifting to evening.

Now it became the only thing she could think about.

"Griffin," she began, her voice low and throaty.

She wasn't sure what she might have said, she only knew
something sparked in his gaze, something hot and hungry that
left her achy.

He leaned toward her slightly and she caught her breath. Just
before he might have kissed her, they heard someone coming
out of the room into the hall where they stood.

His grandmother, Natalie realized with chagrin.

Birdie looked around, her eyes vague behind her thick lenses.
What had she seen?

"Griffin? Are you and Natalie out here?"

"Yes. Right here," he answered, backing away so quickly, she
worried he would run into the wall.

"I was, um, just grabbing some more paper towels," she lied.

"Oh, that's nice of you. Did you get something to eat?"

"Not yet," Griffin said, his voice sounding gruff.

"Well, make sure you grab something before it's gone. I
wanted to let you know there's a free concert tonight at the

church next door, featuring a children's choir from Haven Point. It starts in an hour. A bunch of us were thinking about going."

"That sounds nice."

"Do you think the girls might be interested?"

The girls did enjoy Christmas music and were always singing "Away in a Manger" loud enough to wake the baby Jesus.

"You said it was a children's choir. I'm assuming they're playing music young children might enjoy."

"I think so. The title of the concert is A Child's Christmas Around the World."

"That sounds lovely. I'm sure the girls would very much enjoy it. I'll have to see if I can find something for them to wear."

"I'm sure they're adorable just as they are. You don't need to change their clothes."

"How do you know, Gram? You can't see them." Griffin's voice was dry. "For all you know, they could be wearing swimming suits and snorkel fins."

Birdie made a face at her grandson. "I can see colors perfectly well, and I know they were both wearing red sweaters and red-and-black pants in some kind of pattern I can't see. Use your best judgment of course," she said to Natalie. "None of us plans to change what we're wearing. It's a casual concert. I wouldn't think anyone needs to dress up."

If no one else planned to change, she imagined the girls would be fine. Most of the Shelter Inn residents who had been crafting with them wore cardigans or holiday-themed sweatshirts.

"I'll grab their coats and maybe a fresh sweater for Nora. It looks like she's spilled a little ketchup on hers."

She wasn't entirely sure how much the girls would enjoy the Christmas concert, but she figured they could always slip out. The church was only next door. If attention levels frayed, they could always walk back to the Shelter Inn.

"We can keep an eye on the girls while you get their coats," Birdie said.

While Natalie knew Birdie couldn't actually do that, the others could. She had come to appreciate how all the residents seemed to watch out for Nora and Hazel. The girls lived in a building containing twenty-four apartments filled with honorary grandparents.

And an actual grandfather, she suddenly remembered.

She shifted her gaze to a table across the room, where Steve seemed to be entertaining Liz and a few of the husbands. His hands moved animatedly as he spoke, and his eyes sparkled with laughter.

He did look healthier than he had years ago at McKenna's wedding, she had to admit. He no longer appeared thin, hollow, ravaged by grief for Jeanette.

He must have sensed her scrutiny. He shifted his gaze slightly and met hers over Liz's head. He gave her a tentative smile, looking so much like the father she once had adored that Natalie felt a little light-headed.

He wasn't that man, any more than she was that innocent girl, untouched by tragedy and loss.

She jerked her gaze away and rose, heading for the food so she could grab a croissant sandwich for herself and make up a quick plate for McKenna.

After again making sure the girls seemed to be fine, ensconced at a table with Arlene Gallegos and Calvin and Barbara Wiggins, she carried a couple of sandwiches, a cookie and a covered bowl of soup down the hall to McKenna's apartment.

When she opened the door, McKenna's voice seemed louder than usual.

"Again? This is the fourth night this week you've had to work overtime. You're not the only manager there, Travis. Can't Jorge or Paul handle the late shipment?"

"Jorge was supposed to, but he had a family commitment." She heard her brother-in-law's voice, sounding tinny and distant. He was on a speakerphone, she realized. "I'm sorry, sweetheart. I know how hard this has been on you. But you've got your sister and your dad there to take care of things. If I put in the hours now, it will be that much easier to take my family leave after the new baby comes."

"How do I know you'll even do that?" McKenna snapped.

"I told you that was my plan."

"It's easy to say now, but I'm afraid after the baby comes, you'll just come up with another excuse to work overtime."

"Come on. You know I won't."

McKenna hesitated, as if afraid to voice her next words. When she spoke, her tone was so low, Natalie almost couldn't hear her.

"Sometimes I almost think you don't even want this baby."

She sounded so defeated, Natalie wanted to rush in and hug her. Not now. She was in a weird situation, unsure whether to remain here lurking behind the door or rush in and announce her presence in the middle of the fight.

Her brother-in-law hesitated a moment too long before he answered. "You know that's not true."

"Do I? From where I sit—which is on this blasted bed, where I've been for two weeks now—you are putting on a pretty good impression of a man who cares more about his work than his family."

Natalie couldn't hear his next words. They were muffled as if he spoke to someone off camera. When he returned to the conversation, his voice sounded distant.

"You're seeing things that aren't there."

"That's right. I'm the hysterical, overemotional pregnant woman who has completely lost touch with reality."

"I didn't say that."

"You didn't have to say it. I can pick up on the subtext."

"I'm trying to keep my job, Kenna. You know how strict they can be about mandatory overtime during the holidays. You either work or they let you go. I can't afford to screw this up. In a few weeks we're going to have another mouth to feed. Where would we be if I got fired? We would lose our health insurance and wouldn't be able to pay our bills."

"At least we would still have us."

"We still have that. We'll *always* have that," Travis said. "Look, I have to go. We can talk about this more when I get home, if you're not already asleep. I love you, babe."

McKenna did not say the words back. Instead, Natalie heard a strangled sound like a sob then a crash that made her suspect her sister had thrown something against the wall. Possibly her phone.

She had no choice but to go in now. Natalie cleared her throat loudly to announce herself, then walked into the room.

McKenna looked up, pressing a tissue to her nose. "Oh. Hi." She sniffled and swiped at her nose. "I guess you heard some of that."

"Some. I'm sorry. I wasn't eavesdropping on purpose." She set the sandwiches and the soup onto the hospital-style rolling table that had been set up in the room. "I was bringing you some dinner."

"So now you know. This pregnancy is turning me into a total beyotch."

She sat on the bed and hugged her sister. "Oh, honey. You aren't. It's completely reasonable for a woman in your situation to seek comfort and reassurance from your partner."

McKenna looked miserable. "Everything seems so different this time. Sometimes I wish we'd never tried again after I had those miscarriages. Maybe God was trying to tell us something, that we were supposed to stop at two."

Anything Natalie might have said seemed inadequate so she turned to the universal panacea. Food.

"I brought you some food. Birdie ordered dinner from the Trestle Top Café for everyone."

"Oh, that's nice."

"Birdie and some of the others are heading next door for a children's concert. They thought Nora and Hazel might enjoy it, but if you would rather we stay here with you, I have no problem doing that."

"You don't have to." McKenna gave a watery smile. "I'm sure they would enjoy the concert. We went to one last year around this time, and they were both transfixed. I wish I could go with you."

Natalie couldn't imagine how trapped she would feel if she had to sit here day after endless day. She wasn't sure she would be able to handle it.

"I imagine if you open your window, you might be able to hear the choir, but you would definitely get a little cold. I can record it for you, if you'd like."

"Thanks. That would be nice. It might help me get in the Christmas spirit a little more."

"Eat your soup while it's hot. I'll go refill your water."

She picked up her sister's giant insulated water bottle and returned to the kitchen, where she added fresh ice and cold water.

"Here you go. Do you need anything else?" she asked when she returned to the room.

"An attitude adjustment. Can you give me that?"

"I'm sorry. I wish I could."

Her sister shook her head. "You've done so much already. I'm so glad you're here, Nat. I know I've probably said it a hundred times since you came home, but I don't like thinking about what I would have done if you hadn't come to my rescue."

"Then stop thinking about it. I'm here, and you're doing exactly what you need to for your baby. Focus on keeping that baby in just a little bit longer and think about how he'll be toddling around the house next Christmas, pulling the ornaments off the tree, throwing his baby food at the walls and generally annoying his sisters."

McKenna laughed, as Natalie had hoped.

"I can't wait."

"Are you sure you'll be okay if we leave you?"

She nodded, paper crinkling as she unwrapped her sandwich. "I'll be fine. I'll try not to lay here feeling sorry for myself while you're off enjoying a little holiday spirit."

"And trying to keep two little girls quiet who have a very hard time with that particular concept."

McKenna smiled. "There is that. Good luck."

"We shouldn't be too long. I'll keep my phone on vibrate and we can slip out if you need me."

"I won't. Thanks again."

She was still worrying about her sister as she hurried to the closet and grabbed the girls' coats.

fourteen

Moments like these could make even the most cynical soul believe in the magic of the holidays.

Griffin sat in a hard pew of the historic old church next to the Shelter Inn, listening to the pure, clear tones of the children's choir singing about angels crying and creatures gathering round. On one side of him, his grandmother had her eyes closed, her expression rapt as she focused on the music. On the other side, little Hazel Dodd was swinging her leg in time to the music.

Even as he enjoyed the music, he was intensely aware of Natalie, her features soft and lovely. She sat on the other side of Hazel with her niece Nora on her lap, her head bent to whisper something to the child that made her smile.

Before he could turn his head and focus again on the music, Natalie glanced up as if she sensed him watching her.

Their gazes met and awareness seemed to coil around them like curled ribbon.

She was the first to look away, but not before he saw the color rising on her skin and the slight tremble in her fingers.

They were sitting in a church surrounded by sixty or seventy other people, including his grandmother and Natalie's diminutive nieces. Yet he was completely overwhelmed by the urge to reach over Hazel's head and kiss Nat, as he almost had in the hallway before his grandmother interrupted them.

He had it bad for her.

What was he going to do about it?

Nothing. He answered his own question. He would go on silently aching for her, probably until she left town and he could work on pushing her out of his mind.

"What's happening? I can't see," her niece complained as the choir ended the song and the chorister began pulling out an assortment of different-sized bells from a large decorative box.

"It looks like they're about to play a song with some bells," Natalie whispered to her.

Hazel shifted from side to side, trying to see around the rather large head of hair belonging to the woman seated in front of her. "I want to see. Can I go closer?" she said in a voice slightly on the wrong side of a whisper.

Natalie looked torn. "You need to stay in your seat. That's what you do at a concert."

Hazel heaved an enormous sigh and crossed her arms across her chest, her cute little face glowering. She looked ready to throw a fit any moment now.

"Can I sit on your lap?" she asked after a moment.

He froze when he realized she was speaking to him.

"Um. Sure," he finally said. What choice did he have?

He pulled her onto his lap and she wriggled to get comfortable, then leaned against him, using his chest as a backrest as she probably did often with her own father.

"That's better," she said in that same overloud whisper that drew the attention of more than one concertgoer.

"Remember, you have to be quiet," Natalie said to her as the children in the choir began a festive number with some of the older choir members accompanying them on the bells.

They were good, performing with enthusiasm and delight, if not perhaps perfect musicality.

Hazel seemed entranced by the bells. Her eyes glowed and she hummed under her breath.

He would be hard-hearted indeed if he didn't find the concert more enjoyable because he was seeing it through the wonder and joy of a child.

His son would have been only slightly older than Hazel.

The reminder took the breath out of him as if Hazel had just kicked him hard in the gut.

As the choir shifted from the more energetic bell number to a softer song about the Virgin Mary singing a lullaby to her child, images flashed through his memory.

Holding his son for one brief instant before the nurses took him away.

The tiny, wizened frame inside the incubator in the newborn intensive care unit, hooked up to monitors and machines.

That heartbreaking moment when all the monitors went still.

Helping Tonya dress him for the first and last time in an outfit some kind soul had donated to the NICU for just this purpose.

Chase Griffin Taylor had lived three days after he was born early at twenty-eight weeks gestation.

Even then, Griffin had known his marriage to Tonya was on rocky ground. Neither of them truly had wanted to marry, but had decided it was the best course of action after she found herself unexpectedly pregnant only a few months after they started dating.

He had met her when they were both new doctors, not long out of med school. She had been smart, funny, kind, lovely... but her heart hadn't really been available. She had been in love with someone else, and while he had liked her he hadn't been interested in anything long-term, until fate had intervened.

They shouldn't have married. It had been a serious mistake. He had known it even as he said his vows. But Tonya had been adamant about keeping the baby after she became pregnant when birth control failed. After many long discussions, they had both decided marrying was the best way to share in raising their child, physically, financially and emotionally.

Chase had had a shock of dark hair, a dimple in his chin and a courageous spirit.

They had every reason to believe he would survive after a stint in the Neonatal Intensive Care Unit, until he had caught an infection in the hospital and his tiny heart had failed, despite valiant efforts to save him.

Griffin had thrown idea after idea at the neonatologist. In the end, they had accepted that letting their son go was the best course.

Their shared grief hadn't brought him and Tonya closer. Instead, they had withdrawn into their individual pain. What had already been a shaky foundation eroded more, until they both accepted that while they cared about each other, they weren't in love.

Griffin had never wanted to be divorced, like his parents with their bitter anger at each other. This was different, he knew, but the failure still stung. With a strange mix of sorrow and relief, he had eventually signed their divorce papers nearly a year to the day of their first date.

It had been a surreal chapter of his life, one that often seemed as if it had happened to someone else.

While Griffin had refocused his attention on his residency in California, Tonya had returned to her hometown in Vermont to finish hers. Griffin had been relieved six months later to learn that Tonya had reconnected with the man who had always had her heart, her high school sweetheart.

They married soon after, and she had recently given birth to a healthy son. She was a pediatrician now and had sent him a Christmas card, brimming over with pictures and details of her new life.

He was happy for her. She deserved every moment of joy that came her way.

For the most part, he was able to compartmentalize that loss five years ago. Okay, maybe he still had a gaping hole in his heart, but he had patched it over and managed to get on with his life.

Holding this sweet little girl on his lap, her hair smelling of grape jelly and her hand tapping out the song rhythm on his arm, seemed to shake some of those boards loose.

What would his son have been like? Would he have liked music? Soccer? Dogs?

He supposed every person who had lost a child must wonder about those might-have-beens.

Hazel seemed content to stay on his lap throughout the remainder of the concert. When it ended, she clapped along with everyone else and gave a happy sigh, her hands together at her chest.

"That was amazing!" she exclaimed.

"Amazing," her little sister parroted.

"I wish they could sing on and on."

"I think they would probably get too tired to keep singing all night," Natalie said with an affectionate smile at her niece.

"Also, I think the magic of something like this would be lost if it happened every day," his grandmother said. "If we listened to a concert like this all the time, wouldn't we get a little bored? It would lose some of its beauty and wonder."

"I guess." Hazel didn't look convinced as she slid off his lap and held out her arms again for Natalie to put on her coat.

When both girls were bundled up against the cold, Griffin was warmed when Hazel reached for his hand.

She didn't seem to stop talking as they slowly made their way back to the Shelter Inn, Hazel holding his hand and his grandmother tucking her arm in the crook of his.

Snow still fell lightly, flakes drifting gently out of the sky like sugar from a sifter.

Across from the inn, the Christmas lights in the town square shimmered in the night, a kaleidoscope of bright, cheery colors.

Before they could reach the front door, his grandmother and Nora yawned in concert. A few seconds later, Hazel joined them, giving an ear-popping yawn.

Undeterred, she turned to her aunt as soon as they were inside the lobby. "Can we go swimming?"

"Not tonight, honey. It's already past your bedtime."

"You said we could go swimming later."

"I did. But that was before we went to a concert. We'll go tomorrow, I promise. It's time for bed."

The girl's brow furrowed, and she looked about five seconds away from stomping her foot. "I don't want to go to bed. I'm not a baby like Nora."

"I'm not a baby," the other girl protested.

"Neither of you are babies," Natalie agreed. "Babies are too little to go to fun concerts."

"You have to go to bed or how will the visions of sugarplums dance in your head?" Birdie asked.

"That's only on Christmas Eve," Hazel said sternly.

"Oh, my mistake."

"But Santa's helpers are watching all the time. That's what my mommy says," Hazel said.

"That's right. And they probably want you to go to bed on time," Natalie said.

Hazel sighed. "I guess."

Looking crafty, she reached for his hand again. "Dr. Jingle, can you read us our story tonight?"

He instinctively tried to come up with an excuse, but Birdie gave him a look every bit as stern as Hazel's had been.

"I'm sure he would love that," she said, her tone brooking no opposition. "Griffin doesn't have the chance to enjoy a good story very often."

"We're reading Christmas books now," Nora said.

"Even better," Birdie answered.

Griffin was trapped and he knew it. How was he supposed to resist the combined efforts of two cute girls along with his implacable grandmother?

"I'm off to bed, darlings," Birdie said, gripping her cane. "Natalie, girls, I'll likely see you tomorrow. Griffin, dear, I'll undoubtedly see you sometime soon."

He kissed Birdie's cheek, grateful as always for this woman who had been such a force for good in his life. She had been a rock of stability among all the changing tides of his life.

"I can walk you to your apartment."

"No need. I know where I'm going," she said, her tone implying she wasn't as certain that he could say the same.

"Thank you for spending the evening with me."

"My pleasure," Griffin said. He wasn't lying, but only part of that enjoyment had come from his grandmother's company. The rest had been because of Natalie and her nieces.

"Come on, girls. Let's get you into the tub."

Natalie led the way to the apartment. The living room was decorated with a Christmas tree bearing popcorn garlands and colorful ornaments.

The place had been updated since he used to come here with Jake. He had always thought it was fairly small for a family of five, but then Jake and his sisters had also had the run of the hotel.

Natalie gestured to a chair. "The baths shouldn't take long, if you want to chill for a few moments and check your email or something."

"Sure. I can do that."

Meanwhile, he could also try to figure out how to extricate himself from this woman who had an uncanny knack for wriggling her way under his skin.

fifteen

Both Hazel and Nora were unusually well-behaved as they took their baths. She had discovered over the past week that bath time could be a long-drawn-out affair, filled with much splashing, quibbles over toys, wet towels. Tonight, both Hazel and Nora seemed in a hurry to finish.

No wonder, Natalie thought, when they had Griffin's story time to look forward to.

"We're done," Nora announced after they had only played with one or two of the many toys stored inside a net attached to the tile wall with suction cups.

"Already?"

Hazel nodded for both of them. "We have to pick a story for Dr. Jingle to read to us."

She had wondered if perhaps McKenna might want to read to her daughters. While she was running the bath for the girls, she had opened McKenna's door a crack and found her sister sleeping, the lamp next to her bed still on and a mystery novel Natalie had picked up for her at the library open next to her.

Better not to wake her, she decided, especially when they seemed to have their hearts set on Griffin reading to them.

The girls hurried into their pajamas and waited impatiently for Natalie to brush the tangles from their hair.

"Finish brushing your teeth, then you can go find a story-book in the basket."

"Can we open two books tonight?"

"No. Then you won't have anything to open tomorrow. Only one."

Her sister had followed the tradition handed down from their mother of wrapping up a different holiday-themed book for every night of December.

The girls took turns unwrapping a new book each day, then cuddling for a while with McKenna on her bed while reading that day's story. It was a cute, clever way of counting down the days to Christmas and gave McKenna a few calm, peaceful moments with her daughters.

Tonight it was Nora's turn. Hazel watched impatiently while her sister selected a wrapped book then hopped to the sofa to open it.

"You're already opening presents?" Griffin asked, looking confused.

Hazel nodded and explained the tradition to him.

"That sounds really fun."

"Usually we read with our mommy, but tonight we can read with you," Hazel said.

Nora quickly unwrapped the present while her sister watched with avid interest. Finally, Nora pulled the book free from the wrappings and held it out to Griffin.

"*The World's Biggest Snowman.* Wow. That's a lot of snow."

Natalie thought he seemed a little nervous. He probably wasn't at all accustomed to reading with children.

"Can I sit on your lap?" Nora asked in a voice just above a whisper.

"I wanted to," Hazel complained, not bothering at all to keep her voice down.

"How about this?" Natalie suggested. "Nora can sit there first, then it can be your turn about halfway through the book."

Hazel pouted but seemed to accept the compromise.

Nora climbed onto Griffin's lap. He looked momentarily nonplussed, then adjusted her into a more comfortable position on his knee.

"How's that?" he asked.

"Good," she answered, her voice a little shy.

"Where should I go?" Hazel asked.

Griffin pointed to the cushion next to him on the sofa. "This would be perfect. There's plenty of room."

She gave a put-upon sigh, but cuddled up next to him.

"Will you be able to see the pictures?" Natalie asked.

"I guess."

As he started to read, Griffin's voice was low, as calming as the ocean on a sunny day.

Natalie had to fight the urge to curl up against him on the opposite side from Hazel.

The girls were enthralled with the story, as if they hadn't heard it before, though they most certainly had. All the books were old favorites. This particular one had been beloved by both Natalie and McKenna.

The girls laughed at all the right parts, frowned when the family building the snowman fought about how to make it bigger and sighed happily when he finished.

Hazel was so wrapped up in the story, she didn't even point out the halfway mark so she could have a turn sitting on Griffin's lap.

"Oh, I love that story!" Hazel exclaimed, her features soft and tender.

"Me too," Nora echoed. "I wish we could build the world's biggest snowman."

"Yeah. Why can't we?"

"I'm not sure we have the right kind of magical snow here in Idaho," Natalie was quick to point out.

"Maybe we can build the world's second biggest snowman," Hazel suggested.

"The next time we have a big storm, we can build a snowman. They are best when the snow is fresh." Natalie spoke as if she knew this as fact, though in truth she had no idea what snow would be best to make a snowman.

She had a random memory of building one with her father when she had been about nine and McKenna seven. Probably because they had read this very book.

The memory twisted through her, bittersweet. She could almost feel the cold seeping through her boots, smell the coal Steve had found for eyes from his barbecue grill off their small patio.

Steve had been a good father throughout her childhood. He had been caring and involved, coming to all her softball games, every school performance.

All that changed when Jeanette lost her battle with cancer. Though they had all known her cancer had reached the terminal stage, Steve had seemed completely shocked that she was really gone.

He had spent the first few months in a drunken stupor, then had announced he needed to spend some time living off the grid in Alaska to put his head back together.

It had worked so well, apparently, that he had never come back.

She couldn't forgive him for that. Yes, Liz had stepped up to care for them and manage the hotel. If not for her, Natalie knew her uncle and aunt would have taken them in. It wasn't as if their father had dumped them into the foster care system.

He had been their father, though. The only parent left. Surely he could have stuck it out for a few more years, four at the most, until McKenna finished high school, before running away to "find himself" or nurse his broken heart or give up drinking or whatever the hell he had done up in Alaska.

"Can we have another story?" Hazel wheedled, drawing Natalie back to the present. To this sweet moment, with Griffin and her nieces.

"That one was so short, and I didn't even get a chance to sit on his lap," Hazel went on. "That's not fair."

Her niece was deeply concerned about equity and could be very bossy about it.

"That was a pretty short story," Griffin said. "How about Hazel picks the next story and you two can swap places?"

She wanted to tell him not to encourage Hazel. Natalie had learned that if she gave the girl an inch, Hazel would squeeze every drop out of it until she was too exhausted to argue further and simply surrendered to her demands.

As a life strategy, unfortunately it was working well for Hazel. But if Griffin was willing to read another story to the girls, both of whom clearly wanted it, Natalie didn't feel right about arguing.

Hazel slid off the sofa and hurried to the basket of books that had already been unwrapped. After studying the contents, she pulled out a book that was familiar to Natalie, one of her own childhood favorites.

This was a gorgeous Jan Brett book about a mitten that stretched and stretched to fit a forest full of animals.

"Oh, I like this one." Griffin smiled at the cover. Nora pouted a little as she was replaced on his lap by her older sister, but as soon as he began to read, her frown faded and she listened attentively.

The girls were captivated by the story. Natalie was simply captivated by *him*, foolish as that made her.

"How about one more?" Hazel asked sleepily, as predictable as snow in January.

"Nope. That's enough," Natalie said firmly. "It's been a big day and it's time for bed."

The girls looked as if they wanted to complain but since both of them were halfway asleep, their protests were muted.

"Good night," Hazel said, throwing her arms around Griffin's neck. He hugged her back, though he seemed a bit disconcerted.

"Thanks for letting me read to you."

"You're a good reader," Nora said, leaning her head against his arm.

"Um. Thanks," he answered, looking amused at the praise.

"Can you help tuck us in?"

"Hazel."

The girl gave Natalie an innocent look. "What? I just asked. Our dad does whenever he's here to read to us."

Yes, but Griffin was not their father. He was simply a kind man who had the same hard time saying no to the girls as Natalie did.

"I'll tuck you in, but Griffin can say good-night. How about that for a compromise?"

"Okay."

Nora slipped her hand into Griffin's. "Come see our room." She tugged him down the hall toward the pink-and-purple bedroom Natalie had once shared with her own sister.

As she went through the complicated routine of preparing the girls for sleep, Natalie found herself uncomfortably aware of Griffin leaning in the door frame, watching the process with interest.

After all the blankets had been tucked, pillows turned to the cool side and favorite stuffed animals unearthed from the pile at the bottom of each bed, she kissed the girls on the forehead.

"Good night," she said firmly.

"Will Daddy read to us tomorrow?" Hazel asked.

She tensed, wishing she had a better answer.

"Your dad is super busy right now. He's trying to get all his work done so he can be here when your new baby brother comes."

"I wish he could be here now," Nora said, her voice quavering a little. Tears always seemed at the ready whenever the girls were tired.

"He will be soon," Natalie assured her, doing her best to be the supportive aunt by telling Nora what she needed to hear. It wasn't easy when she wasn't exactly thrilled with the girls' father right now.

"Christmas will be here in only two more weeks. And your brother should be coming a few weeks after that."

"And then Daddy will be home?"

Natalie certainly hoped so.

"That's right. Now go to sleep."

Nora rolled on her side, eyes bleary as she fought the inevitable.

"Night, Dr. Jingle." Hazel gave him a sleepy smile.

Nora opened one eye. "Night," she echoed.

"Good night, girls. Thanks for a fun afternoon and evening."

They gave him angelic smiles, then both closed their eyes, already drifting away as Natalie eased out of the room and closed the door behind them.

When they returned to the living room, Griffin released an exhausted-sounding breath.

"Whew. They are two busy young ladies," he said.

She laughed. "And you were lucky. You caught them on a relatively well-behaved day."

He looked so alarmed that she had to laugh.

"Would you like some toffee? Betty in 292 made it. McKenna is trying not to do chocolate, which leaves it all for me and I have zero willpower."

"Is that right?" He raised an eyebrow.

Natalie could feel herself flush. She meant she had no willpower regarding holiday treats and sweets, but apparently she also had no willpower when it came to Griffin Taylor. She should be ushering him out the door. Instead, she was offering him toffee and hoping that he could stay a little longer.

"Sure," he said. "If I'm doing you a favor. I guess I could probably make a sacrifice and eat a piece or two of toffee."

She took a plate down from the cabinet and opened the metal canister Betty Martinez had dropped off. After piling several large pieces on the plate, she handed it over.

"I said a piece or two," he stated.

"Trust me, it's next to impossible to stop after one."

He took a piece and bit into it. Though she hadn't made the candy herself, she still enjoyed the way his eyes widened then closed in appreciation.

"That is delicious," he said when he could talk again.

"Tell me about it. Thanks for helping me get rid of it."

"Anytime."

He smiled as he went to sit on the sofa again. She let out a breath, reminding herself about all the reasons she couldn't fall for him.

"Thank you for being so patient with the girls. They're having a tough time with this whole thing. Their mother being stuck in bed and Travis working so much overtime, I mean. I think they've been feeling a little bit lost."

"They are sweet girls. I love seeing how excited they are about the holidays. After you grow up, you kind of forget how magical this time of year can be, until you see the wonder reflected in a child's eyes."

"I've had the same thought. It's hard to remember I'm not a big fan of the holidays when Nora and Hazel are chattering every minute about Santa Claus and the baby Jesus and all the things they're excited about."

"Why don't you like the holidays?"

She should have known he would pick up on that part.

"I don't hate them. Not really. It just always seems like so much fuss and bother for a moment that's gone and forgotten so quickly."

"I wouldn't have taken you for a cynic."

Was she? Maybe. She didn't like thinking it, but had to admit there was definite truth in his words.

He had been so kind that day, she decided it was only fair to be honest with him.

"How much do you remember about when my mom was sick?"

"Enough to recall how tough it was on everybody. I'm not sure Jake ever got over it."

He shifted his gaze away, his expression turning somber.

Griffin became edgy every time Jake's name was mentioned, probably for the same reason she always felt this helpless sorrow.

"Our mom loved the holidays. She always put the trees up the first day of November, both in our apartment and in the main lobby. The day after Halloween, all the decorations would come out. My dad... Steve used to give her such a hard time about it."

She said nothing for a long moment, her mind crammed full of sad memories. "That last Christmas, we all knew the end was near. She had been on hospice for three months and we knew doctors had done everything they could. She could barely speak by then. Still, she made us decorate the hotel as if our family wasn't already grieving. She wanted us to go through the motions. The presents, going to look at lights, listening to music. She couldn't go to any performances so the women's choir at church came to our house and gave her a private concert."

"That's nice."

"Everyone was very kind." She released a long, slow breath, the memories as clear as if they had happened yesterday.

"I think it was her love of the holidays that made her hold on as long as she did. She was so sick, so frail, in so much pain. But she still held on."

She was quiet, her gaze fixed on the glimmering lights of the tree. "I suppose I was waiting for some kind of Christmas miracle that would save her life. I prayed and prayed for one. We all did."

"In my experience, miracles are few and far between."

His expression looked dark again, a pain there she didn't understand.

"I thought if anyone deserved a miraculous healing, it was my mother, who was so kind to everyone."

"She was."

"Of course we didn't get a miracle. She died two days after Christmas. Sometimes I think she might have held out a few more weeks, if she hadn't exerted all her energy to make sure that last Christmas was as perfect as she could manage."

His eyes softened with compassion. "I'm so sorry, Nat. Those are hard memories. Your mom was an amazing woman. I always envied Jake for your family. You all seemed so supportive of each other, even during the worst of your mom's cancer treatments."

"She was the glue, you know? Without her, everything fell apart."

"Not everything. You and McKenna stayed close."

"Yes," she acknowledged. "Kenna loves the holidays as much as Mom did. The next year, I didn't want to put out any decorations. Everything felt wrong. Dad was gone, Jake was out at all hours of the day and night. I wasn't at all in the Christmas spirit. So McKenna did it by herself. A few weeks into December, I found her out here late one night decorating the tree by herself and crying."

The memory filled her with shame and chagrin for being so selfish in her own pain, she hadn't realized how much her sister was hurting.

Tears burned in her throat, behind her eyes, but she held them back. "McKenna said Christmas was about hope and joy, and we certainly needed some of that around here. She said Mom was probably looking down, furious that we couldn't even be bothered to put up a tree."

Her sister had been so feisty back then, far more courageous than Natalie.

"McKenna said that if we didn't decorate our house, our mom was probably going to haunt us and send all her fellow ghosts to do the same thing."

"Somehow I can absolutely imagine your mom doing that."

He smiled, and while her throat still felt achy, Natalie couldn't resist returning it.

They gazed at each other, there in the light of the small Christmas tree, and she suddenly felt as light and airy as those snowflakes outside the window.

He glanced at her mouth again and then away so quickly she wondered if she had imagined it.

"Griffin."

At her low voice in the quiet room, something kindled in his eyes, something hot and fierce and hungry, and he lowered his mouth to hers with an inevitability that left her stunned.

His mouth tasted like chocolate and toffee, two of her favorite things. Natalie had a feeling she would never again be able to enjoy those particular flavors without remembering this moment.

Griffin had always been her secret crush. She could admit that now, when his mouth was warm on hers and his hand slid across her skin.

When she was a twelve or thirteen, she had nurtured dreams of him doing exactly this. He had always been so kind to her, even when she acted like a brat.

She had never told anyone. She had never been ashamed of her feelings, she had simply feared that talking about them aloud would diminish the magic somehow.

The reality of his kiss was far better than those childish dreams.

sixteen

Griffin couldn't remember the last time he had kissed a woman so spontaneously.

Had he ever?

All day, he had been fighting the urge to do exactly this, to lick and taste and explore. He had wanted this since the day she showed up back in Shelter Springs. Every single moment he had spent with her since then had only intensified the ache inside him.

Her kiss was delicious—warm, enticing, addictive. He was powerfully drawn to her wit, to her warmth, to everything that made her uniquely Natalie.

The world seemed to fade away, leaving only the two of them tangled together in this moment, with the gleaming lights of a small Christmas tree that spangled the room with color.

He didn't want to stop. He wanted to touch her a hundred different ways.

Some part of him knew this was a mistake. Wrong time, wrong place. Still, he couldn't force himself to ease away.

A moment more. That was all.

The thought hardly had time to register when he heard the distant, prosaic, unromantic sound of a toilet flushing.

She froze, her eyes wide and slightly unfocused.

"Is it Nora or Hazel?" he murmured.

She drew in a ragged breath and seemed to be trying to gather her thoughts. "I... I don't think so. That's the bathroom off McKenna's room. She must be awake."

Her words jolted him the rest of the way back to sanity. What was he doing? He shouldn't have kissed her at all. He especially shouldn't have kissed her here in her sister's apartment, where two children or their mother or father could walk in on them at any moment.

He eased away, trying to catch his breath and do his best not to pull her back into his arms.

"Do you...need to go check on her?"

"She'll text me if she needs me." Natalie blinked a few times. Her dazed, unfocused expression seemed to recede and he could see her defenses click back into place.

"Griffin, I..."

Her voice trailed off as if she couldn't quite find the words.

"I know," he said, his voice gentle. "What were we thinking?"

"We weren't thinking at all. At least I wasn't."

"Neither was I," he admitted. Though he knew it was far from wise, he couldn't resist adding, "Other than thinking about how much I wanted to do far more than kiss you."

She swallowed hard. "You can't. We can't. I'm not... I'm here to help my sister with her kids, not to...to have a fling with the town's hot doctor."

He wasn't quite sure how to react to her words, which left him both uncomfortable and strangely aroused.

"And I'm far too busy trying to establish my practice here in Shelter Springs. I can't have a fling with the town's hottest temporary resident. As much as I might want to."

Her short laugh had an edge of hysteria to it.

"That's settled then," she said.

He sensed she wasn't any happier about the constraints of their situation than he was.

"So what happens now?" she said after a moment. "I mean, I would hate for things to be...weird between us now."

Weird? No. He could think of many words to describe this... thing between them. Incendiary. Intense. Amazing. *Weird* wasn't on the list.

"Why should they? You're leaving as soon as your sister has the baby. I totally understand that, believe me. We can both be cool about this."

"I hope so."

"It's not like we have to see each other every day. I do stop in once or twice a week to see my grandmother. If you would prefer to avoid me, I can always text you a warning in advance."

"Thank you. I appreciate the gesture," she said with a tremulous smile. "But I don't think it needs to come to that, do you? We're both mature adults. We can both agree this was a mistake that won't happen again. I don't see any reason we should go out of our way to avoid each other because of one lousy kiss."

"Ouch. Lousy?"

She glared at him. "Okay, one amazing kiss."

Natalie Shepherd made him smile even as he wanted to pull her right back into his arms. Why did this particular woman have the power to twist him into knots?

Something about her mix of toughness and vulnerability completely did it for him.

All his adult life, he had believed he was somehow immune to falling in love. He and Tonya had married for convenience and circumstance. He cared about her, both when he married her and now, but neither had been heartbroken when their marriage broke down after Chase died.

Griffin thought maybe his father's substance abuse and his cavalier disregard for the desperate efforts of Griffin's mother to keep their family together had scarred something deep inside him, soured him on love and relationships.

Something told him that if he wasn't careful, Natalie Shepherd could test all of his long-held beliefs about his own immunity to love.

He would have to tread carefully here. As appealing as he found Natalie and as much as he enjoyed being with her *and* her adorable nieces, none of this was real.

He needed to remember that, or he might discover how very wrong he was.

After Griffin left, Natalie stood for a long moment there beside the Christmas tree, then slowly lowered to the sofa where he had been reading to the girls.

What on earth had come over her? She was not the kind of woman to give in to random impulses and kiss a man she knew perfectly well was not good for her

She did not do casual hookups. She had friends who had no problem with moving from guy to guy. She had never wanted that. The few serious relationships she'd known since leaving Shelter Springs each had left an indelible mark on her heart.

That didn't stop her from inevitably moving on, though.

Something told her that Griffin would be a very tough man to walk away from, that any imprint he might leave behind would never fade.

That kiss.

She closed her eyes, remembering the taste of him, toffee and chocolate and sexy, delicious man. She hadn't wanted to stop, even knowing McKenna or one of the girls might walk out of their rooms or Travis could return to the apartment at any moment.

What was she going to do about the man?

Despite her best efforts at protecting her heart, she was more drawn to him than ever.

She pressed her hands against her knees and rose. She couldn't sit here all night, angsting about Griffin Taylor.

She had laundry to do, and the dishes from lunch were still in the sink.

She was loading the dishwasher when her sister came out of her room, walking with slow, measured steps.

"Kenna! What are you doing out here?"

She held up her jumbo water bottle. "I needed more ice and I didn't want to bother you."

"You're never a bother," she assured her. "Sit down. I can get it."

McKenna held out the water bottle, and Natalie hurried to the refrigerator and pushed the button. The ice maker clanked out fresh cubes.

"Text me or call me when you need something. Or just call out. I can hear you."

"I needed to move. I'm supposed to walk a bit every few hours, just to keep away the possibility of blood clots."

She knew the doctor mostly meant standing up beside the bed and walking in place, but she didn't argue.

"Anyway, I would do anything not to have to stare at those four walls another minute."

"I can certainly understand that. I can make you some tea, if you'd like."

"Thanks. That actually sounds really good."

She set to work, turning the electric kettle on and finding the specific herbal tea McKenna's doctor had deemed safe for her to drink during the pregnancy.

"Did I hear a man's voice out here earlier?" McKenna asked. "I was sleeping and couldn't tell if it was my imagination or real."

To her dismay, Natalie could feel her face heat up.

"The girls asked Griffin to read them a story tonight. He was kind enough to agree."

McKenna gave an appreciative smile. "He's such a great guy. I don't care what some of the old biddies say. I, for one, am glad he's back in town."

Natalie remembered what he had said in passing, about fighting to convince people he wasn't his father.

What a burden he carried.

"Do people really blame him for what his father did?" she asked.

Her sister shrugged. "Don't get me wrong, most people love him. He's not my doctor because I already see Devin Barrett as my primary care doctor and she's amazing. I have friends who go to him, though, and they adore him. His practice seems to be growing. But you know how small-town gossip can be. I've heard from a few who think he is only dredging up old pain by coming back to town. To some, he will always be the old Dr. Taylor's son, first and foremost."

"That's not fair. He's not responsible for his father's actions. Griffin was away at college when the accident happened. He had nothing to do with it."

"You and I know that. It's not fair, but people can be wrong-headed about these things."

That was yet another reason she needed to do her best to keep her distance. Griffin had enough on his plate, trying to separate himself from his father's actions and their grim consequences.

He didn't need the distraction of a short-term relationship, which was all they could ever have.

"How was the concert?" McKenna asked as Natalie set a steaming cup of peppermint tea in front of her.

She sat across from her sister. "Really nice. The girls seemed to like it. Hazel says she wants to join a choir now. Sorry about that."

McKenna gave a small, wry smile. "My Hazel usually wants to try every new thing that comes along. Dance lessons, violin lessons, soccer, T-ball. I love that she isn't afraid to try things. I wish I could have been more like her, instead of always being a scared baby."

McKenna had been a timid child, she remembered, often

content to watch while Natalie climbed the monkey bars or jumped off the high dive.

Their mother's cancer diagnosis, such a pivotal event in their lives, couldn't have come at a worse time. Natalie had been fourteen, but McKenna had only been twelve, just beginning to figure out her place in the world.

"I'm sorry I didn't get the chance to read to them."

"You were sleeping so soundly when we came back, we didn't want to disturb you."

"You should never worry about waking me up. I always want to wake up for my girls. They are my heart."

"That's because you're an amazing mother," she said, meaning every word.

McKenna made a face, then she winced and pressed her hand to her abdomen.

"Everything okay?"

She nodded. "Just a twinge. I'm fine."

"Are you sure? How are you really feeling?"

"Do you want to know the truth? I'm feeling really tired of people asking me that," McKenna said, her tone tart.

"Fair enough. I won't ask."

Her sister sighed. "I'm sorry. I'm restless and bored and feel like I'm missing Christmas completely."

"You are totally entitled to your bad mood. You're trapped in a tough situation."

A situation made tougher because of her brother-in-law and his complete dereliction of duty when it came to his family, she thought, though decided to keep that particular thought to herself.

"That still doesn't give me the right to take out my cranky mood on you, especially when you've been so great to upend your own life and come to my rescue."

"You know I wouldn't have wanted things any other way. If

you hadn't reached out to let me know you needed help, I would never have forgiven you."

McKenna smiled and sipped at her tea before replacing the cup on the saucer.

"Griffin was so sweet to read to the girls. How did that come about?"

"They asked him and he agreed. They seem quite taken with him. Especially Nora."

"That's unusual. She's typically pretty shy around people she doesn't know."

"I think she sees him as her hero. I mean, after a guy pulls a jingle bell out of your nose, how can you help but have a little crush on him?"

McKenna laughed, though her gaze seemed to sharpen on Natalie. "What about you? How do you see Griffin?"

Why was she asking? Did McKenna know they had done more than talk out here in the living room?

"Griffin is like a brother. You remember how tight he and Jake used to be."

"But he's not our brother." McKenna gave her a pointed look.

Yes. She was fully aware. She remembered again the heat of his mouth on hers, the solid, comforting feel of his arms around her.

"I know that," she said, focusing on her hands. "Since I've been back, he's become a...friend."

And we can just leave it at that, she thought. But of course, McKenna didn't.

"Is that all?"

"You know I'm firmly in the happily single camp. A relationship with someone here in Shelter Springs doesn't fit at all into the life I've created for myself."

McKenna gave a sad smile. "Too bad. If there was something more between you, maybe Griffin would have better luck than I have in convincing you to come home for good."

"That's not going to happen, Kenna," she said gently. "You

know I'm a rolling stone. I'm happiest when I'm seeing the sunrise from a brand-new spot."

"That's the thing about sunrises. Even if you're watching the sun come up from the same spot your entire life, you'll never have the same view."

Darn her sister for hitting her with inescapable logic.

Before Natalie could respond, McKenna pressed a hand to her stomach again, wincing.

"Are you sure you're okay?" Nat asked, trying not to sound as worried as she felt.

"Yes. He's kicking hard tonight, but I keep telling myself that's a good sign. When he stops kicking, that's when I should worry."

Natalie couldn't imagine all the angst that must go into carrying a pregnancy to full-term after two hard miscarriages.

"Maybe you should go back to bed," she suggested.

McKenna sighed. "I suppose you're right, though that's the last place on earth I want to be right now."

She rose, still graceful despite her large abdomen. "Thank you for the tea and the company and for keeping things running here. Are you heading to bed too?"

She should, but she knew her brain wasn't at all ready to shut down, especially after that stunning kiss.

"I think I'll stay up a little longer and listen to my audiobook while I finish another ornament for the market."

She was also trying to finish knitting a baby blanket for her nephew after the girls went to bed each night.

"Good night, then." McKenna gave her a pained-looking smile, then made her way back to the bedroom.

As she suspected would happen, the audiobook failed to capture her attention, though the story about a female spy in World War II was gripping and emotional. After only a few moments, when she realized she had completely missed what was happening in the plot because her thoughts continuously returned to

Griffin, Natalie tapped her earbuds to stop the narration and worked in silence at the kitchen table, felting the little owl ornament with movements that were probably too forceful.

She had just finished forming the face when she heard a key in the door, and a moment later her brother-in-law came inside.

He stopped short when he saw her, dismay on his features that he couldn't hide. He drew in a breath, then moved closer to where she worked at the table. "Hi. I didn't think anyone would still be awake."

Had he waited long enough at the tavern to make sure he wouldn't have to deal with his family or with her? She thought she again could pick up a hint of alcohol coming from him, but she couldn't be certain.

"Yes. We had a late night. I took the girls to a children's concert at the church next door."

"Oh yeah?" He poured some ice water from the refrigerator. "How was it?"

"Nice. The girls loved it. And they were very well-behaved."

"That's good." Travis glanced at his bedroom door. "How's Kenna today?"

For one unguarded moment, she saw his expression twist with raw, painful emotions before he quickly concealed it behind a false smile.

That expression went a long way to deflating Natalie's simmering anger.

"She seems to be okay. I know it can't be easy on her. I think more than anything, she's bored." She paused. "And scared."

"Oh." He sat heavily into a chair across from her, gripping his water glass as if worried it would slide across the table.

"She won't say it, but I know she's petrified she will lose the baby. After everything you've been through to bring a healthy son into the world, I think her heart would be shattered if something happened to him."

His features took on a grim expression. "I know. She had

such a hard time when she miscarried after Nora. It was a dark time. I tried to tell her I was fine with the girls, that we were a happy family and didn't need anything else, but she insisted she wanted to try again."

Natalie set down her felting needle, surprised at the information. For some reason, she had assumed Travis was the one who had pushed for another child.

"I wish I had worked harder to convince her we were happy the way we were." He sipped at his water.

"If McKenna had her heart set on a third child, I'm not sure you could have convinced her otherwise," she said honestly. They both knew McKenna wasn't easily dissuaded when she wanted something.

"She struggled after she lost the other two pregnancies. I don't know if you know how much. She lost interest in just about everything. Your calls were the bright spot in her week."

Natalie squirmed at this. She hadn't been exactly consistent at reaching out to her sister. She tried to call a few times a week, but sometimes when she was on a busy deadline or had traveled to a new job, she let more time slip by between calls.

She had sensed her sister was sad after the miscarriages, but hadn't completely understood the depth of her pain.

"Kenna became obsessed with having another baby."

"*Obsessed* is a strong word."

"It fits, though." Travis curled his hands around his water glass, staring down into it as if it offered a glimpse into the future. "Another baby was all she wanted to talk about. She wouldn't listen to any of my arguments."

He sighed. "The moment we found out she was pregnant, we were both nervous wrecks until she hit fifteen weeks, which was how far along she was when she had the second of her miscarriages. Until she started having trouble a month ago, she's been so happy, convinced we were home free."

"What about you?"

He looked at her, eyes stark with anxiety. "I want to be happy. I'm just so damned scared. I can't lose her."

"Is that why you've been heading to the Saddle and Spur every night after work when your family needs you here?"

He flinched as if she had reached over and poked him with her felting needle. "I don't go every night."

She did feel sympathy for him. Watching the woman he loved suffer must have been heartbreaking. While his words went a long way to helping her understand his actions, she still couldn't condone indulging his fear by neglecting his family.

"You aren't helping McKenna by staying away more than necessary. If anything, you're ratcheting up her stress level."

"I know."

"And the girls need their father."

He grimaced. "Do they? You're here. So are Liz and Steve. They've got plenty to keep them busy in the lead-up to the holidays."

Steve had probably justified his desertion of them using almost exactly those words. Liz was here. So were their other relatives and friends.

But girls needed their fathers, whether they were sixteen and fourteen or five and three.

"We can take care of their basic needs, yes. But not all their emotional needs. They miss you. Do you want their Christmas memories of this year to all be with someone else? They will only remember that you were never here."

He sighed again. "I get your point. It's not all about me and my fears, is it?"

"When you have kids, it can't be."

"I'll try harder to be here for my family."

She smiled and squeezed his hand. Travis was a good man. He clearly loved his wife and children, but was letting his fear rule his actions.

Something she knew entirely too much about.

seventeen

How had she forgotten the unique comfort and joy of being with friends who had known her since grade school?

The day after she took the girls to the concert, Natalie sat on a folding chair she had brought in from the recreation room, listening as the conversation of a dozen women washed over her.

McKenna's bedroom was packed with dear friends who had dropped everything in order to cheer McKenna up with this impromptu baby shower.

"I can't tell you how excited everybody is," Hannah had said on the phone that morning when she called Nat to make arrangements. "After I talked to McKenna yesterday and she told me she had talked to Dr. Reynolds, who said a small, casual gathering in her room would be fine, we decided we would have to do it now, before the holiday market opens tomorrow and everyone gets too busy."

"Good idea." What else could Natalie say, when Hannah and Holly had already started the ball rolling?

To her astonishment, the twins managed to arrange the whole thing in only a few hours. They had brought pastel balloons, a cake, adult drinks for everyone but McKenna, and a platter of bite-sized chicken salad sandwiches they had ordered from the Pine Street Grill.

Steve had happily agreed to take the girls to see the latest animated offering at the theater in town, promising popcorn and soda that would probably keep them up all night.

Now, Natalie sipped a margarita, thoroughly enjoying the laughter, conversation and silly baby shower games.

She had friends from college that she kept in touch with online, but she couldn't remember the last time she had gathered with a large group of friends like this. When she was house-sitting, she did try to work occasionally at the local café or enjoy the entertainment offerings at the neighborhood pub. She had friends around the world she had met in her travels, many who didn't even have a shared language in common.

None compared to this group of a dozen women, Aunt Liz included, who had been so dear to both her and McKenna through the years.

She had missed them dearly.

These women had carried her through her worst moments. The trifecta of pain, she thought of it. Her mother's long, lingering death, her father's abandonment, then Jake's tragic accident.

What would she have done without them?

It warmed her to the core to see they were still supporting McKenna when she needed them.

Feeling a little emotional, Natalie rose from her chair.

"Anybody need more margarita mix?" she asked.

"Me," Holly said, holding out her drink.

"I could use a top off too," McKenna's best friend, Vivi Morales, said.

"I'll go grab the pitcher. How are we doing on sandwiches?"

"You don't need to serve us," Hannah protested. "That wasn't the deal."

"I don't mind. I'm not great at games anyway. You keep playing."

"Since I'm out, I can help you." Amanda Taylor rose from

her folding chair, slim and lovely, with auburn hair and a pale sprinkle of freckles across her nose.

She wanted to tell the other woman she did not need her help, but couldn't come up with any words that didn't sound rude.

In the kitchen, she hurried to the refrigerator for the pitcher Holly had mixed earlier.

"I'll grab the sandwiches," Amanda offered.

"Thanks," Natalie said. Could Amanda sense the stiffness in her voice? Probably. The other woman gave her a quick look, but focused on transferring more sandwiches from the large catering tray to a smaller, more manageable one.

The distance between them made her ache a little. Amanda had once been her best friend. She, Holly and Hannah had been the fearsome foursome.

When they were young, the four of them had bonded over books and silly games and racing their bikes up and down the streets. As they grew older, it was boys and pop music. In high school, they seemed to migrate to the same activities—the debate team, the drama club, the honor society, the yearbook staff.

They had once known everything about each other, from their innermost dreams to their biggest mistakes.

Natalie was grimly aware that she hadn't actually had a conversation with Amanda in years. Probably not since McKenna's wedding, when she had been maid of honor and Amanda had been a bridesmaid. Even then, their conversations had been stilted and awkward.

"How have you been, Nat?"

She returned the large pitcher of margarita mix to the refrigerator. "Good. Busy."

"Kenna tells me you were supposed to do a job in Tenerife. I've always wanted to visit the Canary Islands. Your life must be so interesting."

Somehow her regular life seemed far away from this warm, cozy apartment filled with friends.

"I find it rewarding," she answered.

Amanda's smile was small and tinged with sadness. "You always wanted to go as far from here as you could. I remember how you always used to talk about living in Paris and being a writer. I guess you're doing exactly what you always dreamed about."

"I'm a copy editor and travel writer who house-sits for rich people with more money than they know what to do with. Not quite the romantic image I used to dream about, of being a novelist toiling away in a garret somewhere in Le Marais."

"It still sounds exotic and exciting to me. I mean, I'm living in my grandmother's house and I never go anywhere."

She angled her head to look at the other woman, even more lovely than she used to be.

"I'm surprised you stayed here all these years."

Amanda likely faced the same sort of scrutiny from some circles that Griffin struggled against. Natalie knew she had left town for a few years to attend college. What had compelled her to return?

"I love Shelter Springs," Amanda said, answering the unspoken question. "This is my home. I know it's not perfect, but there's something...peaceful here, even with all the hard memories."

Her chin quivered a little. Somehow Natalie knew she was thinking not about her father, with whom she'd had a difficult relationship, or her mother who had been completely unable to cope with an alcoholic husband. She was thinking about Jake.

"Plus Birdie is here," she went on, "and I didn't want to leave her alone, especially after she started losing her sight. She's always been so wonderful to me and to Griffin."

"I understand you have your own store now. Everyone raves about it."

Amanda's smile seemed more genuine this time. "Yes. The Lucky Goat. It's more of a collective, really. I originally started selling only soaps and lotions that other women in town made, but now we've branched out a little into jewelry, pottery, even some hand-knitted items. You should stop by while you're in town. It's great for holiday shopping."

She did have a weakness for exactly that kind of store. "I'll try. I'm usually pretty busy with Nora and Hazel, but I do still have a little Christmas shopping to do. Maybe I'll try to chance it one day this week when Hazel is in preschool."

"If it's easier, you can bring them to the market. I've got a booth there that offers a good sampling of our inventory. I saw the map the other day, and it looks like the Lucky Goat kiosk will be close to the front as you first walk in."

"I'll check it out."

The others were waiting for more refreshments, but neither she nor Amanda seemed in a hurry to leave the quiet kitchen. She longed for the closeness they once shared, when they would talk for hours, laugh at the silliest joke, tell each other anything.

"So. Are you dating anybody?" Natalie asked. It seemed a logical question, considering Amanda had once been engaged to her brother.

The other woman gave a rueful smile. "I'm afraid the choices are pretty limited here in Shelter Springs. Everybody of an appropriate age is either married or divorced. Or there's a really good reason why they're neither."

She paused, her hands clasping the counter behind her. "If you want the truth," she finally said quietly, "I don't know if I ever truly got over losing Jake."

Some of the anger that had simmered inside Natalie seemed to return in a rush. Oh yes. Now she remembered why she and Amanda had drifted apart.

"Really?" She couldn't contain her skepticism. "I don't know. You seemed to be pretty over him when you broke up with him three days before he died."

Amanda's features went pale, and she straightened from the

counter as if a sharp edge had gouged at her. Natalie instantly kicked herself for the impulsive words.

"I'm sorry. I shouldn't have said that."

Amanda let out a heavy sigh, her eyes filled with pain. "I never stopped loving Jake, Nat. I swear. I only... I only ended things because I hoped I could shake some sense into him. I wanted to give him a wake-up call. Maybe show him what he stood to lose. He was partying so much in those days. You remember, don't you?"

Natalie nodded, recalling nights her brother wouldn't come home at all.

"He was drinking all the time. Anything to mask the pain of losing your mom and his anger at your father for taking off like he did. Jake could go through a twelve-pack of beer during the day and then turn to the hard stuff at night."

"I remember."

She and McKenna had tried to talk to Jake about his drinking. So had Liz, she recalled. He hadn't listened to any of them.

"I couldn't keep going like that," Amanda said, her voice only slightly above a whisper. "Not after everything that happened with my...with my dad."

Right. Of course Jake's partying would hit her hard, after her own father had died in a fiery crash only months earlier that had killed several innocent teenagers.

"I gave him an ultimatum." Amanda had a faraway look, as if remembering that distant conversation. "He told me I wasn't his mother and he wasn't going to stop. I either had to accept it or walk out the door, he said. I didn't know what else to do. So I walked."

"And three days later he was dead."

She didn't say what she had always wondered, what she feared. Had his death truly been an accident? Or had her brother deliberately snowboarded into the dangerous off-limits area, triggering the avalanche that had buried him?

She didn't want to think that, but some part of her had always wondered.

That was the one question she couldn't ask Griffin.

"I know you blame me for his death. Believe me, whatever you think about me is nothing compared to the blame I place on myself. If I hadn't ended things, would he have been drinking so much? Would he have been able to make better choices on the mountain?"

Those were all things Natalie had wondered too. Along with those darker thoughts she didn't want to admit to anyone.

Amanda picked up a tissue from the box on the counter and wiped at her eyes. "As much as I might want to, I can't go back and change anything."

"None of us can, unfortunately."

"I've wondered a thousand times if the outcome would have been different if I hadn't ended things between us. If I had... given him another chance."

There in the warm kitchen with the muted sounds of laughter coming from the bedroom, Natalie had a startling revelation.

Even if Amanda had never broken things off with Jake, he still would have imploded. He had been teetering on a cliff's edge, just waiting for any nudge to topple him.

Amanda may have given him the excuse, but she hadn't pushed him over. Jake had done that all on his own.

"I don't blame you," she finally said, a little shocked that she meant the words completely.

Shock flared in those blue eyes. "You don't?"

"Maybe some part of me has been mad at you for hurting a man who was already in pain. I was wrong to think that, even for a moment. Jake was an adult who was making all kinds of poor decisions. You weren't responsible for his actions that day when he decided to snowboard into the off-limits area."

Neither was her father.

She caught her breath at the epiphany. It had been easy to blame everyone else for Jake's death.

Why had Amanda chosen that time to break up with him?

Why had Steve abandoned his three grieving children who had just lost their mother?

That was only masking her true anger, at Jake himself. She didn't know if he had deliberately snowboarded into that area in hopes of triggering an avalanche or if he had been arrogant enough to think nothing would possibly happen to him. She would probably never know.

Either way, Jake had made choices that had deadly consequences.

She looked up from her thoughts to realize Amanda's head was bowed and she was crying silent tears.

Natalie set down the pitcher and went to her friend, folding her into a hug that was long overdue.

"It wasn't your fault, Amanda. I'm sorry you've carried this guilt all these years and that I contributed to it."

"It was only natural for you to blame me. To hate me."

"I don't hate you. I never did. Jake was on a self-destructive path. We all tried to step in and help him. At the time he wasn't at a place where he was willing to listen to anyone else."

"I miss him so much," Amanda whispered. "He was my first love. My only love. I've never been able to let anyone else into my heart."

She remembered suddenly how much Amanda had dreamed of having a family. When Natalie used to talk about traveling the world and all the exotic places she wanted to see, Amanda had been focused on the future she wanted to create with Jake, the children they would have someday after they both finished college and established their careers, the happy-ever-after that she believed without question was their destiny.

Natalie's heart ached with sorrow for unfulfilled dreams.

"It's been more than a decade," she said softly. "It's past time to move on. I know you loved him, but I also know Jake wouldn't want to you to spend the rest of your life grieving for him."

Amanda didn't look at all convinced. Natalie pressed her hand.

"We need to find someone for you."

"Oh no. Don't you start too. Birdie is always after me to put myself out there."

"You should. Calvin Wiggins was telling me the other day about his grandson who is moving to town in a few months to open a mountain climbing school. He sounds delish, but then I'm not sure you can completely trust anything Calvin says."

Amanda's smile looked slightly less watery, Natalie was happy to see. "I'll have to be on the lookout for Calvin's delish grandson."

"Have you tried dating apps? I have friends who have met some great guys that way."

"Once. It was a big mistake. I met three different guys for coffee over the span of a week, and all three of them seemed offended when I refused to take them back to my house immediately."

"There's someone amazing out there for you. I'm sure of it. My aunt Liz knows everybody in three counties. I can ask her if she can think of any eligible bachelors for you to date."

Amanda snorted. "If Liz knows of any eligible bachelors, she ought to be setting them up with *you*, especially if one of them might convince you to stick around."

Natalie suddenly remembered the night before, when Griffin had kissed her just feet away from where his sister now stood. Her toes curled, and she could swear she suddenly smelled toffee and leather and sexy male.

"Liz knows I am a lost cause. I'm not interested in meeting anyone, unless it's a Scottish laird with a castle on a loch and a bunch of wolfhounds. Mind you, I'm not interested in the laird. I just want to take care of his castle and his wolfhounds while he goes on vacation."

Amanda laughed more genuinely this time and wiped at her lingering tears. "I've missed you, Nat. So much."

Natalie impulsively hugged her friend, remembering slumber parties and boating trips and Friday night fro-yo runs to their favorite spot in town.

"How did we let so much time go by without trying to fix things?" she asked.

"I wanted to reach out," Amanda admitted. "I thought about it so many times, but every time I started to send you a text or an email, I lost my nerve. I... I figured you wouldn't want to talk to me. If you did, you would have reached out."

"I should have. I'm sorry I didn't," Natalie said. "I haven't been a very good friend."

"We'll do better from now on. I don't want to lose track of you again."

"We should probably get back in there. I'm sure people are wondering if we're out here drinking all the margaritas."

Amanda laughed. "By now we've probably missed out on playing pin the diaper on the baby or something equally exciting."

They both picked up the refreshments and carried them back to the chattering group.

While there was something wonderful about being surrounded by a group of good friends, Natalie thought, reconnecting with one dear friend who had slipped out of her life felt completely magical.

eighteen

"Isn't it a beautiful night?"

Griffin smiled down at his grandmother, holding his arm as they walked the few blocks between the Shelter Inn and the Lake Haven Events Center that housed the Shelter Springs Holiday Giving Market.

He was charmed that Birdie still managed to find joy in her surroundings, even with her failing vision.

"It's lovely," he agreed. How could he argue? It was a rare mild December evening, cool but not bitter cold, with no wind blowing off the lake.

Stars sparkled in the vast sky, and every business they passed was lit up for the holidays.

"It was a good idea to walk, wasn't it?" she asked.

"Definitely."

He had been assured by his office staff that parking at the convention center during the market, especially on the opening night, could be a nightmare. It was best avoided, if possible, his office manager, Stacy, had told him.

"I haven't taken time to walk through downtown to see the holiday decorations. Does the jewelry store still have that beautiful Christmas tree in their big window?"

He looked across the street, where a flocked tree appeared covered with brilliant gems.

"It looks like it. Would you like to go closer?"

"Do you mind?"

"Not at all."

Griffin helped her over the curb and they crossed the road and backtracked a short way to the store. She stood gazing at the window, looking fragile and older somehow.

"What can you see?" he asked softly.

"Mostly a blur of colored lights. But it's still beautiful."

The gleaming gems weren't real, but they still made a beautiful display on the small Christmas tree in the window. He would have liked to tell the store owner, but Sam Hollister had lost a son in the fiery crash caused by Dennis Taylor. Griffin doubted Sam would be interested in anything he had to say.

After a moment's contemplation, they walked on, enjoying more of the downtown decorations.

"Is that glow coming from the Saddle and Spur?" Birdie asked, angling her head toward a brick building that featured an abundance of neon.

"Yes. They've put up a big neon Santa on the roof, wearing a cowboy hat and boots."

She chuckled with delight. "Oh, I wish I could see that."

He could only imagine how difficult it must be to lose a little more vision each day, such an elemental part of her life, yet Birdie didn't complain. She faced each day with a grace he envied.

"I don't think we're in for many more mild evenings until spring."

"All the more reason why we need to enjoy this one while we have it." She smiled, leaving Griffin wishing he had inherited her skill at finding the good in any situation.

They were almost to the convention center when he spotted something incongruous on the sidewalk ahead. As they neared it, he saw purple contrasting with gray concrete and realized it was a child's mitten.

He scooped it up and held it out.

"What did you find?" Birdie asked curiously.

"A purple child's mitten with a little pink flower knitted on the back."

She frowned a little. "Where have I seen a mitten like that?"

The answer came to him immediately. "I believe it belongs to Travis and McKenna's oldest girl."

His grandmother nodded. "That's right. Hazel. She made me look at them right after she got them. As I recall, she held them right up to my nose so I could see the flower. Oh, she'll be on a tear, that one. When she's upset about something, everybody in the building knows about it."

"She definitely has spunk," Griffin agreed. "It doesn't look like it's been here long."

"Maybe she dropped it on the way to the market."

"In that case, we'll have to look for her so we can return it."

"You can go ahead and look for her. I'll listen. That girl is a little hard to miss."

"Deal."

If Hazel had dropped her mitten while walking to the holiday market, that likely meant her aunt was with her as well.

Griffin tried to clamp down his eager anticipation at the prospect of seeing Natalie again.

He hadn't been able to stop thinking about her since the night they had kissed.

The memory sent heat rushing through him.

What was wrong with him? He couldn't remember ever becoming this tangled up over a woman.

He knew nothing could come of it. Even if he were looking for a relationship, Natalie was simply not available. She had made that clear.

Kisses were one thing. A relationship was something else. She was not at all interested in sticking around Shelter Springs, and he could not leave.

They turned the corner heading closer to the lake toward the small convention center. It was immediately obvious that the opening night of the market was a Big Deal in town. His office staff had been right about parking. The road was packed with cars jockeying for space. More bundled-up pedestrians were converging from other streets to the events center.

They were almost to the intersection when he spied a woman and two small girls moving against the flow of traffic, toward them.

He immediately recognized Natalie, wearing a pink knit hat and a matching scarf.

She looked like springtime, bright and cheerful. One of the girls walking with her, though, was anything but cheerful.

"We have to find it! Mrs. Wiggins made it special for me. Purple and pink are my favorite colors."

"I know they are. We'll retrace our steps back home, though that will make us miss the rest of the music group we were listening to."

"I don't care. I need my mitten!" Hazel said, half sob and half plaintive demand.

"I told you we would find her," his grandmother said to him. She chuckled a little then raised her voice. "Hazel, did I hear you lost a mitten?"

The girl looked up, and Griffin saw tears streaking down her cheeks. He kind of missed the days when losing a mitten could be considered the most traumatic event to happen all day.

"Hi, Dr. Jingle!" Nora said excitedly. He had a feeling he wasn't going to soon lose that nickname.

When he met Natalie's gaze, he saw she wore an expression he couldn't quite read.

Was she happy to see him? Annoyed? Apprehensive? He couldn't tell.

"Did you say you lost a mitten?" Birdie repeated.

"Yes! My very favorite mitten. It's just like this one." She held out her left hand that sported a mitten that exactly matched the one he had found. "I think it fell out of my pocket when we were walking here."

"Which is why I told you to wear it on your hand, not put it in your pocket, remember?" Natalie asked.

Hazel huffed out a breath.

"You said it looks just like that one? Purple with a pink flower?" Griffin asked, reaching into his own pocket for the soft wool mitten.

"Yes! Can you help me find it?"

"Yes. I believe I can." He presented the mitten to her with a flourish, and her tears seemed to instantly dry up.

"You found it!" she exclaimed. She snatched it from him and put it on her bare hand, then held them both up for his inspection.

"How did you find it?" she asked in a wondering tone.

"We saw something pretty and purple on the sidewalk while we were walking over here," Griffin told her. "My grandmother thought she remembered you having a mitten exactly like this one, so we planned to find you at the market."

"Yay! I was so sad when I thought I had lost it forever."

She had quite the flair for the dramatic. He, like Birdie, found her adorable.

"Yay," Nora echoed.

"Now we don't have to walk back to the Shelter Inn, then all the way back here," Natalie said. "What do you say to Griffin and his grandmother for finding your mitten?"

"Thank you," Hazel said. She threw her arms around Birdie's waist.

"You are most welcome." His grandmother returned the hug.

To his delight, Hazel turned her attention to him and hugged him as well.

"Thank you, Dr. Jingle."

"No problem. I'm just glad we happened to see it and then were able to find you. We could have missed each other on the way."

Birdie, he suddenly realized, was looking between him and Natalie with a crafty expression he didn't like.

"Why don't we all go to the market together?" his grandmother suggested. "I know I'll have more fun seeing everything with some cute little girls instead of only my grandson."

"Wow," Griffin said. "I guess I know where I stand."

Birdie squeezed his arm. "You know I adore you. But Christmas is always more magical with children."

He felt a pang, thinking of the Christmases he had missed with his son.

Though she didn't press, he knew Birdie would love great-grandchildren someday from him or Amanda. He supposed she would have to be happy getting them from her other grandchildren, his cousins.

"We would hate to intrude on your evening," Natalie said. She seemed to be avoiding his gaze and he wondered if, like him, she couldn't stop thinking about their kiss.

"Nonsense," Birdie said staunchly. "It would be delightful to go together."

"Can we, Aunt Nat? Please?" Nora asked. She was already edging closer to Griffin, he couldn't help but notice.

After a moment's hesitation, Natalie nodded. "Sure. That's fine. But remember, you still have to keep your hands to yourself. No touching any of the items unless the person running the store says it's okay."

The girls looked delighted at this, and before he quite realized how she accomplished it, Nora had slipped her little hand in Griffin's.

Natalie looked on with amusement as she took Hazel's now-mittened hand and began walking toward the convention center.

When they walked inside the market, Birdie closed her eyes as if the onslaught of color and noise was too much for her.

She must have been focusing on her other senses. He couldn't blame her for needing a moment to assimilate. While the cacophony of voices, chiming bells and bluegrass Christmas music coming from the small stage at one end of the huge space was overwhelming, the mingled smells of popcorn, gingerbread, sugar cookies and wassail enticed and seduced.

"Are you okay?" he asked his grandmother in a low voice.

She smiled, eyes still closed. "Yes. I just adore the holiday market. Being here brings back so many memories. I was part of the committee that started the very first one. I can still remember how nervous we were that nobody would come. Now shoppers make the trip from as far away as California and vendors apply to participate from every state in the Mountain West. Even from Canada."

"It's really grown since the last time I was home for the holidays," Natalie said.

"I love it," Birdie told her. "This is my very favorite part of the holidays. Don't get me wrong, I love the concert series at the church and I always enjoy the Lights on the Lake parade we do with our neighbors in Haven Point. They have their own craft fair, but it doesn't come close to comparing to our world-famous market."

Natalie didn't bother to hide her smile at Birdie's blatant civic pride.

"I've been to some of the most famous Christmas markets in Europe. Strasbourg, Brussels, Cologne. It's wonderful to have a market this vibrant here in our little corner of Idaho."

"And even better that a large share of the proceeds goes to charity."

"Where do you want to start?" Griffin asked his grandmother.

"It doesn't really matter. I want to see everything."

Hazel looked around Griffin, her features troubled. "But you can't see very good, right? That's what my mom said. That's why you always have your cane and Dash with you. Where is he, anyway?"

"I gave him the night off."

"Were you worried about the crowd?" Natalie asked.

"Oh no. He does fine in the crowd, but I knew I would have my grandson with me this evening to help me get around."

She bent down so she was eye level with Hazel. "You're absolutely right. I can't see very well with my eyes. But I still have my other senses. Do you know what they are?"

"Hear, smell, touch. And one more I can't remember."

"Taste," Birdie said with a cheerful smile. "I plan on using that one plenty tonight. They usually have the very best hot cocoa here with marshmallows shaped like little snowmen."

"Ooh! Can we have some hot chocolate with snowman marshmallows, Aunt Natalie?" Hazel asked.

"I'm sure we can, but why don't we walk through and see what's here before we head straight for the food area?"

"Okay," she agreed happily.

Griffin had moved back to Shelter Springs in spring so had missed the Christmas market the previous year.

While he had visited a few times over the years when he would return home for the holidays, he did not remember it being this crowded or this...fun.

Having the girls along definitely added to the holiday spirit. They were so thrilled at everything, from a selection of handmade marionettes in one booth to knitted dolls in another.

The market was always set up like a traditional *Christkindl-markt*, a German Christmas market with rows of individual wooden kiosks like little huts about ten feet long. The proprietors were slightly raised from the shoppers, their wares displayed on tiered counters at eye level.

As far as Griffin could tell, people were selling a little of everything. Besides every conceivable kind of holiday craft, one stall had an assortment of hot sauce and pepper jellies. Another featured cakes and pies that smelled delicious. Still another had beef, elk and turkey jerky.

He knew many of the vendors, but not all of them.

The girls' favorite stall by far was the one with the large Shelter Inn Gifts sign along the top.

"Grandpa!" Hazel released her aunt's hand and ran to the kiosk, where Steve Shepherd, dressed in a garish Christmas sweater with a Santa hat, stood talking to shoppers. Behind the counter, Natalie's aunt Liz and Sal Ramos seemed to be doing brisk business.

"Look who's here!" Steve exclaimed, smiling broadly as he scooped up Hazel into his arms. "It's my two favorite girls."

Nora giggled and released Griffin's hand to hurry with Hazel to their grandfather.

"Hi, Grandpa Steve," Hazel said. "Guess what? We're going to have some hot chocolate with snowmen marshmallows. Do you want to have some with us?"

"That does sound delicious. I just might do that."

"I really hope I haven't oversold the hot chocolate," Birdie murmured to Griffin.

"I'm sure it will be great," he said, even though he would much rather have a beer.

"How nice of your aunt Natalie to bring you to the market." Steve smiled at his daughter. "Have you found anything good?"

Griffin noticed Natalie had grown tense the moment she spotted her father.

"I want to buy a little of everything," Birdie said.

"I would have to say, you're well on your way." Griffin held up the shopping tote containing his grandmother's purchases.

Birdie smiled. "I have lots of people to buy for. And you'll notice I only purchased from the stalls where more than twenty-five percent of all sales goes to the market foundation. I tried to buy most things from those that give more than that."

"A hundred percent of our sales go to the foundation," Steve pointed out.

"Yes. Isn't it marvelous? I hope you sell out of everything!"

"If we sell out of everything today, what are we supposed to do with our stall the rest of the time?" Steve asked.

"I guess you'll just have to make more wooden cars," Birdie teased.

"He didn't make the wooden cars," Natalie said.

Birdie looked surprised. "Yes, he did. He makes all of them up in Alaska and ships them down here for us to paint."

That was apparently news to Natalie, who appeared flabbergasted.

"Can we get a wooden car?" Hazel asked her grandfather.

"You have a whole box of them at home," Natalie reminded her.

"But we don't have one that looks like Santa Claus is driving it."

There was indeed a wooden car that looked like it had a little figure of Santa Claus behind the wheel. Griffin had to admit it was charming.

"They definitely need a Santa car, don't they?" Griffin said, smiling at Natalie.

She pressed her lips together. "Want? Maybe. Need? Definitely not."

"Oh please?" Hazel begged.

"We'll have to see when we're done walking through the market," Natalie said. "If that's what you really want, we can have Aunt Liz hold it for us."

"It's for a good cause," Birdie reminded her.

Natalie made a face at his grandmother. "You're not helping."

"Sorry," Birdie said, though she was smiling as she said it.

They chatted for a few more moments with Steve and Liz, though the kiosk was crowded with customers. Liz agreed to set aside the Santa car for the girls.

"Can we have hot cocoa now?" Hazel asked after a moment, tugging her aunt's coat. "You said we could a long, long time ago."

They had only been walking through the market for about forty-five minutes, but he imagined it felt like forever to a five-year-old girl.

"Yes. You've been patient enough, I guess," Natalie said. "Are you ready, Nora?"

Her father still had his younger granddaughter in his arms. Griffin noticed she didn't talk to her father, only to the girl.

"Yes!" she exclaimed, wriggling from his arms to the ground.

"All the food vendors are in the center row of stalls," Steve said. "You can buy everything from crepes to calzones to roasted chestnuts."

"And cocoa?" Nora asked.

"Yes. I believe the hot cocoa vendor is all the way near the back."

"Look for the one with the longest line," Liz Cisneros said with an apologetic smile.

"I think I'll skip the hot cocoa tonight," Birdie said.

"You were the one who suggested it," Griffin reminded her, exasperated.

"I know, but I forgot how much hot cocoa gives me heartburn these days. You go ahead with Natalie and the girls. I'll hang out here and visit with Liz and Steve and Salvador."

"You don't have Dash with you, though," he pointed out, hoping she didn't decide to wander the market on her own without her support dog.

"I'll be fine. I have my cane if I need it, but I don't plan to move from this stall. When you're done, you can come back and find me."

He was reluctant to leave her, especially when she was the only reason he had come to the market in the first place. He frowned, about to protest, when Nora slipped her hand into his again.

"I want cocoa, Dr. Jingle."

Steve Shepherd and Salvador Ramos both grinned at the nickname. He decided there were worse names people could call him. And probably did.

Not knowing what else to do, he made sure his grandmother was settled in a folding chair next to the kiosk, then headed with Natalie and her determined nieces for hot cocoa.

nineteen

Natalie hadn't been expecting the chaos and noise of the Christmas market. On this first night, it seemed half the town and many from neighboring communities had come hoping to score the best merchandise.

Back-to-back musical performances had been scheduled on the stage at one end. The bluegrass Christmas music that had been playing when they first arrived had given way first to a Celtic-sounding trio and now a group that was singing "Jingle Bells" in Spanish, accompanied by what sounded like a full mariachi band.

"You mentioned earlier that you've seen some of the amazing original Christmas markets in Europe. This must seem like small potatoes to you."

She glanced at Griffin, then back at the rows of stalls that lined the convention center. "It's a little smaller, maybe, but has an even wider variety. Also, most markets I've been to aren't designed as a fundraising vehicle. Here, you do feel like at least some of your money is going to a good cause."

"It does help ease the sting to the wallet a little, doesn't it?"

When Griffin smiled, she felt as giddy as if she had just eaten a half dozen giant sugar cookies in a row.

She had been trying her best to rein in her reaction to him

all evening, since that moment when she had spied him outside walking toward them, Birdie's hand tucked securely in the crook of his arm. She had felt as if someone had squeezed all the breath out of her. While they walked through the market, she felt as if she hadn't been able to fully take a breath all evening.

The man was too darned gorgeous. It also didn't help that he was incredibly sweet to both his visually impaired grandmother and her own rambunctious nieces.

So much for her resolution not to spend more time alone with him.

How could she possibly resist him for the time she would be remaining in Shelter Springs?

She had no idea.

At least she had a finite departure date. Earlier that day, she had accepted a job taking care of a trio of bichons for a month in a small French village in the Dordogne, along with their owner's three-bedroom house and garden near the village center. She started the first week of February.

The way she figured it, McKenna was due the third week of January but would probably have the baby at least a week early, if not two. That would give Natalie two weeks at a minimum to help out her sister.

By then, their apartment would feel crowded and McKenna would probably be anxious to have her family to herself so she could finish preparing Baby Austin's nursery and settle into her new routine with three children.

Natalie was a little disconcerted at how hesitant she had been to accept the request when she had received the email from the house-sitting agency. She had cared for the very same dogs two years earlier and loved their owner, a lovely widowed Frenchwoman who liked to visit her daughter and grandchildren in Tahiti during the colder winter months.

When Natalie had stayed there previously, she found the house charming and comfortable, with plenty of available day trips nearby where she could take the dogs on gorgeous walks in the countryside.

The woman also paid a generous stipend for the care of her beloved dogs and her house that more than covered the plane ticket, even if Natalie didn't have plenty of frequent flier miles available to use.

How could she refuse?

She hadn't told McKenna yet. She didn't want to upset her sister unnecessarily. There would be time to break the news.

As they wended their way through the crowds, the girls chattering, she thought again how much she would miss Hazel and Nora.

She hoped they would remember her fondly when she left, that she would be able to sustain the new relationship they had forged.

"Here we are," Griffin said as they approached the hot chocolate stall, which did indeed have the longest line she had yet seen.

She should start again, trying to protect her heart from this man whom she found entirely too appealing.

"You don't have to stay, if you're not in the mood for cocoa," Natalie said as they joined the queue.

"I'm good, as long as Birdie doesn't decide to wander around on her own."

"I really don't mind. The girls and I can enjoy our hot cocoa together, if you want to go make sure your grandmother is safe."

He seemed to consider it, then shook his head. "She'll be fine. I'm sure the others at the Shelter Inn booth will take care of her."

"It is quite heartwarming, the way the residents of the apartment building all seem to watch out for each other. They're especially protective of Birdie."

"That's such a relief to me and Amanda."

"It's nice that she found a good place at the Shelter Inn," Natalie said.

"Is our hot chocolate going to be as big as that one?" Hazel asked, pointing to the sign above the booth featuring a giant cup of cocoa topped with frothy whipped cream.

"I don't think I could drink that much," Nora said, a worried look on her face.

"You don't have to worry about that." Griffin looked amused. "I promise it will be sized just right for you. If you ladies want to find us somewhere to sit, I can grab the hot chocolate."

"With marshmallow snowmen. Don't forget that part," Hazel reminded him.

"Naturally."

She didn't feel right about leaving him alone to handle the queue. On the other hand, the girls might be a little easier to contain if they were seated at a table where she could distract them instead of being forced to stand in line, bored and restless.

"There are so many people." Hazel looked around with interest at the crowd.

"Do they all want hot chocolate too?" Nora asked.

"Looks like it."

The line behind Griffin had already grown by at least a dozen more people in only a few moments.

She was distracting the girls with a tried-and-true game of I spy when she heard someone call her name.

"Natalie Shepherd? Is that you?"

She looked up from trying to find something brown that Nora spied, which Natalie strongly suspected was the large sign above the stall with the cup of cocoa. She had been guessing every other small brown thing she could see in an effort to keep the game going as long as possible.

Now she turned to find a woman about Liz's age who looked vaguely familiar approaching the table.

"Yes," she said warily.

"You don't remember me, do you? Louise Arredondo. Years ago, I used to do your mom's hair."

Memory came back to her in a flash, and she was embarrassed she had forgotten.

Louise had been her mother's good friend and longtime stylist. She came to their house every week when her mother was having chemo to help style what was left of Jeanette's hair.

After her mother finally had to turn to turbans and wigs, Louise still came weekly to do her nails, style the wig and make sure Jeanette felt as pretty as possible, under the circumstances.

As clearly as if her mother sat beside her, she could hear the echo of one long-ago conversation.

"If you ever are lucky enough to have a friend like Louise, never, ever let her go, darling," her mother had said. "True friends are a priceless gift."

The memory made her smile, though it also left her a little choked up. "Louise. How wonderful to see you," she said around the sudden lump in her throat. "Sit down. We're about to have a hot cocoa."

"I can't stay. I'm helping out my daughter-in-law. She has a kiosk over near the restrooms, selling her watercolors. I just came to grab us both a couple of drinks." She held up the sodas in her hand to reinforce the point.

"We're having hot cocoa. With marshmallows. Dr. Jingle is getting it for us," Hazel informed her.

Louise smiled at her in a kind way that told Natalie she was probably a wonderful grandmother.

As Jeanette would have been.

"Aren't you lucky?" she said. "That sounds delicious."

She turned back to Natalie. "Are these your girls?"

"Oh no. They're McKenna's. I'm just their fortunate aunt."

"Of course. I can see the resemblance now. They're as lovely as their mother. And you. Look at you. Oh, your mother would be so proud."

Louise's scrutiny made Natalie supremely conscious that her hair was overdue for a trim. One of the downfalls of being a digital nomad was the difficulty in making an appointment with a really good stylist, especially when her time in any one location was limited.

The other woman didn't seem to mind. She gazed at Natalie, her eyes bright with sudden tears. "You look like her."

She appreciated the words, even if she couldn't see a resemblance herself, except perhaps in the eye color they shared.

"Thank you," she said. "I couldn't ask for a better compliment."

"I miss that woman every single day," Louise said with a sincerity Natalie couldn't miss. "She was just about the best person I ever knew. She never met a single soul whose life she didn't try to make a little bit brighter."

"She was good at that, wasn't she?"

That had been the one thing people had said to her most often after her mother died, that Jeanette was one of those people who made everyone feel better about themselves after being in her presence.

Natalie knew she wasn't following in her mother's footsteps in that regard. Jeanette had focused on finding ways she could help other people.

Natalie wanted to think she was a decent person. She loved animals, she recycled, she gave up her seat on public transit for pregnant women and older passengers.

Compared to her mother, who was always cooking meals for someone or thinking up ways to make the Shelter Inn guests feel more at home, Natalie knew her efforts were paltry.

She traveled where she wanted, never putting down roots, never forging any deep connections.

A tumbleweed in her own life.

She knew she had spent most of her adult life running away. What would Jeanette have said about her choices?

You can't outrun the pain. When you feed it, it will always stay with you, following at your heels like a stray dog.

She wasn't sure she had ever heard her mother say those particular words, but she could easily imagine it.

She and McKenna had suffered the same losses, but had
made very different choices. Her sister had stayed here in Shelter Springs, letting others into her heart to help fill the space
left by those they had lost.

Her sister had also opened the hotel up to people who needed
a tribe, senior citizens in search of community and home. She
made a difference in people's lives, as Jeanette had done.

"My mom was pretty amazing," she said now to Louise.

"I miss her every single day," Louise repeated. "I'll never have
another friend like her."

"I remember she loved you dearly and was so very grateful
for all you did for her toward the end."

"She gave me back far more than I ever gave her," she said
solemnly.

What a lovely thing to hear. "It's so good to talk to you,
Louise."

"And you. Make sure you give my best to your sister."

"I'll do that."

The woman sighed. "I should probably go. My daughter will
be wondering if I decided to abandon her and go shopping."

She gave a sudden mischievous smile. "Don't think I wasn't
tempted."

"Good luck. I'll have to take a look for your daughter's stall."

"Yes. Do that. We're three rows over and about five stalls
down."

Before Louise could leave, Griffin returned carrying a tray
with four hot chocolates in insulated cups.

To Natalie's dismay, the woman's friendly, generous expression tightened into one of mistrust and suspicion.

"Dr. Taylor," she said stiffly.

Griffin tensed momentarily, then seemed to paste on a polite
smile. "Louise. Hello. How are you?"

"Fine," she said shortly. "I'm fine."

She abruptly turned away from him back to Natalie. The warmth that had been on her expression was completely gone now, replaced by hard lines, though she seemed to muster a smile for her.

"It really is good to see you again, Natalie. I hope we get the chance to catch up more while you're in town."

"So do I. Good luck with the kiosk. I hope your daughter sells out."

The woman walked away, leaving an awkward silence filled only by the girls squabbling over which hot cocoa belonged to which.

What was that all about?

Natalie suddenly remembered. Louise's nephew Alex had been one of the teenagers killed in Dennis Taylor's drunken accident.

He had been a standout high school athlete with a basketball scholarship to a Florida university, all his potential, his golden future, gone in an instant.

For all her kindness to Natalie, Louise apparently associated Griffin with his father.

She felt a rush of compassion for him, for shouldering a burden that wasn't his to bear.

"Can we have our hot chocolate?" Nora asked, impatience in her voice.

Griffin seemed to collect himself. "Yes. Sure. Here you go."

"Which one is mine?" Hazel asked.

"The cups with the snowman drawn on them are both the same, for you two." He handed each girl a cup. "They added a little bit of cool milk to it so it shouldn't be too hot for you. And by special request, here are your snowman marshmallows."

The girls could not have looked more thrilled as he pulled out a small clear bag and sprinkled several marshmallow snowmen onto each cup of hot chocolate.

Hazel even squealed a little. "They're so cute!"

"Yes. I try to make sure all my food is cute," Griffin said dryly.

The girls sipped at their cocoa with much lip-smacking enjoyment. She couldn't blame them. It really was delicious, thick and rich and decadent.

"Yummy," Hazel declared.

"Isn't it?" Natalie agreed.

They chatted about inconsequential things while the girls drank their hot cocoa and she and Griffin sipped at theirs. While they enjoyed their treat, the girls soon returned to playing I spy.

When she was certain they were distracting each other and not paying attention to them, she finally spoke about what had been bothering her.

"Louise Arredondo didn't seem very happy to see you. I'm sorry. Is she one of the people in town you said weren't supportive of you coming back?"

He looked down at his half-full cup. "She has her reasons."

"Not good ones," she murmured. "It's not right that anyone could seriously blame you for something your father did."

"People who are grieving need somewhere to put their anger. My father inconveniently died in the accident. That puts a target on those of us still here."

"Does Amanda get the same cold shoulder from people?"

"She doesn't really talk about it, to be honest. I have heard through the grapevine that there are a few people in town who don't shop at her store because she's a Taylor. I would like to think that's the exception and not the rule. Fortunately, the tourists don't know or care about something that happened more than a decade ago."

Again, she wondered why Amanda had chosen to open her store here instead of moving even one town over to Haven Point. Natalie only wished she had been more supportive of her friend instead of adding to her pain by distancing herself when Amanda needed her.

Her mother would have been ashamed of her for that too.

She released a breath, grateful they had at least made a start in repairing their relationship.

It was a good reminder that Natalie did not have the monopoly on pain and grief. If she had learned one thing throughout her travels, it was the inescapable truth that everyone faced adversity in some form or other. All those who appeared to have perfect lives, perfect relationships, perfect families on social media were often concealing deep pain beneath the glossy veneer.

"I'm sorry. It's not right," she said to Griffin now. "Neither you nor Amanda deserve to be blamed for your father and his mistakes."

Griffin made a humorless sound. "A mistake is failing to yield in a roundabout. What my father did was so much worse. He stole four beautiful lives, devastating dozens more who loved them in the process. I can't go back and change that. I can't fix it. The only thing I can do is try in my own way to be here for the people of Shelter Springs. I can never completely balance the scale, but I can at least try."

She was very close to falling hard for this man.

The realization, there in the noisy Christmas market with her nieces debating which of them had more marshmallows in their cocoa, left her feeling light-headed.

Or maybe it was the sugar. She would prefer to go with that.

Her thoughts were suddenly interrupted by a large burp coming from Hazel.

"'Scuse me," the girl said with a giggle. "I think I drank my cocoa too fast."

Griffin smiled down at her. "Or exactly right. Sounds like your tummy loved it."

She beamed at him, clearly as besotted as Natalie.

twenty

"I have to say, that is one of the best Christmas markets we've ever had," Birdie declared as the five of them walked back to the Shelter Inn together an hour later. Griffin carried all their shopping bags while he walked through the night with his grandmother's arm tucked through his.

"Amanda told me it was going to be spectacular this year, with more stalls than ever. She was not wrong."

"We already walked so much," Hazel complained from ahead of them, where she trudged along on one side of Natalie while her sister walked on the other.

"There was so much to see," Natalie agreed, the glow from colored lights on a house they passed reflecting in her eyes. "How long has Amanda been on the market committee?"

"Oh, five years or so. She's been the driving force for the past few years. My granddaughter knows how to get things done, if I do say so myself."

"She obviously learned it from the best," Natalie said, smiling at Birdie.

"How much longer? I wish we drove our car," Hazel complained.

Natalie frowned at her niece. "You were the one who wanted to walk earlier."

"I know," she said, shoulders drooping as if she had walked miles instead of a block. "That was before. Not now."

He would have offered to take the girl on his shoulders, but had a feeling Nora would complain and need a ride as well. He couldn't carry them both and help his grandmother at the same time, so he remained quiet.

"Did you have fun?" Birdie asked the girls.

Nora gave a sleepy nod. "I loved the hot chocolate and the dancers with the noisy shoes."

"The tap dancers, you mean?" Natalie asked.

Nora nodded. "I wish I could be a tap dancer."

"Me too," Hazel said. "Where can I get noisy shoes?"

Natalie smiled. "Your mom will have to figure that out. I'm not sure if anybody teaches tap in Shelter Springs."

"They must, or we wouldn't have been gifted with such a stirring tap routine," Griffin pointed out.

"Will Mommy know about the dancing?" Nora asked.

"You can tell her all about it, honey," Natalie said. "We'll go talk to her as soon as we get home."

"She'll probably be sleeping," Hazel said. "All she does is sleep."

"Yeah," Nora said, her voice breaking on the word. "I miss Mommy."

"Me too," Hazel said. Completely out of nowhere, she started to cry, which set off her sister too. Before long the two of them were sobbing.

Griffin fought down sudden panic. He never knew what to do with tears, probably from all the years he had seen his mother cry over his father's drinking.

"And she misses you too," Natalie said. "So much. She would have loved to come to the market with us tonight, but she has to stay in bed to keep your baby brother from coming too early, which wouldn't be good for him."

"Growing a baby is hard work," Griffin said, completely out

of his element. "Your mommy sleeps more than usual because she's tired from helping your brother get big enough to come out."

Both girls looked behind them at Griffin and Birdie with the same skeptical expressions and tears still dripping down their cheeks. They clearly didn't believe him or care about his medical credentials. All of his fellow students in med school should have hung out more with five-and three-year-old girls to keep them humble.

"What if Mommy doesn't love us anymore?" Hazel whispered. "What if she only loves our new baby brother?"

At this, both girls started crying louder. A dog from a house down the cross street howled in sympathetic harmony with them.

"That isn't going to happen, I promise," Natalie said.

She picked up Nora in one arm and pulled Hazel into a hug with the other. "Your mom will never stop loving you. In a few more weeks, you'll get to meet your new brother and you'll see that moms and dads always have more than enough love to go around."

That unfortunately wasn't true, as Griffin had seen too often throughout his residency and now in private practice. Every single case of abuse and neglect weighed heavily on his heart.

"Do you promise?"

"Yes. I pinky swear it," she said. "Do you know that in Japan, the pinky swear is called *yubikiri*. And they say that if someone lies after making a pinky swear, they will have to swallow a thousand needles."

"Ouch. That would hurt!" Hazel seemed momentarily distracted.

"Wouldn't it?"

To Griffin's relief, the girls' tears disappeared as quickly as they had arisen. By the time they reached the inn, they were their usual cheerful selves again, chattering about what they would tell their mother about the market.

Was it all young children or simply these two whose moods could shift so dramatically in seconds?

He suspected it was all children. In his practice, he had learned how to cajole children out of their sour dispositions at having to see a doctor into reluctant smiles and even sometimes laughter. He always considered it a victory.

"It was so fun to spend the evening with you all," Birdie said when they walked into the lobby of the apartment building.

"It was our pleasure." Natalie gave his grandmother a warm smile.

"Bye, Mrs. Birdie," Hazel said.

"Bye," her sister echoed.

"I can take our packages now," Natalie said to him. He set them down on one of the chairs in the lobby and began sorting through them.

"I think that's the last one." She pointed to a small white cloth bag containing the girls' wooden Santa car.

As he handed her the bag, their fingers brushed. He gazed down at her, fighting a powerful urge to pull her into his arms right there in the entryway of the Shelter Inn and kiss her as he had been aching to do all evening.

Wouldn't that be a disaster, especially in front of his grandmother and her nieces?

Instead of pressing his mouth to hers, he merely kissed her cheek in farewell, his lips brushing somewhere near her ear.

She smelled delicious, that subtle, evocative scent of jasmine and vanilla.

If he couldn't kiss her as he would have liked, couldn't he simply stand here inhaling her scent for the next odd hour or so?

Sure. That wouldn't make him weird or anything.

He forced himself to step away. "Good night."

She blinked at him, her pupils slightly dilated. He almost groaned, certain that she was remembering their kiss as well.

"Bye, Dr. Jingle." Nora broke the spell by rushing to him and hugging him around the waist.

He hugged her back and then did the same to her sister. "I'll see you both later."

Natalie gripped her packages and, with a tentative smile toward him and Birdie, she ushered her nieces toward their apartment.

Griffin was astonished and dismayed to realize he immediately missed them.

He was only grateful his grandmother couldn't see the yearning he was quite certain was written all over his face.

"She's lovely," Birdie said as they walked toward her apartment.

He knew his grandmother wasn't talking about outward beauty, which she couldn't see well anyway.

"Yes. She is."

"And those girls are absolutely adorable. They make me laugh every single day. Hazel is so bossy, in the best possible way, and Nora is sugarcoated steel. Sweet on the outside but definitely as strong-willed as her sister."

He punched in her keypad and pushed open the door. They were met by Dash, wagging his tail as if he hadn't seen them for months.

"Where's my good boy?" Birdie reached down to rub the dog's chin, smiling with affection.

When she straightened, she gave him an apologetic look. "I know you gave up your whole evening to escort me to the market, but can I ask you one last favor?"

"You know you can. Anything."

"Would you mind walking Dash for me? Just to the corner and back? He's been cooped up all evening, and I'm sure he would love the chance to stretch his legs. My feet are killing me, or I would do it."

He was tired and wanted nothing more than to go home and pop a batch of popcorn and veg out in front of ESPN for an hour or two, but how could he refuse his grandmother? He couldn't, especially when the alternative likely would mean she would take the dog herself, sore feet and all.

Anyway, what would fifteen more minutes cost him?

"Sure."

"Thanks, darling."

"No problem."

He hooked up the dog's harness and leash and grabbed the clean-up bags, then headed for the front door of the building. Dash suddenly started wagging his tail ferociously and straining at the leash, which was unusual.

Griffin figured out the reason as soon as they reached the lobby when he spotted Natalie leaving the building ahead of them, the pom-pom on her pink beanie bobbing as she walked.

"Hi again," he said.

She turned and a flush of startled color rose on her lovely cheekbones. "Oh. Hi."

"Heading out again?" he asked, stating the obvious.

She made a face. "Yes. Travis is actually home early, and he wants to get the girls to bed and read to them. I figured I would head back to the market to see if they need help closing down the Shelter Inn stall for the night."

He wasn't thrilled at the idea of her walking by herself at night and was about to say so, then checked himself. This was Shelter Springs. While not crime free, it was overall a safe community. Beyond that, something told him Natalie could take care of herself. She traveled the world on her own, doubtless picking up more than a few tricks along the way to protect herself.

"What about you?" she asked.

He gestured to the dog. "Birdie asked me to take Dash out

to stretch his legs and do his business. Mind if we walk with you a bit?"

She opened her mouth and he briefly thought she would refuse, until she closed it again and nodded. "Sure. That's fine."

He had noticed when they were walking home earlier that the night had grown colder. The temperature had dropped even further in only the few moments he had been inside with Birdie. The cold seeped through his coat, and he wondered what Natalie would say if he pulled her closer to conserve heat.

He didn't, of course, only continued to walk alongside her with Dash leading the way, ever enthusiastic.

"The girls must be happy to have the chance to spend some time with their father. I hope we didn't tire them out too much."

"They seemed fine when I left. They were thrilled to see him. Travis is a good father, when he's around. I want to think things will be better after the baby comes."

"But you don't think so?"

She shoved her hands into the pockets of her coat. "I suppose I should be more optimistic, but I can't get rid of this stupid feeling of dread."

He frowned. "What do you fear?"

"That Travis can't handle the responsibility of three children and will leave her or something."

"Why would you think that? He always seems like a good guy in the few interactions I've had with him."

"He is. I told you, I'm being silly. I know he loves McKenna and he loves the girls. We had a good talk the other night, and I know he's mostly been staying away so he doesn't reveal to McKenna how afraid he is for her and the baby."

"Why do you worry, then? Don't you believe him?"

She gave a short laugh. "I don't know. I suppose I do believe him. But then, the men in my life don't exactly have a great track record for sticking around."

Her words didn't sound bitter or self-pitying, only matter-of-fact. His hand tightened on the dog's leash as he fought the urge again to pull her into his arms.

"Then you obviously haven't been around the right men."

This time, her laugh sounded more genuine. "I'll be sure to tell Steve you said so."

He blinked. "Are you talking about your dad leaving or about a slew of boyfriends being jerks?"

"My dad. And Jake, I suppose. For the record, I haven't had a slew of boyfriends, jerks or otherwise. Not serious ones, anyway. What is a slew, anyway?"

He smiled, suddenly glad he had agreed to take Dash for a walk. It was nice to have the chance to talk to her without their respective sidekicks, his grandmother and her nieces.

"I believe a slew means a large number. As in, the Shelter Inn has a slew of inflatable decorations."

"Oh, I thought it was a preponderance. Or simply an excess of inflatables."

"Glut would work too."

She laughed and he thought how lovely she was, there in the wintry moonlight.

"I don't have a slew of ex-boyfriends. Or a glut. Or even a preponderance. I've dated a couple of guys seriously but things never quite worked out. Long-distance relationships are tough, even in the age of video calls and international text plans."

"You never met a guy who tempted you to stick your duffel bag in his closet?"

Why was he asking this, when he wasn't sure he wanted to know the answer?

"I thought I had a time or two, but after a few weeks, I was always ready to take off again."

Griffin didn't need to remind himself that she would be leaving Shelter Springs soon. The knowledge seemed to hover between them every time he saw her, like a frosty puff of condensation.

He would miss her. More than he had any right to.

"What about you?" she asked. "Why isn't there a Mrs. Dr. Taylor?"

He debated how to answer her and finally decided on the truth, though it wasn't something he shared with very many people. His family knew, of course, but few others.

"There was, actually. I was married for a brief time about six years ago."

She stared at him, eyes wide with shock.

"Seriously? What happened?"

He didn't know where to begin so finally decided on the most important part. "We were never a good fit. We married for convenience, after Tonya became pregnant shortly after we started dating. Though we tried to make it work, we didn't have a good foundation anyway and…it certainly wasn't strong enough to survive the death of our son."

She gave a small, hushed sound of distress and stopped walking.

"Griffin! You have a child?"

"Had. Chase. He was a beautiful baby boy, premature but still healthy, until he caught an infection in the hospital and his tiny heart failed. Nothing could be done. He lived three days."

He spoke in a clinical, almost clipped tone, but he could tell by her expression that she wasn't fooled. She reached for his hand with fingers that trembled.

"Oh, Griffin. I'm so very sorry. How devastating for you and for Tonya."

He wanted to sink into her compassion, to wrap his arms around her and let her softness smooth all his jagged edges.

"It was. That is exactly the right word. It changed me. He changed me. I am no longer the cocky young doctor who thinks he knows everything. I like to think I learned how to focus on what was truly important."

"I don't know what to say, other than how very sorry I am."

"Most people don't know what to say. And the loss of a child is not one of those things you can easily bring up in conversation. I learned it becomes easier to avoid talking about it except with people who…really matter."

She gazed at him, her mouth open slightly and her eyes wet with tears.

She was compassionate and kind and wonderful.

And she mattered to him. Deeply.

"It was a long time ago. We divorced about two months after Chase died. Tonya is now married to her high school sweetheart and they just had their second child together. We still keep in touch, and I couldn't be happier for both of them."

"I am so sorry," she said again.

She still held his hand, her fingers cold. If he were smart, he knew, he would walk with her to the events center, take Dash back to Birdie and go home.

But her fingers still trembled in his hand. He pulled them to his mouth and pressed his lips against the soft, cold skin.

"Don't cry, Nat. Please don't cry. I will always grieve for him and for what might have been, but the crushing pain has eased over the years to an occasional ache."

She curled her fingers around his and then brushed them with gentle tenderness across his cheek and Griffin was lost.

He pulled her into his arms, and they stood that way beside the lake for a long time while the Christmas lights twinkled around them with incongruous cheer.

Finally, she eased away from him.

"I'm honored you trusted me enough to tell me about your son."

He brushed a kiss across her forehead.

Yes. She mattered, more than he could tell her.

He had a son, who had lived only a few days.

Natalie did her best to absorb the stunning news, even as

some part of her wanted to stay here wrapped in his arms, her feet freezing to the sidewalk, and block out the whole world.

The night seemed surreal, filled with colored lights and the scent of impending snow. Stray snowflakes danced through the air, and if she strained, she could hear distant holiday music still playing from the events center, still a block away.

She had worried earlier about what she would do if she fell for him.

She didn't need to wonder. She knew. She was falling in love with Griffin.

Not because he left her breathless and filled with yearning, but because of his sweetness with the girls, his gentleness with his grandmother.

And because of the son he talked about with love and tenderness, grief and regret.

She rested her head on his shoulder, her arms around his neck. It seemed inevitable somehow when he leaned down and kissed her with aching sweetness.

Unlike the other night, this kiss wasn't fevered, hungry. It was slow and tender and completely wonderful.

Oh, he was going to break her heart.

He already had.

She drew in a shaky breath. She couldn't keep doing this to herself. Every moment she spent with him, she lost a little more of her heart. At this rate, she would have nothing left to rebuild when this holiday season was over.

She drew away slightly, feeling cold rush in at the separation. "I should tell you I accepted a job in France starting in early February."

He gazed down at her for a long moment, his expression unreadable in the darkness. A few snowflakes shivered in the air around them, landing on his hair, his shoulders.

"You said the men in your life are good at leaving. Is that why you're now the one who always leaves first?"

She had no answer for him. He was right, just as McKenna had been right when she implied the same thing.

She was a coward.

The realization was humbling and demoralizing. She wanted to think she was brave and adventurous. She traveled souks in Turkey by herself; she once hiked into the rainforest in Brazil; she had even ridden a motorbike in chaotic Thailand traffic.

But she was terrified to let anyone too close to her. What kind of joy was she missing out on because she preferred to use the life she had created for herself as an excuse to protect her heart?

"I... I should go. It's after nine, which means the market is wrapping up. And Birdie will be wondering how far you and Dash might have walked."

"I have a feeling she might have a good idea."

She frowned. "Why do you say that?"

"You mean you haven't noticed my grandmother and all the other residents at the Shelter Inn trying to matchmake?"

"No! Absolutely not!"

"Do you really think it was an accident that my grandmother sent us off to have hot cocoa together earlier?"

"That's ridiculous. Surely they can see that I'm the worst possible woman for you."

He studied her through the darkness. "Are you? That's interesting. How do you have so much insight into what kind of woman I need, especially when I don't believe I've ever shared my opinions on the subject with you?"

She released a shaky breath. "You are committed to staying here in Shelter Springs while that is the last thing I want."

He gazed down at her. "You clearly have put some thought into this."

"I haven't had much choice. Since the night I arrived in town, you've been...everywhere."

"Like a bad virus?"

"You know that's not what I mean."

She reached down to pet the dog, finding comfort somehow when Dash rubbed his head against the side of her leg.

"We're all wrong for each other. The sooner I leave town, the sooner we can both go back to remembering that."

Before he could argue, she turned around and hurried into the market, hating herself for her cowardice even as she knew she had no other choice.

twenty-one

For the next week and a half, Natalie was too busy taking care of the girls to focus on anything else.

Hazel caught a cold two days after the market, probably at preschool, and graciously shared it with her sister. Like a miserable wrestling tag team, the two of them traded off sore throats, coughs and sniffly noses.

They were both cranky, wanting only to cuddle with their mother. At first, Nat had tried to protect McKenna from catching the cold, worried about the baby and her sister's health, but McKenna had quickly set her straight.

"I might not be able to do much right now," she had said sternly, "but I can't ignore my sick girls when they need me."

Natalie made sure the girls and their mother wore masks and applied hand sanitizer liberally...and she went in after them, wiping everything down with antibacterial wipes.

She cooked chicken noodle soup, bought Popsicles, read them stories, watched Christmas show after Christmas show.

To Hazel's vast disappointment, they had to miss their dance performance and were even too sick to go to the Lights on the Lake parade Saturday evening, when boat owners up and down Lake Haven would decorate their watercraft and travel from the Shelter Springs marina to their neighboring town of Haven Point and back.

Fortunately, the marina broadcast a live stream of the parade on YouTube so she and the girls settled in with popcorn in front of the gas fireplace and enjoyed seeing all the boat decorations.

By the time she settled them both into bed at the end of each day, their noses red and their eyes still watery, Natalie was exhausted.

She might have thought she would collapse in her bed and fall into a dreamless sleep. No. Instead, all the thoughts of Griffin that she managed to push to the sideline each day always came crowding back.

She didn't see him at all the rest of the week and most of the next. Either their schedules didn't intersect or he was making an effort to stay away from the Shelter Inn so he could deliberately avoid her.

It was for the best, she told herself. Maybe she could avoid him throughout the remainder of her time here in Shelter Springs.

The prospect left her as glum as if she was the one with the stuffy nose and the sore throat.

By the Friday before Christmas, the girls were feeling better. While they both had a lingering cough, they were done with fevers and seemed back to their old selves.

Natalie was congratulating herself for weathering that particular crisis when Hazel hit her with another one.

"We only have three more books to read counting tonight," she said, pointing to the basket containing their storybook advent calendar. "Is that when Santa comes?"

She and McKenna had been wrapping gifts on the sly after the girls were in bed. Natalie had taken them all to the apartment building office, where they waited in the supply closet for Christmas Eve.

"That's right. Today is Friday. Sunday is Christmas Eve."

"We were making presents for Mommy and Daddy this week

at preschool, only I couldn't go because I've been sick. That means I don't have anything to give them."

"I don't have a present too," Nora said, her eyes panicked above the tissue she was using to delicately wipe her sore nose.

Okay. Big auntie fail. She should have thought about the girls' gift giving before now. Her mother had always made sure she and McKenna bought thoughtful gifts for each other and the rest of the family, reinforcing often that Christmas was most fun when they were giving to someone else.

"Well, we can't have that, can we? Do you want to make something for them?"

"Like what?" Hazel asked.

Her brain seemed to blank on anything except the obvious. "You could color them a picture."

"We do that all the time." Hazel quickly dismissed that idea. "A picture is boring."

"I don't think your mom and dad would agree. I'm sure they love your pictures. But okay. Do you have another idea?"

"We should go shopping. I have money in my piggy bank. Ten whole dollars. And Nora has ten dollars too. Grandpa Steve gave it to us to buy Christmas presents."

Natalie didn't want to think about her father. She had been fortunate enough to avoid him for the past few weeks, since he suffered with a cold of his own the week before and had stayed away for McKenna's sake.

Purely because she knew her mother would have wanted her to, she had dropped off a container of the chicken noodle soup she made for the girls. She didn't really want to talk to him, though, so had texted him to let him know she had left it on the front porch.

She knew Steve was feeling better, since she heard him telling McKenna in one of their frequent video calls. She also knew he had been busy this past week filling in at the Shelter Inn market stall for other apartment residents who had come down with the same thing.

"That was very nice of him," she said now to the girls.

"Do you think we should get Grandpa Steve a present too?" Hazel asked.

"What a good idea," she said, swallowing her first instinct to say no.

"Will we have enough money?"

"I don't know. What do you want to get everyone?"

They brainstormed ideas for a few moments and finally decided on some lotion and lip balm for their mother from the holiday market and warm socks from the local department store for their grandfather and father.

"Can we go shopping now?" Hazel asked.

Natalie looked out the window. "It looks like it's snowing again," she said.

The snow had been fairly relentless over the past few weeks. Though it was only an inch or two a day, that quickly added up. She also knew weather forecasters predicted a much nastier storm to hit the area around Christmas Eve.

"It's only snowing a little," Hazel said. "You can drive us to the market. And then maybe we can go to Target for socks."

Someday her oldest niece would make a very good military officer or maybe a Fortune 500 CEO. She had no problem telling others what to do.

Natalie loved that about her as much as she loved Nora's tender heart.

She had come to love these girls so much over the past few weeks, even when they were sniffly and cranky.

She felt the familiar pang that hit her every time she thought about how hard it would be to leave them in a few short weeks, when her time here was done. How would she go back to being a long-distance aunt?

"Okay. Let me tell your mom what we're doing."

"You can't tell her what we're getting her, though," Hazel said.

"Right. My lips are sealed." She mimed locking her mouth and throwing away the key, which made Nora giggle.

McKenna's door was open to allow the girls to wander in and out through the day. She knocked on the door frame, and her sister quickly hid something under her flowered quilt.

McKenna had taken up knitting while she was stuck in bed, watching YouTube tutorials to figure it out, and Natalie suspected her sister was making her something for Christmas. A scarf, perhaps, or maybe a hat.

Even during her difficult pregnancy, McKenna was thinking about someone else. She was so much more like their mother than Natalie could ever be.

"The girls asked me to take them Christmas shopping this evening. Would you mind being alone for a few hours?"

"Not at all. I hope they're not getting something for me."

"No comment," Natalie replied.

McKenna made a face. "Seriously, I don't need anything. They could color me a picture and I would be happy."

"I told them that. Apparently, Steve gave them a little bit of cash to go Christmas shopping."

"It's only a few days before Christmas. All the stores will be so crowded!"

"We'll survive. We're tough Shepherd girls."

She hoped her sister would smile at that. Instead, McKenna rested a hand on her baby bump. "This Shepherd girl doesn't feel very tough right now. I wish my pregnancies weren't so hard. On me and everyone else around me."

At her dispirited tone, Natalie reached for her hand and squeezed her fingers. "I know it's hard, but you're doing great, sis. My hero. A few more weeks, and this will all feel like a surreal dream while you're holding your beautiful son."

McKenna sighed. "I'll have to take your word for that."

"We shouldn't be gone too long. I'll keep my phone on me, and we can be back here in a few minutes if you need anything."

"I'll be fine. Have fun."

Her sister was already reaching for her knitting again as Natalie left the room.

When they walked into the holiday giving market, the scents and sounds assaulted her, as they had on opening night when they had visited last.

While it wasn't quite as busy as that first night, it was still a Friday night, the final Friday before the holidays. A band played live music from the small stage at one end, and the hall smelled of popcorn, cinnamon and rich dark chocolate.

Natalie had always found scents a powerful memory trigger. When she smelled apples, she thought of her mother's shampoo. When she smelled paprika, she remembered walking the food markets of Hungary.

This particular combination of scents instantly brought back the memory of the previous visit, when they had come with Birdie and Griffin.

She remembered how sweet he was to his grandmother and how patient he had been as he carried their bags.

And how she had kissed him later on that magical moonlit night.

She gripped the girls more tightly by the hands so they couldn't slip away in the crowd. This wasn't the time for dwelling on all the things she couldn't have. They had things to do, a strict mission to find gifts for their mother and father and grandfather.

She stood for a moment to catch her bearings, then headed with the girls in the direction of the Lucky Goat kiosk, where Amanda sold her handmade candles, soaps and lotions.

Her old friend wasn't there. Instead, a college-aged woman with a trio of piercings in each ear, a diamond stud in her nose and a name tag on her shirt that said Scarlet stood behind the counter. She gave them a polite smile.

"How can I help you?"

"We need some lotion," Hazel announced. "A good one. Not too stinky. Our mom doesn't like stinky lotion."

The young woman's smile broadened. "I think we should be able to help you with that. What kind of scent does your mom like best?"

Hazel's brow furrowed. "I don't know. She always says she likes the smell of rain."

"Flowers," Nora said.

Hazel nodded. "She does like flowers. Do you have any lotion that smells like flowers and rain?"

The clerk gestured down the counter at the neatly arranged baskets filled with lotion bottles. "I imagine we can find something for you."

She held out various offerings for the girls to sample. To Natalie's amusement, they seemed to know exactly what they wanted. Or at least what they didn't want. They turned down at least a half dozen options, until Scarlet looked as if she was running out of options.

"This one actually is one of my favorites," she finally said, pulling out a lotion with a purple label. "It's mostly vanilla, like sugar cookies, with a little hint of lavender."

"I love cookies," Hazel announced.

"I do too," Nora quickly said, not to be outdone.

"We have lavender in our garden in the summer," Hazel said. "That's a flower."

"Right. More of a shrub, but yes."

"Last summer Nora and me broke some off and gave it our mom to put in her vase and she said she loved it."

"There you go. Do you want to try a little?"

The girls held their hands up and Scarlet handed the sample bottle to Natalie so she could put a little dab on each girl's hand.

They rubbed them together and held their fingers up to their nose.

"I like that one," Nora announced.

"Me too. How much is it?" Hazel asked. "We have twenty whole dollars."

Scarlet smiled. "You're in luck. We have a sale going on right now. Twenty percent off, since we only have one more day left of the holiday market. You have more than enough for a bottle of lotion."

"Do we have enough to get some lip balm too?" the older girl asked.

"You certainly do. Those in our selection here are all fla-vored like Christmas treats. Does your mom or your aunt have a favorite? Gingerbread? Chocolate chip cookie? Toffee? Snick-erdoodle?"

"Snick-o-doodles," Nora said firmly.

"That's my favorite too," Scarlet said. She rang up the gifts and carefully handed back the change to the girls.

"Would you like me to gift wrap them for you? It's free."

"If you have time."

"I have time. We're not super busy right now and this shouldn't take long."

They waited while Scarlet wrapped up their gifts in pretty blue paper with sparkly silver ribbon.

"Can I carry them?" Hazel asked.

"I wanted to," Nora said.

Natalie could feel a fight brewing between the girls. They were good at finding anything to bicker about. To head it off, she handed Hazel one present and Nora the other.

"Okay. That's all we need. That was fast."

"I wish we could have hot cocoa again," Hazel said.

"If we do that, we won't have time to shop for your dad and grandpa."

The girls sighed in disappointment.

"We have hot cocoa at home. I'll make you some tomorrow, I promise."

"But we don't have snowman marshmallows."

"No. But you know what? We have mini marshmallows. You can make your own snowmen with them."

She remembered a few wintry mornings when their mother would set all three of them at the dining table with a box of toothpicks and a bag of mini marshmallows to see what three-dimensional objects they could create.

They were close to the Shelter Inn stall so she decided to stop and say a quick hello to her aunt. She had hardly seen Liz during this trip back to Shelter Springs and missed talking to her.

"Hey! It's Grandpa!" Hazel announced loudly when they approached the stall.

She looked up and, sure enough, there was her father behind the counter with Aunt Liz.

They looked deep in conversation, gazing into each other's eyes. Her father laughed suddenly and kissed Liz right on the lips. Not a casual peck either, but with the look of a man who had plenty of practice kissing this particular woman.

Natalie felt a little unsteady, as if the room had suddenly started a slow spin. Her father had just kissed her aunt. His late wife's sister.

And Liz hadn't looked at all like she minded.

What was happening in her world right now?

Maybe she should just grab the girls' hands and go back the way they had come. The thought hardly had time to register before Nora and Hazel took matters out of her hands by rushing to the stall.

"Grandpa! Hi, Grandpa! Hi, Aunt Liz," Hazel shouted.

"Hi," Nora said, waving energetically.

The two of them stepped apart quickly. She saw Liz sway a little and her father reach a hand to the small of her back to support her.

She had suspected something between them when she saw them at the concert.

It was one thing for them to show up at a few events in town together. That could easily have been a couple of friends, a man and his late wife's sister looking for companionship and company.

But kissing. That took things to a whole new level.

On the other hand, she had kissed Griffin and they certainly weren't dating.

That was different, she told herself.

"Hi, girls," Steve said. "What are you up to?"

"I could ask you the same thing," Natalie muttered.

Her father's gaze sharpened and Liz cleared her throat, looking disconcerted.

"We're Christmas shopping," Hazel announced cheerfully. "We bought something for Mommy and now we're going to find something for you and for Daddy."

"We got her lotion. And lip balm that tastes like snick-o-doodles," Nora said.

Hazel frowned. "You're not supposed to tell."

"Why not?"

"Because presents are secret!"

"We won't say a word," Steve said.

"Nope," Liz said. "I'm sure she will love whatever you got her."

She knew McKenna had already bought gifts online for the girls to give Liz, books she had been wanting. Natalie had helped her sister wrap them only a few nights earlier.

"Have you had a break at all since the market opened?" Natalie asked her aunt.

Liz shrugged. "I'm not here from open to close, if that's what you mean."

"You're not supposed to be on your feet so much. I thought we worked out a schedule of volunteers to help fill the time slots at the market."

"We did. But half the Shelter Inn residents are sick. Those of us who are healthy have to fill in where we can. Anyway, I'm not standing all of the time. I have a stool up here and when things are slow, I do plenty of sitting."

She had been so busy taking care of the sick girls that she hadn't really lifted her head up to look around and see what else was happening in the family.

"I'm doing fine," Liz assured her. "Since he's been feeling better, your dad has helped a ton and makes sure I spend plenty of time off my feet."

"That's good," she answered, though she didn't like the idea of her father being so solicitous.

"We only have one more day, anyway. The market ends tomorrow."

"And you've promised you're going to spend the week between Christmas and New Year's sitting in a comfortable chair and letting everyone else take care of you," her father said.

By *everyone else*, did Steve mean himself? Natalie didn't want to think about it.

"It's been our most successful market ever. We've sold more than any other year, and every cent goes to charity. People have been amazing. When they find out all our proceeds are being donated, they often purchase extra items to give to neighbors and friends."

"That's very nice."

"And we completely sold out of the felted owl ornaments on the second day. I could have sold thirty more, easily. I'm so glad we were able to pull it off this year. It wouldn't have happened without your help, Nat. And yours, of course."

The smile she gave Steve was intimate and warm and left Natalie in no doubt that they were dating.

Had Liz forgotten everything? How he had left them devastated when he took off? Had she forgiven him, like McKenna, who had drawn him into her daughters' lives?

Was Natalie the only one who couldn't seem to let go of the hurt and betrayal?

She let out a breath. Was *she* the problem here? Steve genuinely seemed to be trying to do his best to be a good grandfather to Hazel and Nora. Why couldn't she focus on that instead of how lost and alone she had felt without her father, especially with Jake wasted half the time?

She determined to try a little harder. She could at least be polite. "Thank you for giving the girls some money for Christmas presents. They're having fun spending it."

"I remember doing the same thing for you and your sister," he said with a soft smile. "You couldn't wait to go to the dollar store and see how far you could make your money stretch."

Sometimes it was physically painful for her to remember what a wonderful father he had been before her mother got sick.

Steve used to love taking all three of his children skiing in the winter and fishing on the lake in summer. He would come to all their sporting events and cheer loudly, not just for them, but for everyone on both teams.

When her mother got sick, everything changed. Jeanette's cancer had taken over everything. Her parents still tried to do their best for them, but she knew her mother was worn-out all the time from the chemotherapy and her father was exhausted from running the inn and taking care of his wife too.

She pushed down the dark memories. They were always there, but she didn't have to dwell on them. This was Christmas. The time of hope and joy and renewal. She would be far better off if she could focus on that instead.

"We'll see you later. We've got a little more shopping to do."

"We're not telling you what we're getting, either," Hazel said.

"That's exactly right. I want to be surprised," he said. He picked her up and hugged her tightly, then did the same to Nora. For some reason, the gesture made Natalie's throat feel tight and achy.

"I should be able to help you take down the kiosk tomorrow night after the market closes," she said to her aunt.

"Thanks, honey." Liz smiled. "I'm not sure if we'll need you since everybody seems to be feeling better, but I'll let you know."

"You know we're supposed to have a big storm coming in Sunday, right?" Steve said. Some things didn't change. Her father had always been obsessed with weather reports.

"I've heard," she said.

"They're saying two to three feet by Christmas Day."

"Yay! Snow!" Hazel exclaimed.

"Having a white Christmas never seems to be a problem in Shelter Springs," Liz said ruefully.

Natalie couldn't remember a year they didn't have snow on the ground, likely because of their high elevation.

A customer asked a question of Liz then, and Natalie waved farewell to her aunt. "We have to go. We'll see you later."

"Christmas Eve for sure," Liz said, already busy helping the shopper.

"Bye, Grandpa," the girls said in unison.

"Bye, ladies."

She couldn't think of anything to say so Natalie simply smiled and ushered the girls away for the next stop of their evening.

twenty-two

"Are you sure you don't mind picking up a few things for me? I can't believe my online order isn't going to make it here before Christmas."

"Of course not," Griffin said into the phone to his grandmother. "I'm happy to do it."

It wasn't precisely true. He was exhausted after a long day of work. Though his clinic had been closed for an hour, he was still in his office, going over patient records.

But if Birdie needed him, he would do what he could to help her.

"Thank you, my dear. I would have asked your sister, but she's down with that cough that's going around and hasn't left her bed all day, poor thing."

He hadn't talked to Amanda for a few days and hadn't heard she was ill. It didn't surprise him. He felt as if he had treated half the town.

"How are you on groceries?" he asked. "Can I grab anything else for you while I'm out? You know a storm is coming, right?"

"Oh, you're such a sweetheart. I'm the luckiest woman in town to have such a thoughtful, handsome grandson."

He rolled his eyes. "What do you need, Grandma?"

"If you want the truth, I forgot a few things for the side dish

I'm making for our Christmas Eve dinner. Why don't I text you my list?"

"Sounds great. I'm just finishing up here, and then I'll head to the store."

"No rush on my end."

He entered the last patient notes into the computer, then shut down for the night.

He walked out into the December evening and headed to the only vehicle left in the parking lot, his pickup truck. He was so tired, he thought as he climbed inside. Not only had the bug racing through the community kept him hopping at work, but it didn't help matters that Griffin hadn't had a decent night's sleep in days.

He usually wasn't one to suffer from insomnia. Maybe an occasional bout, but not for longer than a week.

He knew why.

He was restless.

For so long, his focus had been geared toward exactly this moment, establishing his own practice in Shelter Springs. At every step along the way, he had kept his attention on the goal.

Now he had achieved everything he had worked so hard for since he was eighteen years old. He had a busy practice, a condo overlooking the lake and the mountains, good friends and family in town.

So why did he feel so...empty?

He was lonely, as pathetic as that sounded. He wanted a family. Not necessarily kids, at least not right now, but someone who cared about him, who wanted him to be happy, with whom he could share his small triumphs and frustrations of the day.

He tried to convince himself the restlessness had nothing whatsoever to do with Natalie Shepherd. Wouldn't that be a waste of his time, when she had made it clear she wasn't interested in settling down, in Shelter Springs or anywhere else?

Still, he couldn't stop thinking about her. Somehow thoughts of her seeped into his mind at the most inconvenient times, especially that moment right before he was about to fall asleep.

He couldn't stop thinking about the night they went to the market with Birdie and her nieces, when he had told her about Chase and she had kissed him with aching tenderness.

A few stray snow flurries brushed his windshield as he drove to the business district of Shelter Springs, where most of the national chains had been built.

The parking lot of his destination was packed with vehicles on this last Friday evening before Christmas. He had expected nothing less.

Better to find the nonperishables first, he decided, grabbing a shopping cart and heading straight to the men's department. Birdie needed socks for his aunt's stepsons, who all worked construction.

He turned the cart into the aisle he needed, then suddenly heard a high-pitched squeal from the shopping cart ahead of him.

"It's Dr. Jingle! Hi! Hi!"

The woman pushing the cart turned, eyes wide, and Griffin felt his heart give a kick. Of course it would be Natalie and her nieces, standing in front of the long rack of men's socks.

What were the odds that of all the stores in Shelter Springs, they would find themselves in this particular one, in this department, at the exact same moment in time?

Under other circumstances, he might have suspected Birdie of arranging the whole thing. It seemed like something his grandmother might have come up with in her devious, matchmaking mind—except she couldn't possibly know Natalie would be here at this exact moment. Could she?

He wouldn't put anything past Birdie.

"Hi," he said, forcing a smile. He was dismayed to find he was slightly breathless.

He couldn't tell by her expression whether she was happy to see him or annoyed.

He had to hope she didn't suspect him of stalking her or something. If she could guess how often he thought about her on any given day, that probably wouldn't seem like a completely unreasonable suspicion.

"Hi," she said with a smile that seemed slightly forced.

"We're buying Christmas presents for our mom and dad," Hazel informed him. "We already bought lip balm and lotion that smells like cookies and flowers for our mom, and now we're buying warm socks for our dad so his feet don't get cold while he's at work and for our grandpa, who lives in Alaska where it snows a *lot*."

"Those sound like some excellent gifts."

"What are you buying?" the girl asked him, peering at his empty cart.

"I'm helping my grandmother with the last few things on her list. Oddly enough, she needs socks too, for my uncle and cousins."

"We don't know which socks to get. Can you help us?" Hazel asked.

"Me? I'm afraid I'm not really a sock expert."

"You're a guy who wears socks." Natalie's voice was dry. "That makes you more of an expert than any of us."

He couldn't argue with her about that.

"Which ones would keep our daddy's feet the most warmest?" Hazel asked.

He looked at the socks they were considering and finally pointed to high-performance wool socks that wicked away moisture and held in heat.

"This is what I wear when I go skiing. My feet never ever get cold. I think that's what I'll get too."

"Do we have enough money?" Nora looked worried.

"You do," Natalie promised. "Do you want to buy two pairs for your dad and two pairs for your grandpa? That way you can each wrap up a pair to give to them."

"Yes!"

"What color?" Hazel asked.

"You can't go wrong with any of them," Griffin said. The selection wasn't exactly vast. Gray, brown and black.

The girls settled on gray and black, and Hazel happily plopped them into their cart.

"Okay, I think that's all we need. We should get out of Dr. Taylor's way so he can finish his own shopping."

He suddenly didn't want them to go.

He had missed them. Not just Natalie, but her sweet nieces too.

Before he could come up with some excuse to prolong their time together, Nora, sitting in the seat of the cart, coughed into the sleeve of her coat. It sounded deep and raspy, similar to several of the other respiratory conditions he had treated that week.

"Oh no," Griffin said, giving her a closer look. "That doesn't sound good."

"I got a cold," she informed him. "Hazel gave it to me."

"And I got it from my friend Lucy at preschool. And she got it from our other friend named Jaden. We've been so sick, we couldn't do our dance show and I couldn't even go to preschool this week."

"Oh dear. I'm sorry. It seems like everybody has the same cold. I think I've seen half the town this week."

"We just came from the market," Natalie said. "My aunt had to fill in at the Shelter Inn booth all week because many of the volunteers who were supposed to be staffing the kiosk have been sick."

"Amanda's got it too. Which is why I'm the designated last-minute shopper for my grandmother."

He held up his phone to show his grandmother's list that she had sent him with her voice to text program.

"Can we help you pick up anything?" Natalie offered. "We're done with our shopping."

"That's very nice of you."

"The girls love to shop. Don't you?"

"Yep," Hazel agreed. They both beamed at him and Griffin was aware once more of that ache inside him, the imprinted memory of the son he had lost.

"It's a win-win," Natalie said. "They help me shop, and we work on colors and letters at the same time."

She was amazing with her nieces, though he had a feeling she would probably argue the point.

He really didn't need their help, but he was also reluctant to say goodbye.

"I only have about twenty items, mostly in the grocery aisles. It shouldn't take me long."

"You know what they say. Divide and conquer."

He copied half his list and texted it to her.

"Can we have a race to see who gets done first?" Hazel asked.

"I love that idea," he said, surprised to realize the exhaustion weighing on his shoulders earlier had all but disappeared.

"It's not fair, though," Hazel said. "We have three people on our team and you only have one. Nora should go with you. Then it's even."

He had already figured out that equity was an important principle to Hazel. Everything had to be fair.

"What do you say, kiddo? You want to help me?"

"Yes!" The younger girl held her arms out, and he lifted her from the cart and set her in his.

"Okay. First group done, wait up by the checkout. We'll meet you there," Natalie said.

As they made their way through the store, Nora chattered about anything and everything.

At random intervals, they would spy Natalie and Hazel hurrying through their own list, and Nora seemed to find that completely hilarious and would tell him to go faster.

Because of the impending storm, he also stocked up on some of the basics his grandmother hadn't added to her list, just in case she started to run out and couldn't make it to the store. Milk, bread, butter, a few canned soups, toilet paper.

He finally added a dozen eggs to the cart and looked at his list again.

"Nora, my girl, I think that's it. We picked up everything on our list and then some."

"Yay! Did we win?"

"I don't know. We'll have to go to the front to find out."

He hurried to the checkout area, only to find Natalie and Hazel approaching from two aisles over at exactly the same moment.

"Looks like a tie," he said as they met in the middle.

Natalie looked amazed. "I'm not sure how that happened. I thought you would have been waiting for us a long time. We had to make an unexpected trip to the bathroom."

"I had to pee," Hazel informed him.

"Well, we added a few extra things that weren't on our list, didn't we, Nora?"

"Yep. Because of the snow."

"I bought a few extra provisions so Birdie doesn't run out if we get hit as hard as they're saying we will," he explained.

"Right. When we went shopping yesterday for the things we needed for our Christmas dinner, we stocked up on extras. Though I think everybody's making a big fuss about nothing. I spent my entire childhood in Shelter Springs and don't remember ever being snowed in. I think we only had one school snow day when I was in elementary school, and I happened to be home sick anyway that day. It seemed totally unfair."

She looked so disgruntled, he had to smile, fighting the urge to reach over the carts and tug down her beanie, just because.

"I don't remember many snow days off from school either, though I think a few times we had a delay in the start of school so the buses could get around. They're saying this storm is different. Maybe a hundred-year event, especially with the cold coming down out of Canada."

"Better to be ready, I guess. Do you want to transfer our groceries to your cart or just take the two carts? All we have are the socks."

"I can unload them both."

She pulled their socks out of the cart. "Okay, girls. Let's go pay."

"You go ahead of me, since I've got more to unload," he said.

"I can help you unload," Hazel offered. "That's my favorite part."

Natalie went ahead of him to purchase the socks while Hazel helped him pull items out of both carts and set them on the conveyer belt.

The checker turned out to be one of his patients, not an uncommon thing in a small community like Shelter Springs. Brynn Wallace, he knew, was a single mother who had recently moved to town to be closer to her sister.

"Dr. Taylor." Brynn beamed at him. "Hi. Merry Christmas. Is this your family? Your girls are adorable!"

She must have seen them talking together before they entered the line. He gave a polite smile he hoped concealed his sudden yearning.

"No. I only borrowed them for the evening," he said, not wanting to go into any long explanations.

She looked confused and slightly wary, as if this was some strange Shelter Springs custom she hadn't heard about yet, people borrowing other people's families. "Um. Okay."

"Griffin, er, Dr. Taylor and I are friends," Natalie explained. "And these are my nieces. We happened to bump into each other tonight, and we offered to help Griffin finish his shopping."

"How fun," Brynn said. "I'm Brynn, by the way. He's my

doctor and my boys just love him. He's been so kind since we moved to town this fall."

"That's great. Welcome to Shelter Springs. I'm Natalie. I grew up here, but don't live here anymore. But my sister does."

They chatted easily while she rang up his groceries. By the time Brynn finished, she and Natalie seemed like old friends.

When they walked outside, the night still felt mild, almost pleasant. He had a hard time believing a storm was coming soon, though he certainly knew how fast the weather could change when one lived next to a mountain lake.

When they walked to the parking lot, they found their vehicles were parked next to each other.

"This is yours?" Griffin asked, surprised.

"My sister's."

"I can't believe I haven't thought before now to ask, but what happened to your rental?"

It seemed forever ago that he had found her stranded by the side of the road.

"The rental agency sent someone to pick it up a few weeks ago. They offered to bring me another one, but I decided I really didn't need a car, since Kenna can't drive right now anyway while she's on bed rest. I'll take a shuttle when I head back to the airport in a few weeks."

Did she deliberately say things like that to remind him that she was leaving soon?

Or was she reminding herself?

"Need help putting the girls into their seats?"

"No. Hazel manages her own, basically, and Nora goes in hers easily. But thanks. I guess we'll see you back at the Shelter Inn when you deliver Birdie's groceries."

"Right."

He loaded the groceries on the rear seat of his pickup and then started up the engine and headed for his grandmother's place, humming the Christmas song that had been playing in the store as they checked out.

He never would have guessed that a trip to the store for his grandmother would turn into the highlight of his week.

twenty-three

Friday night traffic in downtown Shelter Springs could be hectic, especially right before Christmas. By the time she managed to make her way through the crowded streets and pull into the covered parking stalls at the Shelter Inn, Natalie couldn't wait to put the girls to bed and unwind in her room with a good book.

She had no idea that keeping up with two young children could be so physically and mentally exhausting.

"Look. There's Dr. Jingle," Hazel said, pointing to Griffin's pickup truck, pulling into his grandmother's stall. "We should help him with his food."

Natalie instinctively wanted to argue that Griffin was a big, tough man and could carry a few groceries by himself, but she caught herself just in time. Hazel wanted to do something nice to help someone. How could Natalie discourage that?

"Great idea," she said instead. "That's a very nice thing to do."

Griffin looked surprised when they joined him at his truck.

"Can we help you carry food?" Hazel asked. "It's a very nice thing to do."

He caught Natalie's gaze, and the amusement in his expression warmed her to the core.

"It *is* a very nice thing to do. Thank you very much. Can you carry the toilet paper?"

"It's light."

He handed her the multipack, which was almost taller than she was.

"I can carry something too," Nora insisted.

Griffin looked through the bags and finally handed her one that held only a few small items.

The girls beamed and raced toward the front door, leaving her alone with Griffin.

"I can help too."

"You have your own things."

"One small bag containing a few socks, some lotion and some lip balm. Let me carry something. You know me. I'm always looking for something nice to do."

He laughed and handed her a few bags, then pulled the rest out himself. "That's it," he said, closing his pickup truck's door with his free hand then locking it with his fob.

"Thanks again for helping me with the shopping today," he said as they headed for the building. "It's not my favorite task, and you saved me a lot of time, since I'm not super familiar with where everything is in that store."

"Where do you usually shop?"

"I usually don't. I use a grocery delivery service. That's what I probably should have done tonight, but I was worried they would be out of some of the basics, since people tend to stock up before big storms."

"I learned to really love going to the market every day when I was living in Europe. It became part of my routine, wandering through every morning to buy fresh vegetables and fruit straight from the grower and warm, crusty bread right out of the oven."

"You make it sound lovely."

"Shopping the market can be chaotic too, but that's part of the charm. I wrote an article about it, in fact, for one of the travel websites."

"I'll have to look it up."

"I can send you a link."

"I'd like that. Thank you." He smiled, sending her a sideways look. "You really love it, don't you? Exploring the world?"

"I do. At first my only motivation was to get away from here, and then I fell in love with the fun of discovering new places. There's always something unique and wonderful around the corner. That goes for everywhere."

"Even Shelter Springs?"

He reached to hold the door open for her, and she saw the girls racing down the hall to Birdie's apartment.

"Yes, actually."

What would he think if she told him *he* was among the wonderful things she had discovered here?

"I really haven't lived in Shelter Springs for any length of time since I graduated from high school. I always took summer jobs somewhere else or had internships. And I haven't been here during the holidays in many years. I forgot how serene the lake is this time of year, with the blue shining through the ice along the shore and the mountains always looming in the background."

She had actually found herself stunned almost to tears by the beauty of it on the few rare moments she had risen before the girls did and took a quick walk along the lake trail.

"I also forgot how *good* people here can be," she admitted. "I have certainly learned you can find decent people everywhere, but there's something different about folks here. I don't know what it is."

"It's not a bad place. In fact, we have plenty of digital nomads who move here for all those things you mentioned."

He spoke in a casual tone, but she sensed something deeper in the comment.

She didn't have time to puzzle it out before they reached Birdie's door, where the girls greeted them loudly.

"What took you so long?" Hazel asked.

"We had a few more bags to carry than you did," Natalie answered. "And we're old and don't move as fast as you two can."

The girls both giggled, but didn't disagree.

"Why didn't you knock?" Griffin asked.

"We waited for you," Nora said. "Can I ring the doorbell?"

"Sure."

She reached on tiptoe to push it and a moment later, Birdie opened the door, Dash at her side.

"Hi, Dash! Hi, Birdie," Hazel sang out as she hurried into the small apartment. "It's me, Hazel, and my sister, Nora, and my aunt Natalie and Dr. Jingle."

Griffin's grandmother looked amused. "Hello. What a nice surprise to find two cute grocery delivery girls on my doorstep."

Nora giggled, dropped her bags on the floor and gave his grandmother a giant hug.

"It smells delicious in here, Gram. What are you making?" Griffin asked.

"Oh, I remembered how much you used to love my shortbread. I thought I would make up a batch for you to take home with you."

"How do you find the stuff to cook with when you can't see very good?" Hazel asked.

Natalie winced at the bluntness of the question, though she found herself curious too.

"I have various ways," Birdie confided. "I can still see colors, so I put all my cooking ingredients in different size containers with different color lids. I also write the letter of what's inside in a special marker with raised ink that I can feel with my fingers. Sometimes I use my nose. Cocoa smells different from baking soda, for instance. Sometimes I have a friend come over and help me find things. Today I ended up doing a video call with my granddaughter and had her read the recipe for me, as it's been a few years since I made it."

Natalie had nothing but admiration for this woman who

didn't seem to let her deteriorating vision get in the way of living a full, rewarding life. She even played pickleball using a special light-up ball as her guide and not caring at all if she missed it completely.

"You must stay and have some shortbread. I'm about to take another batch out of the oven."

"Can we?" Hazel and Nora both asked at the same time.

Every moment Natalie spent with Griffin was filled with more things she would have to try to forget later.

She didn't know how to say no to the girls, though. And, she had to admit, she adored shortbread.

"Sure. A few minutes. We can't stay long, though. It's past your bedtime."

The girls took a seat at the table in Birdie's warm, richly scented kitchen, and she handed them small plates with a cookie each.

"Do you mind grabbing that batch out of the oven?" she asked Griffin, who had gone to work putting away the groceries in what was clearly a well-organized refrigerator and pantry.

"Sure. No problem." He grabbed an oven mitt and slid the cookies out of the oven, setting them atop the range to cool for a few moments before they were transferred to the cooling rack on the counter.

"May I have a drink of water?" Hazel asked.

"Of course, my dear."

"Don't get up," he told his grandmother, and reached into the cupboard for three cups, which he filled from the ice maker and handed over to them.

"Thanks," Hazel said.

"Thank you," Nora said, then primly nibbled another bite of her shortbread.

"You're very welcome."

He smiled at them, and it was clear both girls were completely besotted.

He would have been a wonderful father.

The thought made her heart ache again as she imagined him holding his son for one last time.

She hoped he could someday have the chance to raise a child of his own, though that would mean finding someone else.

Picturing him with another woman, becoming a father to her children, left Natalie depressed and vaguely queasy.

The girls finished their cookies and sweetly thanked Birdie—and Dash, for some reason—with hugs.

"All right, girls. Time to go."

Though they complained a little, it was obvious both girls were tired.

Hazel opened Birdie's outer door and they both raced out, heading toward their own apartment.

Griffin walked Natalie to the door. "I told my grandmother I would take Dash for a short walk tonight. After you get the girls settled in bed, would you like to come with me? This might be our last mild night around here for months." He sounded hesitant, as if he wasn't quite sure whether to ask the question.

Every instinct warned her that spending more time with him was a mistake, that she would wrap up this holiday season with a lovely bow made from the strings of her broken heart.

She was weak, though, and couldn't seem to find the words to refuse.

"A walk would be good," she heard herself say.

She wanted to bask in his bright smile.

"Stop by when the girls are in bed," he said. "We'll be ready."

She nodded and walked down the long hall toward her sister's apartment, unable to quite believe she had agreed to spend more time with him.

What was wrong with her? Yes, she was weak. But was she also completely self-destructive?

"Should we ring our doorbell?" Hazel called out.

"No. I'm coming. I'll open it with the code. You don't want

your mom to feel like she has to get out of bed and come to the door, right?"

"Oh right." Hazel huffed out a breath. "I can't wait for our baby to come."

While Natalie wanted that for her sister, she also knew that the baby's arrival would mean McKenna would no longer need her help and Nat would have to go back to her real life.

Get to, she corrected herself, though the words seemed hollow.

Much to her relief, after she punched in the code and they entered the apartment, she found Travis home at a decent hour again. He was in the kitchen heating food in the microwave while McKenna sat in a chair looking swollen and uncomfortable.

The girls shrieked and hugged their father, as if they hadn't seen him in months.

He hugged them back. "Where have you guys been?"

"We can't tell you," Hazel said, her shoulders hunched as she gave him a mysterious look.

"We were just doing a little last-minute Christmas shopping," Natalie answered. "Hazel, can you take this to your room?"

She held out the shopping bag containing the gifts they had purchased. Hazel hurried to hide it behind her and backed out of the room so her parents couldn't even catch a glimpse of the packaging.

"How are things?" she asked her brother-in-law.

"Good. Only two more days until Christmas, and then things will finally slow down."

McKenna made a little sound that Natalie thought at first was disbelief, then she realized by her sister's wince it was from discomfort.

"Are you okay? Are you sure you should be up?"

McKenna gave her a dark look. "If I have to stay in that bed another minute, I'm going to scream."

"I'm sorry."

"Why are you apologizing? It's not your fault."

"I'm sorry you're going through this."

"It will be worth it. Or so I keep telling myself."

She shifted and gave a small moan that she tried to quickly disguise into a cough.

"Seriously, are you okay? You look like you're hurting."

"This is as okay as I get right now. I'm more than eight months pregnant. My back is killing me, I've had bad heartburn the past few days and tonight I've been having random contractions at odd moments."

Travis's features seemed to pale. "Contractions? Why didn't you say anything?"

"Because they're mild and because I know they're not real yet. Dr. Reynolds was just here yesterday and said I'm still dilated to two centimeters, like I have been for weeks. She told me to call her if the contractions become more intense or more regular."

"Maybe you need to lie down again," Travis said, still nervous.

The girls came out before McKenna could reply.

"Okay. We hid all the presents," Hazel said with a gleeful expression. "Nobody will ever find them."

"Yeah. Nobody will find them," Nora echoed.

Natalie had to smile at their delight. This was exactly the way Christmas should be, that thrilled anticipation around giving the perfect gift, savoring the secret and imagining how the recipient would react.

"Just remember where you put them so we can open them on Christmas," McKenna said.

"We remember. Don't worry," Hazel said.

Nora went to her mother and hugged her, protruding abdomen and all. "You will love your present," she said.

"I'm sure I will." McKenna ran a hand down Nora's hair, a gesture so maternal and tender that it made a lump rise in Natalie's throat.

"Don't tell her what it is," Hazel warned her sister sternly.

"I wasn't going to!"

"Let me finish my dinner, and then we'll get you both into your beds," Travis said, setting the plate of fettucine alfredo Natalie had made the day before on the table. "It's Friday night. You should go dancing with your girlfriends at the Saddle and Spur or something."

Natalie could imagine few things she would enjoy less. Not the suggestion about hanging out with her girlfriends. She would love that. But fending off drunk cowboys wasn't her favorite thing.

Even in college, she had never been one for the party scene.

"I, er, told Griffin I would help him take Dash for a walk while the weather is still mild, before the storm comes in this weekend."

McKenna eyes widened with interest. "Did you?"

"Yes. And you can take that smug look off your face right now. Griffin is a friend. That's it."

"I have no idea what look you're talking about." McKenna grinned, looking completely unrepentant.

"We helped Dr. Jingle do his shopping," Hazel announced. "We had a race. I helped Aunt Natalie find things on his list and Nora helped Dr. Jingle. And guess what? We had a tie! Nobody won."

"We all won," Nora said. "That's what Dr. Jingle said."

McKenna looked even more interested at this information, and Natalie was quick to shut down the subject before her sister got any more wrong ideas.

"Regardless of who won, it was really fun," Natalie said.

It had been. She had loved seeing Griffin look so lighthearted as he teased the girls. The man carried far too heavy a burden on his shoulders.

"And then we helped him take the groceries to Birdie. That's his grandma," Hazel said. "And she gave us cookies that were so good."

"Shortbread," Natalie said.

"Nice." Travis gave an appreciative smile. "I love those. My grandma, your great-grandma, used to make them. I bet my mom still has the recipe. Maybe I'll give her a call and get it from her. We could make shortbread cookies one day when I'm home with you, after the baby is born."

It was a reminder again that her sister wouldn't need her much longer. Once she gave birth, Travis planned to take three weeks of family and medical leave. Natalie did not want to be in the way.

"You go on your walk and have fun," McKenna said. "We've got bedtime."

"Bundle up, though," Travis advised. "It might be unseasonably warm, but the wind is starting to blow off the water."

She still hadn't taken off her coat or her hat. She added her scarf and mittens, said good-night, then left the apartment, certain she was making a huge mistake.

twenty-four

Why had he possibly thought asking Natalie along when he walked the dog might be a good idea?

It seemed foolish in the extreme to spend more time with her when he was already having such a tough time resisting her.

He had invited her, though, and he couldn't back down now. While he had only seen her a half hour earlier, anticipation sparkled through him as he waited for her to return to Birdie's apartment.

He loved being with her, and not only because of the physical attraction simmering between them. Natalie had a unique way of making everything seem more interesting and fun. Even buying socks and toilet paper.

When the doorbell to Birdie's apartment rang out a few moments later, he and Dash both stood up at the same time.

He was aware of Birdie looking on with interest, but decided to ignore her.

"Um. Hi," she said when he answered the door. "Travis was home so he's handling the girls' bedtime."

She looked so lovely, warm and bright and vibrant. He wanted to stand here and gaze at her for a while, like admiring the night sky full of stars, but had a feeling both women would find that more than a little odd.

"Great. Let me find Dash's harness and leash."

The dog seemed to perk up before Griffin even reached for them beside the door. His tail began wagging fiercely and didn't stop moving the whole time Griffin put on the harness and attached the leash.

After donning his own coat and gloves, he kissed his grandmother's cheek. "We'll see you later, Birdie. We won't be long."

She waved him off. "Take your time. I'm going to pop some popcorn and watch a Christmas movie. Listen to it, anyway. Every year I try to catch *Miracle on 34th Street*, and I haven't gotten around it yet this year."

"That used to be one of my mom's favorites too." Natalie gave a small smile that was tinged with sadness. "I'm afraid I haven't been able to watch it since she died."

Birdie's features softened and she reached for her hand. "Oh, honey. I'm sorry."

Natalie seemed embarrassed to have had revealed that much. She was a woman who liked to keep things inside.

"Thank you," she murmured to his grandmother.

"Your mother was a lovely woman. You are very much like her, you know."

He could tell she wanted to protest, but she remained quiet. Why didn't she like being compared to her mother? Yet another mystery about this woman who intrigued him so much.

When they walked outside, he guessed the temperatures had to be in the high forties, positively balmy for Shelter Springs in December.

Most of the snow of the past few weeks had melted, though he knew the landscape would be covered in white again soon.

It seemed forever ago that he had helped Natalie put up the inflatable decorations that bobbed gently in the light breeze blowing off the lake.

"I hope your inflatables survive the storm," he said.

"Me too, though they're not my inflatables."

She lifted her face to the sky. "It's beautiful out tonight. It feels even warmer than it did earlier when I took the girls to the market."

"I always find it interesting how the weather sometimes turns uncommonly mild right before a big storm, as if everything in nature is holding its collective breath."

She gave him a sidelong glance. "Look at you, all poetic and stuff."

He grinned. "You're the English major. I'm just a humble man with a medical degree and a stethoscope."

Her smile seemed brighter than all the Christmas lights in the town square put together.

Natalie Shepherd was a dangerous woman. He wondered if she had any idea.

They walked as if by unspoken agreement away from the lights of the square down a much quieter residential street.

"How are things with your dad?" he asked after a few moments of walking.

She hesitated before answering. "I haven't seen much of him, if you want the truth. The girls were sick all week and couldn't have visitors, and then he was sick and stayed away to protect McKenna and the baby, so our schedules haven't really meshed very well."

They walked past a house where a forlorn-looking snowman had melted with the warming temperatures into a shadow of its former self.

"I saw him this evening kissing my aunt Liz."

He blinked, surprised. He very much liked Liz Cisneros. She was smart, funny and compassionate. Much like her niece.

"Did you?"

She looked at the sidewalk ahead of them. "I didn't know what to say. I'm not sure they even knew that I caught them. I don't think they did."

She spoke matter-of-factly, but he could sense her tone concealed a flurry of emotions.

"How do you feel about your dad dating your aunt?"

She shoved her mittens in her pocket. "I have no idea how I'm supposed to feel. It doesn't seem right to me, somehow. I didn't tell McKenna."

"Why not?"

"I didn't have a chance, for one thing. The girls and Travis were there. And to be honest, I sort of tried to put it out of my head all evening, until you brought up my father."

"Sorry to remind you."

"McKenna and I haven't really seen eye to eye on our father for a few years now, really since her wedding when she invited him to walk her down the aisle. She's much more forgiving than I can be, apparently."

At her words, a cold wind seemed to knuckle its way beneath his coat. How could she ever forgive him for not being able to save her brother? Was that hovering somewhere in the back of her consciousness now, as they walked past houses with gleaming Christmas trees in the windows? Was that the reason she seemed determined to keep distance between them?

"I honestly thought he would come back after Jake died," she said, almost as if she guessed the direction of his thoughts. "Even losing his only son didn't bring him back to town or stop him from being so caught up in his own pain that he didn't spare a moment to think about ours."

He wasn't consciously aware of reaching for her hand until he felt her cool skin against his. To his relief, she didn't pull away. He wasn't sure what he would have done if she had. They walked past a few more houses, their hands linked, and Griffin was quite sure this might be one of the most romantic moments of his life.

He didn't want to let go.

"One of the most important lessons I've learned over the years is that everyone handles loss and grief differently," he finally said.

"That's very true."

The warmth of her hand in his finally gave him the strength to talk about a subject that weighed heavily on him, one they had danced around since she returned to town.

"I used to be so angry with Jake for the way he handled your mother's death. Your dad left physically. Jake left mentally."

Her fingers tightened in his, and he thought for one breathless moment that she would pull her hand away. To his relief, she finally relaxed her fingers.

"He spent a year engaging in every possible kind of self-destructive behavior," she said quietly.

He nodded, the pain in her voice echoing his own. "I didn't really understand until he was gone, that peculiar mix of grief and guilt."

She stopped walking to stare at him. They were near a small lakeside park, and the glow from the small lamplights lining the path reflected in her eyes.

"You have no reason to feel guilty about his death."

"Don't I?"

Griffin released her hand, feeling the cool air eddy in where her warmth had been. He wanted to keep walking, but forced himself to stop as well.

"Why do you feel guilty?"

He had to tell her, the secret he had been hiding from her for years. The truth he had been hiding from everyone.

"It was my fault he died."

She stared at him. Dash, sensing the sudden tension, gave a small whine and planted himself near her feet.

"Your fault. How was it your fault?"

This was so hard. Harder than he ever imagined it would be. He didn't want to dredge up the past, but he had to tell her.

"You know I was there that day."

"I know you dug him out with your bare hands after the avalanche buried him. The ski patrol guys said you risked your own life to stay on the mountain and keep searching until you found him."

That day. That horrible day. It replayed itself in his nightmares. Their bitter conversation, the words he had flung at his friend, then his helplessness as he watched Jake snowboard into the out-of-bounds area, despite his shouts at him to stop.

And then the horror of that wall of snow swallowing him.

In vivid detail, Griffin remembered how desperate he had been to find Jake, frantically digging for what felt like hours through the snow with his soaked gloves, with no shovel or spade or anything. He had finally found him after ten or fifteen minutes of searching.

By then, it was too late.

It had been small comfort to know that Jake had likely been dead before the avalanche even devoured him. The snow pouring down the mountainside had slammed his head into a boulder, and he likely hadn't known what hit him.

He looked down at Natalie, the words sour in his mouth. He had to tell her, no matter the fallout.

"He never would have gone that way if not for me. We had… words while we were on the ski lift. I was so furious with him. It was 11:00 a.m. and he was already wasted, and he wouldn't stop. He brought along a flask full of something, I don't know what, and kept pulling it out of his parka and drinking from it. On our way up the mountain, I told him I'd had it. That our friendship was done."

He knew even as he yelled at his friend that he had reacted badly. He couldn't seem to help it. He was furious with Jake for all the tears Amanda had shed over him, as angry as he had been at his father for drinking his life away. Somehow everything had jumbled together in his mind and Griffin had been a bubbling hot volcano, spewing his fury all over his friend.

"I told him I couldn't stand by while he self-destructed. He was acting like a whiny, self-indulgent child, and it was past time he got his act together."

His words had been cruel, but completely on the mark.

"He was furious. He threw a punch. Missed, of course. He was too drunk to see straight. I told him he needed to get off the mountain before he hurt someone. Next thing I knew, he started heading for the off-limits area. I tried to stop him, but he called me a name and went past me, a pissed look in his eyes, heading into the trees."

He couldn't look at her, certain she must be looking at him with hatred and disgust. He should have told her this a long, long time ago. Instead, he had let her and everyone else think it had been a tragic accident.

"I should have stopped him. I never should have let him get on the slopes."

"How could you have stopped him? Tied him to a tree?" Her voice sounded ragged, strained.

"If I had to."

She let out a long breath. "That wouldn't have worked, Griffin. You know it wouldn't. He would have found something else reckless and stupid to do the next time."

To his amazement, she sounded sad, but not angry with him.

"I wasn't thinking, or I would have waited until we were at the bottom of the hill before I yelled at him. Jake had been my best friend since we were in kindergarten. I certainly knew him well enough to be certain that the moment someone told him to do something, he would immediately do exactly the opposite."

"He could be such a pain in the ass, couldn't he?"

She made a small sound that could have been a laugh or a sob. He wasn't sure. Either way, he couldn't help reaching for her, half-afraid she would push him away and stalk back to the Shelter Inn.

Instead, she sagged against him, her face buried into his chest.

"I'm so sorry, Nat. I should have told you. I guess I...didn't want to add to your pain."

She didn't cry, she simply held on to him, trembling a little in his arms. He wanted to hold her close and keep her safe from anything hurting her ever again.

He was in love with her.

The truth didn't hit him like a bolt of lightning. It settled over him like a soft, gentle, cleansing rain.

He loved her.

What the hell was he supposed to do about that?

"You were not responsible for Jake's actions that day or anytime," she said, lifting her head away from his chest to meet his gaze. "You were always a good and loyal friend to him, and that's what you were being when you called him on his bad behavior."

"I wish I could have stopped him."

"So do I. But I would never blame you for the choices he made that day. If you want the truth, I'm actually a little relieved that you told me what happened that day."

"Relieved? Why?"

She gave a heavy sigh. "It's better to think of my brother being drunk and reckless than the possible alternative that has haunted me all these years."

He frowned, not sure what she meant.

She looked away. "I've wondered for a long time if Jake might have had a death wish and deliberately took that out-of-bounds trail not despite the extreme avalanche danger, but because of it. Because he knew it would be quick and relatively painless."

He stared. "No. Dear God. No."

"You can't really know that."

"I knew your brother. He was drunk and not thinking clearly at the time, but I swear on Birdie's life or anything else you want that he was not deliberately suicidal."

She looked into his eyes as if trying to measure the truth of his words. After a long moment, she closed her eyes, sighed and nodded with a deep, heartbreaking relief.

When she rested her cheek against his chest again, he was stunned at the complete trust in the gesture.

He rested his chin on her hair, wishing they could stay here the rest of the night.

Natalie closed her eyes, listening to his heartbeat through his sweater. She knew she would remember this moment for a long time, possibly forever.

His arms felt warm and comforting around her, and the scent of him engulfed her. He held her with a gentle tenderness that made her throat tight and her eyes burn.

She felt...safe.

Dash snuffled at something on the sidewalk, and the sound seemed to break the spell.

"We should probably head back," he said, a reluctance in his voice that matched her own.

She nodded and stepped away. She was thrilled and relieved when he wrapped his fingers around hers. Their hands remained linked as they walked back toward the Shelter Inn.

When they reached the parking lot, he pulled her into the covered parking space where he had left his truck.

"I'm sorry," he murmured. "But I've been dying to do this all evening."

Before she quite knew what he intended, his mouth was on hers and the intensity of the kiss left her breathless and achy.

She wrapped her arms around him, thrilled when he pulled her against him again. The heat of him warmed every part of her, all the cold, fragile places she hadn't even realized were there.

They both wore bulky coats, but had left them open in the mild night. He slid his hands inside her coat to the small of her back so that he could pull her more tightly against him.

"You taste like shortbread," he murmured. "And I really, really love shortbread."

She laughed softly, unable to resist him. "You taste the same."

Who knew shortbread could be so sexy?

His tongue brushed her lips and she shivered, every part of her aching for more. His truck was right there and he had a back seat. They could climb inside and neck like they were back in high school.

Come to think of it, why did they have to resort to that? He had a condominium not far away that probably had a perfectly lovely bed.

Her brother-in-law had told her to go out and enjoy the night. She couldn't imagine anything she would enjoy more.

"What would a guy have to do to persuade you to stick around Shelter Springs a little longer?"

His words against her mouth seemed to blow through her like an icy wind off the lake.

She froze and, though it was painfully hard, she eased away from him.

"I know I have no right to ask you to stay. But I care about you, Nat. I would love to see where this thing between us might lead."

His eyes were warm with that tenderness that seduced her as much as his kiss did.

She was tempted. So very tempted.

For an instant, her imagination went wild, imagining how their lives could mesh together here. She could work from anywhere, even here beside the lake.

She thought of the girls and the close relationship forged with them these past few weeks and of her new nephew on the way. Wouldn't it be wonderful to become a regular part of their lives?

She had already accepted a job starting in February, but the agency that had arranged the position could certainly find someone else between now and then. Who wouldn't want to stay in a charming French village with a trio of cute dogs?

She opened her mouth to tell him she wanted that too, more time with him to explore these new and fragile feelings growing between them.

She couldn't seem to find the words.

Before she could speak, fear stole over her, cold and mean and relentless.

She thought of her father, so devastated at losing his love that he had completely walked away from his life.

Shelter Springs had taken so much from her. What if she stayed and things went wrong between them?

She couldn't risk it.

She eased farther away from him. "I'm not… This won't work between us, Griffin."

"Why not?"

"I told you before. I can't be the woman you need. We would make each other miserable. I would hate that."

"I'm getting pretty tired of you telling me what I need, Nat. I do have my own ideas about that. Right now, I can't imagine needing anyone like I need you."

"Yes, we're attracted to each other, but it's only physical. How long would that last?"

"Why are you so determined to run away from me?"

She swallowed, unable to face him. "Because that's what I do, Griffin," she said, her voice low. "Haven't you figured that out yet?"

Before he could argue, she turned and hurried into the Shelter Inn.

The apartment was quiet when she walked inside. The door into McKenna and Travis's room was closed, but she could hear them talking quietly inside.

She hurried to her own small room, whipped off her coat and sat on the edge of the bed, hot with pain and regret.

Oh, how she wished she were pet-sitting right now. She wanted nothing more than to bury her face against a soft puppy's neck and cry out her pain.

Why was she such a coward? Everyone around her, even her nieces, had more courage than she did. Hazel had soared down that mountainside the day they went sledding like she was steering a bobsled in the Olympics. Nora hadn't even flinched during a frightening medical procedure.

Her sister was so brave, she was willing to put her own life on hold for weeks in order to make sure she delivered a healthy child.

Not Natalie. She ran from any risk, any threat to her hard-fought independence and self-sufficiency.

She liked to think she didn't need anyone, but that was laughably ridiculous. She needed people. She simply refused to let them in.

She was no different from her father.

No. Not true. She was worse than her father. Steve had made efforts to reconnect. He had tried over the years with Natalie and had succeeded with McKenna, rebuilding a relationship with her and creating a new one with her family.

All Natalie could do was run.

twenty-five

The storm hit Shelter Springs around noon on Christmas Eve with a ferocity nobody expected, despite all the dire warnings from weather forecasters.

"Wow, it's really coming down out there." Keri Palmer, the nurse on duty with him at the urgent care clinic, looked with wide eyes out the window after an hour of steady snow. "I hope I'll be able to dig my car out when we close in an hour so I can make it home."

The vehicles in the parking lot were already covered with two or three inches, and the wind was blowing drifts against the low stone wall surrounding the clinic.

"I've heard the highway patrol is talking about issuing a no-travel order if we end up getting as much as they're saying," he said.

"It's Christmas Eve!" she exclaimed. "Can they do that?"

"I don't remember it happening before, but I suppose there's always a first time. The big worry is the cold. It's supposed to drop well below zero with a windchill below even that. They don't want a bunch of stranded motorists stuck in those kind of temperatures."

"Well, I hope I can get home before they decide to close the roads. No offense, Dr. Taylor, but I really don't want to spend

Christmas trapped at the urgent care with you and a couple of coughing patients."

He made a quick executive decision. "Go ahead and put a sign on the door that we're closing an hour early. We'll see these final two patients and then get you on the road."

"Thanks." She beamed at him and grabbed the chart of one of the patients.

He had just sent the last patient home with a prescription to treat her sinus infection when his cell phone rang.

He answered it as he was electronically signing a few more prescriptions that had been called in.

"Hi, Birdie. Merry Christmas Eve."

"I'm calling off dinner tonight," she said without preamble. "It's not safe for everyone to drive here from around the lake. They're saying there's black ice and whiteout conditions, and it's only going to get worse. Even if they don't close the roads, I won't put the family in jeopardy for a Christmas party."

He frowned. She had been planning the large extended family Christmas Eve party for weeks and had reserved the recreation room at the Shelter Inn as the only space large enough to fit everyone comfortably.

"Without the party, you'll have to spend Christmas by yourself."

"I won't be by myself. I have Dash and my friends here at the Shelter Inn."

Including Natalie Shepherd.

His chest gave a hard twinge when he thought of her walking away from him two nights ago, shutting him out completely.

"We're closing up here now. I'll come spend Christmas Eve with you there."

"You don't have to do that. What if you're stranded here?"

"Would that be so terrible? You have an extra bedroom. At least we won't starve. You have plenty of food. And I should know, since I bought it for you."

The memory made his heart hurt again. He swallowed, remembering the fun of shopping with Natalie and her nieces.

The last thing he wanted to do was spend Christmas with her just down the hall, but he couldn't bear the idea of Birdie being on her own during the holidays.

"I'll feel better if I can make sure you're okay during the storm, in case the power goes out or something. I can also help you with Dash, since you won't be able to take him out on your own in a blizzard."

His grandmother seemed to be weakening. "But what about your sister?"

"I checked on her this morning and she's still feeling crummy. She wouldn't have made it to your Christmas Eve party anyway. I know she's worried about giving her illness to you, since it hit her so hard."

"She told me. And I made it clear she shouldn't waste her time worrying about me. I'm as strong as an ox."

Birdie might be healthy, but she was still nearly eighty. Amanda was right to be concerned. This particular respiratory virus mutation was hitting older people hard. He had seen six patients with it at the clinic that day and had sent two of them to the emergency room.

"As her medical adviser and yours, I would have told her she's doing the right thing by staying away. Better safe than sorry."

"But it's Christmas. She shouldn't be alone on Christmas."

If he had been in a better mood, he might have laughed at the irony. She had just been assuring him she didn't need him to stay with her during the holidays, and now she was worrying about Amanda being alone.

He had spent plenty of Christmases on his own while he was living away from Shelter Springs. He had usually offered to work a double shift at the emergency department of whatever hospital he was working at, filling in so those with families could enjoy Christmas with them.

A few years back, he had gone on a medical mission overseas during the holidays and had loved every minute of the experience.

Too bad he hadn't arranged another one this year.

There was the second irony of the day. Now that he was back in Shelter Springs, surrounded by his family, he felt more lonely than he ever remembered.

He knew the reason. Because this was the first year he yearned for something different.

He wanted a future with Natalie.

She had made it clear that wasn't on the table, but he couldn't stop wishing he could change her mind.

"Amanda can always join us virtually, if she feels up to it," he told Birdie. "I can set up a video call. In fact, if you want, we can have one with the whole family. We can do all the things you usually do at your Christmas party, just virtually. Read the Christmas story, sing carols, even play your favorite Christmas bingo, I guess. If we have to. You can keep track of the winners and give out the prizes later."

She chuckled at the suggestion. "You love my Christmas bingo. You know you do."

Griffin had to admit that his grandmother's Christmas Eve party was usually the high point of the season when he was younger.

He had never really enjoyed the holidays, except for that party.

On Christmas Day, when his nuclear family was forced to interact, the house would be filled with tension. His father would start drinking early in the morning, his mother would usually end up in tears and he and Amanda would pretend to have fun with their Christmas gifts, waiting for the moment when they could escape to a friend's house.

He had a sudden memory of one Christmas Day afternoon and evening when he had slipped away to the Shelter Inn to hang out with Jake.

That Christmas stood out as one of his best. They went swimming for a long time, then dried off and played board games for hours. After feasting on leftovers, they all bundled up and went for a walk around downtown to look at all the holiday lights.

He had loved every minute of it and had been filled with envy for what he saw as Jake's perfect life.

A few years later, Jeanette Shepherd had been diagnosed with cancer, a harsh reminder that no life was without hardship in one form or another.

He had learned that if a person seemed like they had no troubles, that only meant he hadn't learned about them yet.

After sending the staff home, Griffin closed up the urgent care and spent a good fifteen minutes scraping the windows of his pickup truck.

Before heading to Birdie's, he decided to stop at his condo to grab a few things. On the way, he saw a few accidents that looked like minor fender benders, but for the most part it appeared the people of Shelter Springs had heeded the advice of authorities and stayed home.

It took him about three times as long as normal to make it to his condo. Grateful for the underground parking garage, he hurried up to his place. It seemed barren, suddenly, without even so much as a Christmas tree.

He filled a duffel with his razor, toiletries and a quick change of clothes, then loaded another bag with the gifts he had purchased for Birdie.

After a moment's hesitation, he added the presents he had impulsively bought earlier in the week. Griffin hoped the girls would enjoy the snowman-making kit he had purchased for them, as well as the small stuffed animals.

The other one was an artisan-made bracelet made of semi-precious stones from the local area that he had seen Natalie admiring when they shopped at the market together.

While she had been distracted by the girls, he had gone back to purchase the bracelet, thinking it might give her some connection to Shelter Springs during her roving life.

Perhaps while he was spending Christmas with his grandmother he might find an opportunity to deliver the gifts. Or maybe he would simply drop them off anonymously so Natalie wouldn't feel obligated to give him anything else in return.

Keeping two girls entertained on Christmas Eve when their anticipation was ramped up to fever pitch had turned out to be a bigger chore than Natalie expected.

"I don't want to color right now," Hazel informed her from the floor of McKenna's bedroom, where the girls had brought in their art supplies.

"Why not?" their mother asked. Though McKenna smiled, it seemed strained.

"It's boring," Hazel said. "I want to go sledding."

They had been over this already, several times, but apparently a five-year-old wanted what she wanted.

"We can't right now," Natalie said. "I've explained that to you. Right now we're having a big storm and it's super-duper cold. It's not safe to be outside in this weather."

"We can wear our snow clothes. Then we will be warm," the girl pointed out.

"I'm afraid even your warmest snow clothes won't help you when the wind is blowing so hard and the temperature is so cold." The voice from the doorway had them all turning their heads.

"Hi, Aunt Liz!" Nora, who had remained coloring on the floor during Hazel's protest, jumped to her feet and embraced the older woman.

"Hello, darlings."

Liz seemed to be getting around much better, Natalie was happy to see. She was off the crutches, with only a cane for occasional support.

She looked lovely in a red sweater with her short hair styled more than usual. She wore lipstick and mascara, something else that wasn't typical.

She was glowing. Natalie knew the reason why. She was in love.

She found it highly unfair that being in love made her aunt seem even more beautiful than usual, but made Natalie feel frumpy and exhausted.

"Merry Christmas Eve."

"Same to you," McKenna said. She mustered a smile when Liz reached down to kiss her cheek, but Natalie couldn't help thinking again that her voice sounded strained.

McKenna had been more quiet than usual all day, though she assured Natalie she was fine every time she pressed.

"How did you get here?" Natalie asked their aunt.

"It wasn't easy. The roads are horrible. I heard on the radio they're closing off the canyon roads now and are ordering a mandatory curfew to keep people off the other streets."

"Santa Claus doesn't need to drive," Hazel said. "It won't be too cold for the reindeer because they live in the North Pole, where they have cold all the time."

"Excellent point," Liz said with a smile. "Unfortunately, I *did* need to drive. The roads were bad but I drove slowly. I didn't want to miss Christmas with you all. I also thought it would be a good idea to sleep on the cot in the office so I can be on hand in case the power goes out or we have some other weather-related crisis here at the Shelter Inn. I don't want you to have to worry about anything."

"Oh, good thinking. I didn't even think of what we will do if the power goes out." McKenna looked troubled.

"It won't," Liz assured her, squeezing McKenna's hand.

Natalie was overwhelmed with gratitude again for this woman who had stepped up to care for them. What would they have done without her?

"You might be stuck here for a few days," Natalie warned her. "The last report I heard said the storm will continue on through tomorrow and even into Tuesday."

"That's fine with me. I packed clean clothes for two or three days."

"Well, you certainly don't have to sleep on an uncomfortable cot. You can have my bed. I'll sleep on the sofa."

Liz looked as if she wanted to argue. When she saw the resolve in Natalie's expression, she sighed instead. "You're as stubborn as your father, do you know that? Fine. Thank you. I'll stay here, then. It gets very drafty in that office, right next to the front doors, even if people aren't coming in and out all day."

"Speaking of Dad, how is he? Have you seen him?" McKenna asked.

Liz looked away, a blush creeping over her high cheekbones. "Yes. I've seen him. He's fine. He's feeling much better. He helped me take down the booth last night at the market."

"Oh no! I just realized that if they close the road, Dad won't be able to make it here to spend Christmas Eve dinner with us!" her sister exclaimed.

"Too bad," Natalie muttered.

"It *is* too bad." McKenna looked distressed. "The girls were so looking forward to seeing him, especially since he's been too sick to spend much time with them."

Not too sick to kiss Liz at the market. Natalie had not yet told her sister about finding the two of them in an embrace at the market.

She hadn't talked to Liz about it, either.

"The storm won't last forever," her aunt said. "The girls will still be able to see their grandfather after the storm dies down. We can always FaceTime with him too."

"I guess. It won't be the same, but I suppose it will have to do." McKenna still looked distressed. "I feel terrible for all our residents who were planning family gatherings today or tomorrow. Some of them will be all alone for the holidays now."

"They won't," Hazel said. "They have us."

Her niece's innocent words gave Natalie a sudden idea. She remembered a small village where she had stayed in Greece one unforgettable holiday season, where the residents had all celebrated Christmas Eve together, one huge communal party. They had even invited her to join them and had welcomed her freely into their midst to dance and drink and eat.

"You're right!" Natalie exclaimed. "They do have us. We might all be stuck here, but that doesn't mean we can't celebrate Christmas together. We should have a party."

"A party?" McKenna looked intrigued by the idea, even as she winced again.

"Sure. Why couldn't we do a potluck Christmas dinner? Since everyone has had to cancel their celebrations for the night, I'm sure they have leftover food they can't use. We can all put our dishes together and have one giant feast."

Liz clapped her hands together. "That is a great idea! I wish I had thought of it. Just because the storm is canceling plans right and left doesn't mean Christmas is ruined. A party would definitely help lift people's spirits."

"You could have Hazel and Nora draw an invitation and then make copies and take them around to everyone," McKenna suggested.

Natalie grinned. "Brilliant! I love it. Let's do it."

They quickly put the girls to work drawing a picture of a Christmas tree with presents while they worked out the details, then McKenna added text asking people to meet in the large recreation room at the time they decided would work best.

"I can make copies in the office," Liz offered.

"Great. The girls and I will deliver them. Come on, kiddos."

Hazel and Nora were only too happy to have something to

do. They raced along, singing "Jingle Bells" at the tops of their lungs as they all made their way to the office.

While Liz made copies, two to a page, the girls twirled each other around in the office swivel chair, one of their favorite activities.

Natalie went to work cutting apart the invitations. She was finishing the last invitations when Liz spoke to her in a low, serious voice that the girls couldn't overhear.

"I'm glad to have the chance to talk to you. I wish you would try to make things right with your father," Liz said abruptly.

Natalie blinked, taken completely off guard.

"Whatever you might think, he loves you and your sister very much."

"I don't know if I can do that. Some things are hard to forgive."

Liz nodded. "You don't have to forgive him for the choices he made after your mother died. You can't be any harder on Steve than he is on himself. I'm only asking you to think about figuring out how to move forward. I know he desperately wants a relationship with you now."

"And I desperately wanted a father in my life when I was a teenager. We can't always have what we want."

Liz gave her a stern look. "You and I both know your mom would not have wanted you to ostracize him like this."

Natalie could feel the hold on her temper fray. "You're a fine one to talk about what my mother would have wanted. How do you think she would feel about the two of you carrying on?"

Liz paled, quickly looking over to be sure the girls were still busy playing. "We're not carrying on, as you put it," she said, her voice just above a whisper.

"I saw him kiss you at the market last week."

Liz sighed and closed her eyes. "I was afraid of that. That wasn't the way we wanted you or your sister to find out."

"To find out what?"

Her aunt hesitated. "Okay. If you want the truth, your father and I are...dating. I don't know what other term to use. We have been for about a year now."

Natalie stared. "A year? Why am I just finding out about it now?"

"Because we felt like our relationship wasn't anybody's business but ours."

"How can you just pretend like nothing happened? He dumped me and McKenna on you and took off from all his responsibilities like he was some kind of college student going backpacking across Europe. How do you get over that?"

Liz's mouth tightened. "I was angry with him too. You know I was. I carried that anger for a long time. As the years passed, I started to see how much he regretted giving in to his pain. He never, ever stopped loving you or McKenna, he just didn't think he was capable of being a good father to you until he dealt with his own pain. He felt like he was doing the best thing for you both."

"That sounds very noble, doesn't it? But it was just the excuse he gave. It didn't feel like the best thing for us when McKenna used to cry herself to sleep for missing him."

Or when I find myself incapable of committing to anyone because I'm afraid they're going to leave me too.

Liz looked at her for a long time, as if she understood exactly what Natalie couldn't say.

"I should tell you, your father and I...love each other."

She fought the childish urge to cover her ears with her hands and start chanting so she didn't have to hear the rest.

"We're talking about a future together," Liz went on. "I didn't want to say anything until after McKenna had the baby, but since you know, I thought I might as well tell you the rest of it. Given your feelings about your father, I don't want it to come between us."

They loved each other.

Natalie felt as if she had been punched.

Liz was the closest thing she had to a mother figure now. She didn't want to lose her. But what if that meant having to accept her father fully back into her life?

"Aren't you afraid he'll leave again?" she finally asked.

Liz's lovely features softened. "Oh, darling. I didn't expect any of this. After my divorce, I thought that part of my life was over. I accepted it. I planned to spend the rest of my life alone. I never, ever expected to fall in love again. But somehow I did. And I discovered that at some point, love has to be stronger than fear."

She smiled softly, sadly. "Your father is a good man who lost his way for a few years after your mother died. He regretted leaving you a long time ago, especially after Jake died, but by the time he came to his senses and thought about coming back, you and your sister were moving on with your lives. You were both in college, away from here, and Steve decided to stay in Alaska. That all changed after McKenna got married and had the girls, when he truly realized how important his family is to him."

Natalie didn't know what to say as a hundred different emotions chased through her.

She loved her aunt and wanted her to embrace the life that brought her joy. If that life included Steve, how could Nat possibly stand in the way?

"I truly hope you can find it in your heart to accept the two of us together," Liz said, her voice earnest. "I love you and want you to be part of our lives. Both of our lives. But if you can't accept the two of us together, I have already told your father I will somehow figure out a way to have a relationship with you that doesn't include him."

"You would do that?"

"Of course. It won't be easy, but we'll make it work."

"Are the invitations ready yet?" Hazel asked, looking slightly green from twirling in the chair too much.

"They are," Natalie said, picking up the stack and holding it out to her.

She turned to meet Liz's gaze. "Thank you for telling me. I can't say I am ready to completely let go of the past, but you're too important for me to let this come between us."

"Oh, darling. I feel the same way."

With a watery smile, Liz embraced her and Natalie rested her head on her aunt's shoulder for a moment, wishing she could spill all her own heartache to the other woman in return for some of her usual sage advice.

This wasn't the time, though, when they had an impromptu Christmas party to throw for an apartment building full of senior citizens.

twenty-six

Birdie's face lit up with joy the moment Griffin walked into her apartment, snow still covering his hair and parka, despite the care he'd taken to shake it all off before he let himself into the Shelter Inn.

"You're here!" she exclaimed. "I was so worried about you. I can't believe you made it through that storm. We haven't had a blizzard like this in years."

Her living room was warm and cozy and smelled of roasting potatoes and gingerbread, an odd but comforting combination.

He set down his bag filled with presents near her small table-top Christmas tree and the unlit menorah and carried his duffel to her second bedroom.

"I barely made it, if you want the truth," he said. "They closed the road coming down from my place right behind me. I'm afraid you're stuck with me for a while, since I won't be able to get back home until the weather clears."

"I'm glad to have you here as long as you want. You know that. But you didn't need to risk your life to come here. I would have been fine. Spending one Christmas alone out of nearly eighty certainly wouldn't have been the end of the world."

"Now you don't have to be alone. Can I help you with anything?"

She glanced at Dash, who was waiting patiently for Griffin to acknowledge him.

"Dash could probably use a trip outside. He's been very patient all day. I took him out before the wind became so fierce, but it's been a few hours."

"I can do that."

"Thank you."

He found the dog's leash, grateful he hadn't yet removed his coat. He didn't bother with Dash's harness this time since they wouldn't be walking anywhere, only going far enough outside for the dog to do his business.

He opened the door and stopped short.

Someone was on the other side. Three someones—Natalie with her two nieces.

She looked beautiful, in a green holiday sweater and dangly snowflake earrings. He wanted to drink in the sight of her like fine champagne.

Judging by her expression, she was equally as stunned to see him.

The memory of that last magical kiss they had shared seemed to shiver in the air between them.

"Hi, Dr. Jingle!" Hazel said, tugging on his coat. "Guess what? It's Christmas Eve! Santa will be here *tonight*!"

He tightened his hand on the leash to keep from pulling Natalie into his arms. All of them, really.

"I had heard that rumor. Are you two ready for him with your cookies and milk?"

They both nodded vigorously. "And carrots," Nora said with her adorable lisp. "For the reindeer."

"Very smart."

He finally met Natalie's gaze fully. "Hi. Merry Christmas."

Her cheeks seemed pink, but he couldn't be sure.

"Hi." She gave an uncertain smile. "I didn't expect to see you here. I heard the roads were closed."

"I made it through in the nick of time. I didn't want Birdie to have to spend Christmas by herself."

"Oh. That's nice." She glanced down at her nieces. Hazel held out a piece of paper to him, which he saw at first glance seemed to be some kind of hand-drawn invitation.

"That's actually why we're here," Natalie went on. "Since everyone here at the Shelter Inn is stuck, forced to cancel family parties and visits, we thought it might be fun to have our own impromptu Christmas party potluck."

"Oh, what a good idea."

Griffin hadn't realized his grandmother had joined him at the door until she spoke. She smiled at Natalie and the girls.

"I made more shortbread this morning and can certainly bring that to share, as well as a ham and some mashed potatoes. It won't feed everyone, but we can make it stretch if everyone brings something."

"Thank you." She smiled warmly at his grandmother. "That would be wonderful. You're the second person who has a ham, and Barbara Wiggins said she cooked a turkey that will go to waste since her grandchildren aren't coming now and she and Cal don't like turkey anyway. That should be plenty of food."

"I also have all the paper products you might need," Birdie added, "since we were planning to have our family party here tonight."

"Perfect!" Natalie exclaimed. "I hadn't even thought about plates and utensils."

"I'll have my grandson take them to the recreation room after he's done walking Dash."

Natalie gave Griffin a worried look. "You're going out in this weather?"

"Only to the parking lot," he assured her. "I don't expect Dash will want to linger long in a blizzard when he has a cozy bed back here."

"Smart dog."

She petted the golden retriever with affection, and Griffin tried not to be envious of a dog.

"Eating together is genius," Birdie said. "I'm so glad you thought of it, otherwise all this food would go to waste."

"Just keep your fingers crossed the power stays on."

Birdie chuckled. "I don't mind eating in the dark, since I can't see what I'm eating anyway, but I don't like cold food."

Natalie smiled at her. "Girls, we'd better go so we can take around the rest of these invitations. We'll see you in an hour or so."

She ushered Hazel and Nora down the hall to the next apartment. Griffin watched after them, overwhelmed with yearning, until Dash tugged pointedly at the leash.

As he braved the icy cold and biting wind, Griffin couldn't escape one inevitable conclusion.

He was completely in love with Natalie Shepherd.

If he had any lingering doubts, they had disappeared when he had seen her standing outside the door. Had everyone seen the joy and pain and longing he knew must be on his face? It was certainly in his heart.

He loved her and there was not one single thing he could do about it. She had made it clear she didn't feel the same way.

The only thing left for him to do was figure out how to go on without her.

Apparently, throwing a last-minute Christmas party for fifty senior citizens could be chaos. She should have known.

Natalie set out the paper plates and plastic cutlery Birdie had provided, listening to the chatter of a dozen different conversations over the sound of Bing Crosby singing about a white Christmas on the Bluetooth speaker someone had provided.

The party wasn't set to start for another half hour. At least that was the time McKenna had written on the invitation her girls had drawn. That hadn't stopped virtually everyone in the apartment building from arriving early, and now the common room was filled to bursting with conversation, music, even a raucous game of cards in one corner.

Despite the raging storm outside, or maybe because of the enforced intimacy it necessitated on this unusual Christmas Eve, everyone seemed almost giddy.

The girls, she saw, were having the time of their lives, running around talking to all their honorary grandparents.

She glanced out the window, where the snow had piled up to at least eighteen inches. Snowdrifts in places had to be two to three feet deep, and it was still coming down hard.

To her vast relief, Travis had arrived shortly after they finished handing out the invitations and was with McKenna now. Natalie had begun to worry he would have to spend Christmas Eve stuck at the delivery service warehouse.

She was trying very hard to keep her gaze away from Griffin, who was helping a few of the other men set up extra chairs and tables. She had heard him fielding a steady barrage of medical questions with his usual polite calm.

She was setting out serving utensils for all the food items when Mabel Mulcahy clumped over to her with her walker.

"This was a good idea," she announced in her no-nonsense tone.

Natalie looked over the room of cheerful residents. "It worked out, didn't it?"

"You've brought Christmas spirit to a bunch of old codgers. Including this one."

"I'm glad," she said sincerely. "No one should have to be alone at Christmas, unless they want to be."

Mabel harrumphed. "I've spent plenty of holidays on my own. At one time in my life, I told myself that was exactly what I wanted."

Laughter erupted from the card players, and Mabel turned to look at them. When she shifted her gaze back to Natalie, she was stunned to see what might have been tears in the older woman's eyes behind her thick glasses.

"I was wrong," she said abruptly. "We need each other. All of us. Whether we want to admit it or not."

She turned and shuffled away before Natalie could respond.

Okay. That was odd. Why did Mabel Mulcahy feel compelled to give her that particular advice?

She shook her head slightly, and her gaze happened to catch Griffin's. He was watching her with a stark expression that made her catch her breath.

"I think everything is ready." Liz surveyed the tables, bulging with food. "Shall we eat?"

"Definitely," Arlene Gallegos said. "I'm starving."

"Do you mind if I say a blessing of gratitude first?" James Johnson asked in his deep, calming voice.

"Please." Liz gestured for him to go ahead.

When the others quieted, he bowed his head and began to pray, asking for safety for all those out in the storm and giving thanks for the food and for family, both near and far, and expressing that Christmas wasn't about the presents or the delicious food, but about the healing grace of love.

Natalie pressed her lips together. Hearing this kind man utter such heartfelt, sincere words made her throat feel achy and tight. When he finished, she opened her eyes and again found Griffin watching her.

The ache inside her intensified, and she wished with all her heart that she could take back everything and start over with him from this moment.

"Okay. Let's eat," Liz said.

Before the first residents could make their way to the buffet table, they all heard the front door open with a blast of wind and cold, and a person dressed in layers of outdoor gear staggered inside.

Natalie stared, stunned, as the stranger removed a snow-encrusted beanie and scarf to reveal familiar features, now red and cold-chapped.

"Dad!" she exclaimed.

Liz's mouth sagged open. "Steve! What are you doing here? I thought the roads were closed!"

She rushed to him, and Natalie was astonished when she kissed him right there in front of all the residents of the Shelter Inn—much to their delight.

"I borrowed Dave's snowmobile and bundled up in my warmest gear."

"Oh! I can't believe you took such a risk! Why?"

He shrugged as he pulled off more layers. "I was sitting alone in Dave's house, worried sick about all of you here on your own. Finally, I decided there was no point in fretting about it. I needed to take action. I've spent enough Christmases without my family. I didn't want to spend another one, if I could help it."

He gave an apologetic smile. "I would have been here earlier, but I found a couple stranded in their car and gave them a ride to the fire station, where they've set up a temporary shelter for travelers. Good thing I came along. They were almost out of gas. Not sure what would have happened if I hadn't."

Liz slipped her arm through his. "I'm not happy that you risked your life, but it sounds like you were meant to find them."

He looked around the recreation room, which had grown noisy again as people resumed their conversations.

"Looks like you're having a party without me."

Hazel and Nora finally had noticed the arrival of their grandfather and had rushed over to hug him.

"We're having a lucky pot," Hazel informed him.

"Potluck," Liz corrected her with a smile. "We should grab something to eat while it's warm."

"I need to go hang my wet things somewhere."

"I'll take care of it." Natalie stepped forward and took his coat and hat. "There are hooks in the office."

She hurried from the room and had just hung up the coat when her father joined her.

"Sorry. I just realized I left my phone in the inside zip pocket of the coat," he said, reaching for it so he could root through and find the device.

"You shouldn't have risked your life like that," she couldn't resist saying. "The girls don't need to lose their grandfather. McKenna doesn't need to lose you again right now."

He sighed. "I know. It wasn't smart. I thought I was doing the right thing by coming here to help out, but anything could have happened to me. I could have gotten lost in the whiteout conditions. The snowmobile could have had mechanical trouble. I could easily have run into something, with zero visibility."

Her father hesitated, then gave her a long, steady look. "Sometimes my choices don't always have the consequences I want."

She gave him a wary look, sensing he wasn't talking about going out into the storm. His next words confirmed it.

"After your mom died, I was a mess." Steve ran a hand through his hair, tousled from the beanie he had removed. "Even though we knew for a long time what was coming, I just…fell apart. I didn't want you girls or Jake to see me like that. What kind of example was I setting, drunk most of the time, wild with grief when I wasn't wasted. I thought I would spend a few months on my own getting my head on straight, but then… I don't know. It was easier to stay away. I knew Liz was taking good care of you, and I just figured you all were better off without me."

"We weren't."

She folded her hands together, not wanting him to see they were trembling. "We had just lost our mother and now our dad couldn't be bothered with us, either."

"That wasn't it. Oh, Nat. That was never it. I loved you all so much. I was just afraid I couldn't be your father and your mother at the same time."

"So you chose to be neither."

A muscle in his jaw worked. "Yes. I'm not proud of it. If I could go back and change one decision in my entire life, it would be that one."

"You could have come back after...after Jake died. Instead, Kenna and I had to deal with that all alone."

His face twisted with pain. "I know. I could say I'm sorry every day for the rest of my life, and it still wouldn't be enough."

He was silent, looking as if he wanted to reach out to her, but feared she would push him away.

"When I found out about Jake, I wanted to die too," he admitted.

They were both silent, lost in hard memories.

Finally, her father touched her cheek with a soft tenderness that made her want to throw herself into his arms and cry like she was Hazel's age.

He dropped his hand. "I know you can't forgive me. To be honest, I don't think I'll ever be able to forgive myself. But know this. I never stopped loving you. Or Jake. Or Kenna. I kept a picture of you all with me, no matter where I was. I try to read everything I can find that you write online, and I'm so proud of you. Your mother would have been too."

She closed her eyes against the rush of warmth his words stirred.

"I've been wanting to tell you that for a long time."

"Thanks."

He studied her. "I know it's a big ask, but...maybe I could call you once in a while and you can tell me about what you're working on, where you're living."

Could they start over, as she had just thought she wanted to do with Griffin?

A week ago, she would have told her father no, that the pain he had caused was too big to climb over.

But this was a season of hope, of peace. And she was so tired of carrying the burden of her anger.

"I suppose a phone call wouldn't hurt once in a while."

Joy split his face, so bright it made the Christmas tree out in the common room pale in comparison. "That's enough for now."

He hugged her then, just a brief, awkward embrace, but it seemed like a huge hurdle.

"I should probably tell you I'm thinking about moving back to Shelter Springs."

"Because of Liz." She said the words as a statement, not a question.

He looked shocked. "You know about that?"

"Dad. I saw you kissing her at the holiday market, and five minutes ago she kissed you in front of the whole building. Even if she hadn't, I imagine most of the town knows by now."

"What do you think about that?" he asked warily.

She shrugged. "I think it's weird. I probably will for a while. But if the two of you make each other happy, I guess I'll have to adjust."

"We do." He sounded like he couldn't quite believe it.

"What about Alaska? I thought you loved living in the wilderness."

"At the time, that was what I needed. To be on my own, where I could cry all night if I wanted, talk to your mother without people thinking I needed medication, howl in the forest where only the bears and the moose could hear me."

She felt a pang of sadness at the picture he painted, imagining him alone with his grief.

"That's what I needed then. But people change. Circumstances change. I'm not the same person I was then. I'm a better person. A happier person. And I need something different now."

"Aunt Liz."

His face widened into a broad, joy-filled smile. "And McKenna and those kids of hers. I love being a grandfather to Nora and Hazel, and I can only imagine I'll love her new little one just as much once he comes along."

People did change, she thought as they returned to the party.

Maybe *she* had changed. Maybe the perfect life she had created for herself no longer met her needs as it once had.

Maybe, just maybe, she was ready for something else—if she could find the courage to reach for it.

twenty-seven

The holiday Griffin thought would be a disaster due to the ferocity of the storm and the fallout from it was turning into something that he never would have expected.

Something rare and precious and wonderful.

He sat on a folding chair at one of the tables with Nora on his knee and Birdie beside him as Mabel Mulcahy played Christmas carols on the piano and Calvin and Barbara Wiggins hummed along.

Not everyone had stayed after the delicious, if hodgepodge, dinner they had shared. A few said they were going back to their apartments to have video calls with their children or grandchildren and one or two just left without explanation. But about twenty or so of the residents remained in the Shelter Inn recreation room, talking softly and enjoying each other's company.

The wind howled outside and hurled snow against the windows, and every once in a while the power would flicker. So far, the lights had stayed on, though.

"Does anybody else have any traditions they're missing out on tonight?" Birdie asked.

"We always read the Christmas story," James Johnson said. "It's our way of reminding our family that Christmas isn't just about Santa Claus and presents. Does anyone mind if we do that?"

"Not at all," Birdie said. "Especially if you can read it in that wonderful voice of yours."

He must have had scriptures on his phone because he scrolled through for a moment until he found what he wanted, then he began to read.

Nora nestled back against his chest, perfectly content.

"Can we sing 'Silent Night'?" Hazel asked after James finished reading about angel choirs and abiding shepherds. "That's my favorite."

Natalie smiled at her niece, and Griffin felt the jolt of it through his entire body.

"One more song, and then we need to go home and see if your mom is feeling better."

"And get ready for Santa," Hazel said.

"That's right."

They all sang the familiar song together, the perfect way to end the evening.

"All right. Let's go," Natalie said to her nieces. "Tell everyone good night."

Nora slid from his knee. "Night," she said, giving Griffin her sweetest smile, a gift he knew he would treasure.

They turned to leave, but before they could take more than a few steps, Travis Dodd rushed into the recreation room, his face pale and his eyes hollow with fear.

"Oh, thank God you're here," he said, going straight to Griffin. "We need you. McKenna's water just broke."

Natalie gasped and Liz made a small sound of distress.

"What do we do? The roads are closed and the blizzard is even worse. We have no way to get her to the hospital. You're a doctor. You have to help her!"

Griffin stared at him, his mind suddenly blank of anything but the memory of the tiny, frail body of his son, cold and still.

Icy panic clutched at him. He couldn't do this. He would carry McKenna to the hospital himself through the blinding snow, but he couldn't deliver her baby.

He opened his mouth to say as much, then saw the expression in Natalie's eyes as she looked at him, one of complete and utter faith.

He sucked air into his lungs and shoved away the memory to focus on the crisis at hand.

"Someone call 911," he ordered. "See if there's any chance an ambulance can get here through the snow."

"I will," Liz said.

"Girls, why don't you stay here with me?" Natalie's father reached his hands out to his granddaughters. "We can sing a few more carols and maybe even play a few more games."

"What about Santa Claus?" Hazel asked, brow furrowed. "We have to go to bed or he can't come."

"Don't you worry. He won't be here for hours," Birdie assured her.

Natalie gave her a quick hug. "Everything will be all right."

"Is Mommy okay?"

"Perfectly fine."

"Go help your sister," Birdie said. "We've got this."

The weight of responsibility was heavy as Griffin raced down the hall with Travis at his side, aware of Natalie and her aunt right behind them, Liz talking to the 911 dispatcher.

The door was open and they rushed inside. A moan came from the bedroom at the rear of the apartment. He followed the sound, where he found McKenna Dodd, her face pale and contorted with pain.

She released a cry of distress when she saw them. "What am I going to do? What am I going to do? I can't have this baby now. It's too early!"

"It's not that early," Natalie reminded her calmly, going to her younger sister and gripping her hand. "Only a few days. You told me yourself that you'll be thirty-seven weeks along at the end of the week. That's full term."

"I wanted more time."

"I know. I'm sorry."

She moaned again and Griffin saw Travis sway.

"Don't pass out," Griffin told him.

Travis shook his head, eyes determined. "I won't. We've been through this before."

"He's coming," McKenna wailed. "I can feel it."

Griffin moved closer to the bed. "How long have you been having contractions?"

"A few days. Not regular. Maybe five minutes apart at times, then I wouldn't have another one for an hour or more. When can the ambulance get here?"

Liz shook her head, her cell phone still pressed to her ear. "Not for at least an hour. All the ambulances are out on other calls right now."

McKenna gripped Natalie's hand. "I don't think we can wait that long. This baby is coming."

While he wanted to say his truck was a heavy-duty four-wheel drive and he would drive her to the hospital himself, busting down any roadblocks in their way, Griffin knew that wasn't the answer.

If she was as close to delivery as she seemed to think, it would be far too risky to take her out into the blizzard. Better to give birth here in her warm bed with her family around than in the back seat of his truck, especially with the very real chance they could be stranded on the way to the hospital.

"Tell them to get here as soon as they can," he told Liz.

"What can I do?" Natalie asked, giving him a look of complete trust.

How many babies did she think he had delivered in a private bedroom at a retirement community in the middle of a freaking blizzard?

"The usual things you see on TV. Boil water in case we need to sterilize anything and bring in as many clean towels as you've got."

He turned to Travis. "I have an emergency medical kit in my truck."

"I'll get it." The man looked relieved to have something to do.

He handed over his key fob. "Thanks. It's the blue Chevy King Cab. I'm parked in my grandmother's assigned spot. The kit is in the storage space under the rear bench seat."

"Got it."

"Be careful. I wouldn't ask anybody to go out in that storm if this wasn't an emergency."

Travis nodded, rushing out of the room. Griffin could only hope the man remembered to grab his coat on the way.

"McKenna, I need you to move sideways on the bed since the footboard will only be in the way."

"I'll help," Natalie said.

"Take off my quilt first," McKenna ordered her sister. "Travis's mother made it for us and it's my favorite."

While Griffin scrubbed his hands thoroughly in the en suite bathroom, Natalie helped her sister rearrange the bedding so that the pillows were on one side and she stretched across it.

McKenna had another contraction that had her gripping her sister's hand hard.

When he moved into position, what he saw increased the urgency exponentially. The baby was crowning, just the top of his head appearing.

"Wow. Okay. You're right. We're doing this now. You've got a head coming out there. I'm afraid there's no chance of waiting for the ambulance."

"I can feel it," she wailed.

Griffin forced his mind back to his obstetrics rotation, which he had gone through right before Chase had been born.

He knew what to do. That didn't make it any easier.

"I have to push!"

"Hold on for just a moment, if you can. Do you have a bulb syringe?"

She looked disoriented at the question. "Yes. I... I think so. In one of the drawers of the changing table over there."

"I'll grab it."

Natalie rushed to the table and started rooting through drawers. "I don't know what I'm looking for," she finally admitted.

"It's blue," McKenna panted. "Looks like a small onion with a stem."

After another second, she held it up, victorious.

"That's it," Griffin said. "Rinse it in water as hot as you can get it."

They didn't have time for her to boil it. She hurried to the bathroom just as Travis burst through the door with Griffin's emergency bag.

He reached in with relief and pulled out masks, surgical gloves, sterile gauze and the packet containing sterilized Metz scissors.

"It hurts," McKenna wailed. "Where's my epidural?"

He forced a smile, doing his best to portray a calm he wasn't close to feeling as he gloved up and handed masks to Natalie and Travis. "I'm afraid I don't have one of those in my emergency kit."

"Breathe," Travis said to his wife. "You're doing great."

She whimpered, obviously feeling the opposite.

"You've got this," Griffin said, fighting for calm. "Now with the next contraction, I need you to push."

He held his breath, his heart racing. He saw a contraction ripple over McKenna's face as her whole body seemed to twist into an agony of exertion.

"You're doing so great. What a rock star. Come on, one more."

She groaned, her features contorted with pain. She gripped Travis's and Natalie's hands and pushed with all her might.

Natalie held her sister's hand, but also moved to an angle where she could see what was happening. He spared her a quick look to find her face was pale and set.

"Sit down if you need to."

She shook her head. "It's amazing."

It was. Miraculous, agonizing, beautiful, messy, amazing. The perfect metaphor for life.

"Almost there. One more," he told McKenna.

With one more superhuman push and a raw, guttural groan, she strained with all her might and suddenly the baby slithered out into the world and into Griffin's hands.

The cord was wrapped around his neck and his tiny face was covered with membrane and mucus.

He wasn't breathing.

All of Griffin's panic that he had set aside to focus on the moment returned with thundering force.

No. No! This couldn't happen.

With adrenaline bursting through him, he relied on his training. Clear the airway. Clear the damn airway.

He peeled away the mucus and membrane and uncoiled the cord, then picked up the bulb syringe, using it to clean out the tiny mouth and nasal cavities.

Still nothing.

Desperate, he picked up a towel and wrapped the baby in it, still attached to McKenna by the umbilical cord, and began rubbing his blue skin briskly.

He was just about ready to reach into his kit for his manual resuscitator bag when the baby inhaled with a sharp gasp and then let out a small, feeble cry, then a stronger one.

Everyone gathered in the bedroom seemed to sag with relief. Griffin's throat was tight and he closed his eyes, an unspoken prayer in his heart, then he set to work cleaning off the baby with more towels.

"Is he okay?" McKenna craned to have a look.

"Perfect," Griffin assured her. He handed her the baby, whose cry had turned into a steady whimper.

Natalie handed him a soft receiving blanket from the nursery supplies in the corner, and Griffin draped it over both mother and baby.

Travis was crying, he saw. Tears rolled down the big man's face, and he looked at his wife and child with sheer adoration.

"He's beautiful." Natalie gazed at her nephew with an expression of wonder and love.

Griffin didn't have time to deal with the flood of emotions washing over him. He pushed everything away to focus on the job at hand as he cleaned up the afterbirth.

"Do you want to cut the cord?" he asked Travis after he tied it off with a strip of gauze he found in his bag.

The man's hands shook, but he took the sterile scissors from him and cut through the connection between mother and child.

"You did so great," Griffin said to McKenna.

She smiled at him, sweat-soaked hair clinging to her face. She looked utterly exhausted, but radiant with joy.

"Is he okay? He's early."

"His color looks good now, and he's breathing great on his own. I think he'll be fine, but the pediatrician on call at the hospital can do a complete assessment as soon as you get there."

The ambulance crew arrived moments later, stomping off their boots and covered in snow.

Keep it together, Griffin told himself as the medics asked him for a situation report.

He shoved down his emotions for the next few minutes as they assessed her, on the phone apparently with her ob-gyn.

"Nice work, Doc," one of the medics said, his voice gruff.

He knew this man, Griffin realized with shock. Rafe Arredondo was the assistant fire chief and also the son of the woman who had basically snubbed him at the holiday market.

Rafe's cousin and best friend had been one of the teens killed in that fiery accident.

When Griffin first arrived back in Shelter Springs, Rafe had been on the ambulance crew of a couple of calls that had come in when Griffin had been working in the emergency department. The other man had always been polite but cool, avoiding anything but necessary communication.

"McKenna did all the work. I only handled a few of the technicalities," Griffin said now.

"It was a good thing for both of them that you were here," Rafe said.

Griffin didn't know what to say, embarrassed that such mild praise could make him feel the same as the time he hit a three-run homer to win the state tournament in high school.

"Will you be able to make it to the hospital?" he asked the crew.

"It's a real mess, but we'll get her there," Rafe promised.

The paramedics began the transport, but McKenna looked stricken as they passed through the living room. "I can't believe I won't be here for Christmas Eve. Who's going to put out the stockings for the girls?"

"Don't worry," Natalie said. "We'll take care of everything, and we'll FaceTime you through the whole thing."

"Thank you. I wish I could see them before we go."

As if in answer to her plea, Hazel and Nora hovered in the hallway, both looking scared and confused at the hubbub.

"I know we need to go," McKenna said to the paramedics, "but can you give me thirty seconds so my girls can meet their baby brother?"

Rafe nodded to the rest of the crew, and they paused there so that McKenna and Travis could hug their daughters.

"Where are you going?" Nora whispered, her little face tight with fear.

"I have to go to the hospital for a few hours so that doctors can make sure everything's okay with me and the baby. I'll be back before you know it."

"But it's Christmas Eve!" Hazel somehow managed to look both uneasy and outraged. "You can't go to the hospital on Christmas Eve."

"I'm afraid I don't really have a choice. But your aunt Nat and Liz and Grandpa will be here to take care of you. I promise, before you know it, we'll all be home together and I won't have to stay in bed anymore."

"Whew!" Hazel exclaimed.

"Do you want to see him?"

The older girl looked undecided but Nora nodded shyly and stepped forward to peer into the tightly wrapped bundle. After a moment, Hazel joined her.

"Why is his face so squishy and red? Is he broken? Is that why he has to go to the hospital?" Hazel asked.

To Griffin's shock, she was asking him, considering him the obvious medical authority in the room.

He personally thought the boy was absolutely perfect, but he could see why a five-year-old might have a different perspective.

"Um, that's the way babies sometimes come out," he finally said.

"Do you know what? You and Nora looked almost exactly the same when you were born," McKenna answered with a soft, exhausted smile.

"Was I all red like him?"

She nodded and hugged her again.

"We got a baby brother for Christmas," Nora announced in an awed tone.

"That's right," McKenna said, wiping away a tear. "A beautiful baby brother. What a precious gift for all of us."

Her words made Griffin think of James reading the original Christmas story earlier that evening in his deep, wonderful voice, reminding them of another baby born long ago.

"Can I hold him?" Hazel asked, apparently deciding she might like him after all.

"After he comes home from the hospital, you can hold him all you want and help me burp him and even change his diaper."

Hazel screwed up her face, so disgusted by the idea that even the paramedics smiled.

"We should get going," Rafe Arredondo said. "It's turning into a pretty busy night for us."

"I'll follow in my truck," Travis said.

"You'd better ride with us. I'm not sure you'll able to get through on your own. Someone can give you a lift back home when the snow lets up a little."

And then in a flurry, they were moving McKenna into the ambulance that had been pulled up to the front doors of the building.

The crowd of residents who had gathered to watch all the excitement seemed to give a collective exhale.

"Well, that was a little more excitement than I was expecting this Christmas Eve." Liz Cisneros shook her head. "Girls, let's get you into the tub, and then we'll read a story and you can go to bed."

"And then will Santa come?"

"I hope so," Liz answered.

She and Steve ushered them down the hallway to their apartment.

Natalie turned to Griffin, her features bright and happy.

"Thank you." She gave him a tremulous smile. "I'm not sure what we would have done if you hadn't been here."

All of the emotions he had been fighting down for the past hour surged back. He gazed down at this woman who meant so very much to him, the one he couldn't have, and he knew he couldn't stay here a moment longer.

He grunted something, he wasn't sure what, then escaped as if the howling winds were chasing him.

twenty-eight

Unease rippled through Natalie as she watched Griffin walk quickly down the hall.

He didn't go to the recreation room or even toward his grandmother's apartment. Instead, he pivoted and moved into the small room off the lobby used by the residents as a comfortable, quiet reading room as well as a board game and book lending library.

She remembered that brief, heart-stopping moment during all the chaos earlier when he had looked blank with panic.

Something was wrong.

She cared too much about Griffin to let him suffer alone. She followed and found him standing just inside the darkened room, gazing out the window at the howling snow.

"Griffin? What's wrong?"

He turned at her voice, startled, and she saw again that same look of raw pain. He looked away as if to conceal it but it was too late.

"Sorry. I didn't hear you. I'm fine."

He was lying. Even Hazel with her five-year-old wisdom could have figured that much out. She moved farther into the room and touched his arm.

"What is it? What's wrong?"

He said nothing, only looked at her with such an expression

of torment on his features, she could do nothing but wrap her arms around him. He released a long, shuddering breath, folded his arms around her tightly and sagged against her.

Fear crawled across her skin. "Is there something you're not telling me about McKenna or the baby?"

She felt the movement of his head shaking against her. "No. Nothing like that. I just... I haven't helped at a delivery since..." His voice trailed off.

All at once, she understood and wanted to kick herself for her insensitivity. "Since you lost your son," she finished for him, her voice low. "Oh, Griffin. I'm so very sorry. I didn't think."

Helping McKenna deliver a healthy baby must have been painfully hard for him, she realized, dredging up everything he had lost. Yet he had done it anyway with a confident calm that had steadied them all.

Was it any wonder she loved this man with all her heart?

"I've learned to compartmentalize my grief," he murmured, his arms still holding her tightly. "Most of the time I handle it. But sometimes I remember and feel that same helpless pain of just standing by, knowing I couldn't save him. Like I could never stop my dad from drinking. Like I couldn't save Jake."

Natalie closed her eyes, feeling his pain as if it were her own. She wanted to absorb it, take it into her, if that would ease his burden.

She loved him with a fierce intensity that was almost physical.

This was where she belonged, she realized in that moment. Here, with Griffin.

Somehow she managed to find her voice, despite the torrent of emotions.

"Stop it. You are an amazing doctor and an amazing man. But that's the key word. You're a man. You're not God. You cannot hold yourself responsible when you can't fix everything."

He shifted so their gazes could meet, as if he needed to read her expression to absorb the comfort of her words.

His eyes were dark with emotion. "That's a hard thing to accept," he said, his voice low.

"I know. But you have to or you won't be able to do your job, Griffin."

He nodded against her again, and they stood that way for a long time until his breathing steadied.

He finally blew out a breath. "Thanks. I think I'm okay now."

"Are you sure?"

He nodded and mustered a smile. "Yeah. It helped that you were there during the delivery. I wasn't sure I could handle it, but you looked at me with so much faith, I didn't want to disappoint you."

"You could never do that."

She leaned up on tiptoe to brush her mouth against his, a soft, tender kiss that carried all the love inside her. He gave a sharp intake of breath, and then he returned the gentle kiss, his mouth warm, whisper soft on hers.

"I wish you could stay."

At first she thought she had imagined the words, that her own longing had conjured them, but when she opened her eyes, he met her gaze with a look of such yearning, she felt tears burn in her throat.

She loved him and she belonged here. She had never been more sure of anything in her life.

"Why?"

"Because I'm in love with you. Isn't it obvious?"

She had handled the chaos and beauty of her sister giving birth with aplomb, but his simple words staggered her.

"No, it's not obvious. At all."

He gave a rough laugh and kissed her again. "Seriously? I swear, everyone else at the Shelter Inn has figured it out. Birdie certainly has."

"Why?"

She had to ask again, mostly because she couldn't quite believe what he was saying and also couldn't find the words to tell him she felt the same.

"You didn't give me much choice, did you? You blew into town like that blizzard out there. You were smart and funny and kind and I didn't stand a chance."

He rested his forehead against hers and they stood together that way for a long moment inside the cozy little room, the rest of the world as distant as the mountains while the storm raged outside.

"I love you, Natalie," he said at last. "I understand that travel is who you are, what you love. I suppose that sense of adventure is part of what I love about you. But even the most intrepid adventurers need a home base."

His words wrapped around her, plain and lovely in their simplicity.

She smiled softly. "I'm a digital nomad. One of the best things about that is that I can set up shop anywhere. Even in the small Idaho town I once couldn't wait to leave."

"You don't have to give up everything you find rewarding. We can figure something out. You can come visit, and I can always take a week or two off to join you wherever you are."

Touched that he would even consider the idea, she tightened her arms around him.

"I started traveling because that sense of adventure and discovery fed my soul. After coming home to help McKenna, I discovered other things can do the same thing. Holding a sleeping child. Being part of a community holiday market. Falling in love. Life is the adventure, Griffin. Not sticking another stamp on my passport."

His gaze warmed at her words and he kissed her again, until they were both breathless.

"You mentioned falling in love," he murmured after a long while.

She drew away. "Actually, I shouldn't have said that. It's not exactly true."

Confusion and hurt flashed in his eyes. "Oh. Right."

She shook her head. "More accurately, I should have said, finally admitting to myself that I've been in love with my brother's best friend for most of my life."

He looked at her as if he didn't quite believe her, but she didn't mind. She had the rest of her life to convince him she meant every word.

She kissed him again, with all the love in her heart, and he gave a small, strangled laugh and pulled her tightly into his arms.

What a wonderful Christmas, she thought some time later. She had a new nephew and he and McKenna were both doing well. That would have been miracle enough, but this, being in Griffin's arms and finally feeling free to tell him of her feelings, was better than anything else she could have imagined.

She would have to cancel the job in that French village. Or maybe she would take one more trip, since she had already purchased her plane ticket and the homeowner was counting on her.

She and Griffin could talk on the phone as often as possible, or maybe he could take a week away from the responsibilities of his practice to join her. He would love the peaceful charm there, the delicious food and the kind people.

"Merry Christmas," he murmured. "I do think this might be the best Christmas I've ever had. Even better than the year I got a BMX bike, skis *and* a new skateboard under the tree."

"Wow. That's a lot to live up to."

"I don't think you need to worry." He gave a rather wicked smile, and she shivered at all the possibilities that stretched out ahead of them. Too bad they were trapped here at the Shelter Inn, with virtually no privacy in a building full of senior citizen chaperones.

At least the girls would be thrilled to have their Dr. Jingle with them for Christmas, she thought.

And possibly longer.

The reminder of Nora and Hazel made her straighten. "Oh dear. I need to go. My dad and Liz were settling the girls to bed, but I would like to tell them good night on Christmas Eve." She paused. "I also need to put out their stockings and their presents from Santa. I wish we could wait to have Christmas until McKenna and Travis were home with the baby, but I think we all know the girls won't have the patience to wait for that."

"I believe you're right," he said with a smile she felt clear down to her toes.

She reached for his hand. "Want to come with me?"

"Anywhere," he said, his voice gruff.

As they walked toward her sister's apartment and the holiday joy that awaited them, she was suddenly certain they would share many more adventures of their own, both abroad and here in Shelter Springs. Laughter, tears and everything in between.

Their journey was only beginning.

epilogue

"It's my turn to hold the baby," Hazel declared decisively. "You've had her long enough."

Nora made a face at her sister and tightened her arms around Sophie Alberta Taylor, who offered up her toothless smile to both of her cousins equally.

"I have not. You always get to hold her longer than me," Nora argued.

"Because I'm older and I know the best way."

"You do not. I'm holding her okay, right, Aunt Natalie? Tell Hazel she doesn't know everything."

Natalie was quick to intervene. Most of the time the girls, eight and six now, were the best of friends. But they could also argue about every single thing under the sun, from how to cut out a paper snowflake to whether regular popcorn was better than kettle corn.

"You both hold her exactly right. Thank you so much for your help with her today. I don't know what I would have done without you. The last batch of cookies is almost done, and then we can start decorating them."

"Can I have a cookie?"

A bundle of constant energy, their brother Austin—who

would be three in only a few days, which she couldn't quite believe—wandered over to see what was happening.

Austin could never bear the idea that he might be missing something.

"Not yet," she told him, adoring this boy with his curly hair and insatiable curiosity. "We need to put the frosting on first."

"I like them without frosting," he declared.

"No, you don't." Hazel rolled her eyes at him. "You just want a cookie now."

"They smell good," he said, then immediately leaned over the baby on his sister's lap and made a silly face. "Hi, Sophie. Hi, Sophie. Look! She smiled at me! She likes me. Can I hold her?"

"It's my turn next," Hazel said. "You can hold her after that."

Natalie thought it was a very good thing Sophie was sweet and easygoing and that she already loved her cousins.

What had Nat been thinking when she had offered to watch all the children for a few hours on this Saturday afternoon before Christmas so Travis and McKenna could finish their holiday shopping?

She knew the answer. She had been thinking that she missed them and didn't see nearly enough of them these days.

Though the house she and Griffin had built in the mountains overlooking town and the stunning lake beyond wasn't far from the Shelter Inn, the past four months of becoming a new mother had been hectic and challenging and wonderful.

In addition to trying to figure out what she was doing with Sophie, Natalie was still working and was busier than ever, freelance copyediting and writing articles, especially now that her first nonfiction book about traveling with purpose had been published right before her daughter was born.

The timer on the oven went off, and she hurried to the kitchen to pull out the last batch of sugar cookies.

"Yay! Now can we decorate them?" Nora asked.

"Soon. They have to cool first."

"Then I'm going to eat them all," Austin declared.

"You can't," Hazel told him sternly. "They're for the party."

"Most of them," Natalie agreed. "But I'm quite sure we'll have plenty and can spare one or two."

She was taking the children back to their home that evening for the annual Shelter Inn holiday party, a potluck event that had become a cherished tradition among the residents, commemorating the year they had all been snowed in.

"Can I hold her now?" Hazel asked.

"I need to put her down for a nap so she'll be happy for the party. I promise, you can hold her all you want when she wakes up."

Hazel and Austin both pouted at that, but didn't argue when Natalie scooped up her daughter from Nora's arms.

"Go back to watching your movie for a few minutes, okay? When I come back, we can decorate the cookies. Hazel, can you be in charge?"

"Yes!" Her older niece looked as if all her Christmas wishes had just come true as Natalie hurried to the nursery nook just down the hall from the kitchen.

She left the door ajar so she could hear them while she changed and fed Sophie then transferred her to her bed.

She had just closed the door to the nursery when she heard a deep voice speaking to the children and their delighted shrieks as they greeted their beloved uncle Griffin.

When she walked into the great room and saw him on the sofa with a girl on either side and Austin on his lap, everything inside her seemed to sigh with happiness.

Three years later, she loved this man more than she ever believed possible.

"You're early!" she exclaimed.

He smiled, setting Austin down before crossing the room and sweeping her into a dramatic kiss that made the girls giggle and made Natalie's pulse rate accelerate as if she had just climbed Heartbreak Peak.

"The urgent care was slow today. We only had one patient in the final hour and he was easy." He grinned. "Plus I didn't want to miss all the fun here."

"Great. You can help us decorate the cookies."

"I'll help you eat them, anyway. Where's our girl?"

"I just put her down for a nap."

He looked so crestfallen, she had to laugh. Griffin was an amazing father, as she knew he would be. Sometimes in the night, she would wake up to feed Sophie only to find him in the nursery already, holding their daughter and whispering stories to her that she was years away from being able to understand.

The past three years had been happier than Natalie ever could have imagined, filled with priceless memories and cherished experiences.

They had traveled together four times for medical trips overseas, where he had helped out in local clinics providing care to people who otherwise couldn't afford treatment.

Both of them had been so buoyed up by the experiences, she knew they would have many more.

As she returned to the kitchen to set out the cookie decorating supplies, she reflected on how her life had changed over the past three years.

She wouldn't change anything about her journey. Once, her nomadic life had been exactly what she needed. Rich, textured, adventurous. She would always cherish those experiences.

In this house she and Griffin had created, filled with love and laughter and family, Natalie knew this was exactly what she needed at this season of her life.

She couldn't have designed it better.

★ ★ ★ ★ ★